Early Praise for
The Slide

"The theme is American Home, that place that lesser writers sentimentalize and satirize. Kyle Beachy writes with bracing melancholy in a voice that is all his own, and his St. Louis, like Cheever's Westchester, is populated with isolated, self-aware characters, each of whom is new to us. His hero, Potter Mays, is great company."

—Jincy Willett, author of *The Writing Class*
and *Winner of the National Book Award*

"With *The Slide*, Kyle Beachy turns the coming-of-age story on its ear. There's the decay of both the American city and the American nuclear family, the painful inevitability of friends and lovers growing apart, and the ongoing difficulty of denying one's base appetites. Plus baseball. Lots of baseball. Beachy has emerged in his debut fully formed. His writing is propulsive, unique without being forced, and eminently readable."

—Ron Currie, Jr., author of *God Is Dead*
and *Everything Matters!*

"[*The Slide*] is at once hilarious, strange and uncomfortable."

—*Publishers Weekly*

the slide

a novel

Kyle Beachy

THE DIAL PRESS

THE SLIDE
A Dial Press Book / February 2009

Published by The Dial Press
A Division of Random House, Inc.
New York, New York

Book design by Wesley Gott

The Dial Press is a registered trademark of Random House, Inc., and
the colophon is a trademark of Random House, Inc.

Library of Congress Cataloging-in-Publication Data
Beachy, Kyle.
The slide : a novel / Kyle Beachy.
p.   cm.
ISBN 978-0-385-34185-1
1. College graduates—Fiction.   2. Self-actualization (Psychology)—
Fiction.   3. Psychological fiction.   I. Title.
PS3602.E235S65   2009
813'.6—dc22   2008029631

Printed in the United States of America
Published simultaneously in Canada

www.dialpress.com

10 9 8 7 6 5 4 3 2 1
BVG

For Neil Beachy and Harry Brown,
two men I wish I could have known

Now I'm gonna be twenty-two, I say oh my and uh boo hoo.

Iggy Pop, "1969"

the slide

june

one

What was good about the road was that the road's decisions were already made. For two full days I'd watched it emerge on the horizon and disappear beneath me. I saw it change colors, from black to gray to brown, and sometimes felt the seams between them, a clunk against the steady tremble. Los Angeles giving way to glittery Vegas, Martian Utah, and a blind nighttime passage through the Rockies. Then a fresh morning of eastern Colorado fading into prodigious fields of Kansan wheat, forever-sized and flat like nothing you've ever seen, until finally Missouri, blunt and dark, a series of brake lights to guide along the final leg. I surrendered to the road. Only once did I pick up my phone and call Audrey. After eight rings I heard her voice mail, and here I likely should have made some gesture, but everything had already been said, repeated, thrown around like rolled-up socks.

Then I was back in the driveway, engine idling, wondering just what in the shit to do now. There was a new addition to the house jutting into what used to be side yard. I could imagine my parents in the living room, quiet and mostly still, cozy within that special silence of the long-married. If I unfastened my seat belt, the car would beep at me.

Soon enough the front door opened to reveal parents silhouetted against the yellow glow of home. I cut the engine, stepped into the night, raised a hand, and smiled. Hello. The air felt and tasted heavy and wet. A hug, a hand pressed flush against cheek, and even though it wasn't a week since we'd all been together at commencement, I sensed relief in them both. During her second hug my mother swayed and spoke quietly to the air, *our boy, our boy, our boy.*

"Makes more sense to unload now," my father said. "Twice the hands."

She said to make a pile of laundry and she'd take care of it in the morning. "Are you hungry? I've got salami."

Car unloaded, shoes off, I sat on the counter above the dishwasher and chewed a sandwich. My parents watched. I always needed this, when they would stand as a pair, sharing the same frame. *These are my parents,* these two adults. *I am their only remaining child.* My brother, Fredrick Alan Mays, drowned at the age of five when he chased his rubber four square ball into the leaf- and tarpaulin-covered swimming pool at the Sheldon Woods apartment complex. At the time my mother was spoon-feeding a ten-month-old me special prescription formula. My father was at work, making his way through a small mountain of legal briefs. There were no witnesses. Freddy falling onto an ancient, heavy tarp improperly anchored to the pool's deck and becoming entangled, sinking beneath fetid off-season water while my mother ensured I was taking to the new formula. One splash, then many more as his arms flailed, little puddles on the deck, ball bobbing, Freddy sinking. This took a moment of active deliberation: I was their son who didn't drown. To their credit, my parents understood. They remained side by side and gave me a second.

"Our boy," Carla said, beaming as she wrapped up the rolls and the meat.

I could see my father preparing to talk. He was examining his hands, pulling his frame slightly inward, revving. Richard stood over six foot and was handsome the way people found reassuring. His hair, full and gray, embraced age without submitting to it. I watched him shrug slowly and look up from his hands.

"How's the car running?"

"It's a great car," I said. "I love the car. Thank you guys, again, for the car."

"Be sure to check the oil tomorrow. You know how to check the oil?"

"Of course, Pop."

"Of course you do," he said. "Well, give it a check tomorrow. And then what else? Is there a plan? You check the oil and I'll poke around if you like, find something for you. Not to say hurry up and decide. Not to pressure. Your mother and I are just glad to have you around for a while. Aren't we, Carla? But will it hurt to start thinking about things? No it won't. History of the world, nobody's ever died from giving a little thought. Not a single bruise caused by thinking things over. Really: we're just glad to have you back. Wait—I'm in Cleveland this week. Back on Thursday. Poke around then."

I smiled and he seemed to smile kind of, and this was good, then he nodded and looked back at his hands.

My mother moved to my father's side. "The important thing is there's food here whenever you want it. Chicken wings, toasted ravioli, twice-baked potatoes."

I climbed the stairs to the second floor. I stepped into the newly redecorated bathroom and watched myself brush teeth, then spent minutes leaning onto the sink, examining my reflection. In the bedroom, I opened and closed the wardrobe and several dresser drawers. I was continually impressed by the sturdiness of my parents' furniture, dark old wood that hinted at permanence. My poster of Ozzie Smith mid-dive hung over my bed and my sheets smelled of some theoretical sunny and breezy afternoon, the middle of a field. I lay down, closed my eyes, and breathed. Sleep, lately, was becoming an issue.

Some time later, I tossed back sheets and stood. Downstairs, I moved from one room to the next, turning corners with soft steps. Every few years my parents would hire crews of men to come and hang sheets of translucent plastic, rip up floorboards, and push walls outward. Two years ago they furnished the

basement. Before that they lengthened the patio into the backyard, then they added the sunroom, where nobody ever went.
The living room had once been the family room. I stood where
the current living room used to end and looked into the most recent addition. The office, Richard called it. The computer room,
Carla called it. I touched picture frames and ran fingers across
new plaster. I leaned against the enormous desk and waited.

A timer made the rooms go even darker than before.

Back upstairs, the house grew colder and I crawled deeper into
the bedding so that soon only my face was exposed. I may have been
acting like a child, but in this room it was sanctioned. It was *okay*.

Audrey was on an airplane. Or she'd already landed.

Where was it. Paris.

There was noise directly above me, the scraping of some creature in the attic. Plural creatures. From inside the fabric-softened
and spring-breezy cocoon I watched shadows of branches dance
across the wall. Rain.

Breakfast was two eggs fried into the middle of hollowed-out
pieces of toast. My mother poured orange juice, moved about
the kitchen, disappeared, then came back to write onto a Post-it
she stuck to the phone.

"I think there might be squirrels in the attic," I said.

"Squirrels?"

Before retiring, my mother had been a universally loved
second-grade teacher. She won annual awards and was showered
with Christmas gifts by the parents of her students. It took very
little effort to imagine her leading a class. That short, wavy
brown teacher hair, the full-length single-color dresses, flats—her
whole package was perfectly educational, a surplus of maternal
energy.

"We just had a man here for bees. And now squirrels?"

When she retired, much of that teacherly vigor was diverted
into her garden. In the fall she disposed of annuals and cut back

perennials, covered soil with manure as one would ice a cake. She spent entire springs on her knees, dual wristbands to wipe away full days of sweat. It was her passion, basic and earthy in every way.

"How are you for cash?"

"Me? Fine. I'm fine."

She left the kitchen and returned a few minutes later in her sleeveless shirt and denim shorts. Her purse was under the phone. She pulled out her wallet and removed an uncreased bill. She laid the bill next to my orange juice, kissed my forehead, and stepped through the side door into her garden. I walked immediately to the phone and called Stuart Hurst.

"This is Stuart."

"Stubes. So formal."

"Potter Mays! Home again home again. Jiggedy jigg."

"I'm working on two hours' sleep and would like to get out of my house."

"Makes sense. Incidentally, this was my last night in the pool house. I'm out: onward, forward. I'll come pick you up and we'll drive over to the new place. Sneak peek before tonight's welcoming event. You just wait right there."

We'd become friends after my parents left the apartment complex and its pool behind, moving into the desirable Ladue public-school district. That first day of third grade, stepping onto a morning bus full of boys and girls I had never seen, and among all of the eyes sat Stuart the fourth grader, waving me over to his rubberized seat.

"Lookit," he said, opening his palm to reveal a small brick of staples. He picked one off from the rest, put it onto his tongue, and swallowed. "One at a time, they go down easy. Try."

I sat on the front porch and waited. The pool house in his parents' backyard wasn't more than ten minutes' drive, plus whatever time it took to overcome his immense personal inertia. I stood and walked circles through the grass of the front lawn, my head poring over the idea of distance: the mile, a single clean figure that broke down into a mess, those five thousand two eighty feet. I stopped circling and looked at the matting of grass beneath my shoes. Audrey deemed it a terrible waste to not go shoeless whenever she could, and her feet were callused and tough for it. Then one afternoon last spring, as I was packing the car for a camping trip with friends, mine, her right foot found a stray nail hiding in some grass, and I spent the afternoon wrapping her foot, touching her hair, driving to the emergency room, and waiting for a tetanus shot because she couldn't remember ever having one, placing lips to her hand as the needle entered, laughing as she limped back to the car. Saying *of course.* Saying *you're welcome.* All the while the resentment building, growing, this beady-eyed and sharp-toothed troll of resentment making home in my stomach. Delirious wonder if maybe she'd found the nail on purpose, that it was all secretly on purpose. Resentment as appalling as it was amazing, a sheer force I had no choice but to embrace. I moved from grass onto driveway. I had been saying *I love you* for the past four years and meaning it every time as far as I knew. Her flight went Portland to O'Hare to London Heathrow to Charles de Gaulle. Three weeks.

Finally I saw him. Despite limitless wealth, Stuart continued to drive the first car his parents bought him, a mid-nineties Ford Explorer variously dented and run-down. He viewed himself as the unique product of convergent psychocapitalist forces, so driving his big dumb American truck car until it died was a way to both honor these forces and assert his individuality. When I opened the door, he was nodding and not smiling.

"And so begins what might be the worst year of your life."

"Start simple, please, and tell me how," I said.

"Can't," he said. "Your version won't be anything like mine. What do you know about Cambodia? Don't get me wrong, this is going to be difficult. I promise. But not Cambodia."

After graduating from Brown the year before, Stuart went straight from the baggage claim to his parents' pool house for a swim and a beer. Weeks passed and he decided he might as well live there and avoid the potential explosions with his father and stepmother at the main house. And so he stayed. He inhabited the pool house as if it were some sort of womb, subsisting on the runoff luxury that trickled from John and Deanna Hurst's massive home. Details of his year were sparse. He admitted to devoting a fair chunk of his time to open-ended thought, and he also mentioned blowing the occasional line of Talkative.

"Situations came up." Stuart rolled through a stop sign. "Some of them involved women who won't enter a room unless there's Talkative inside."

Now Stuart had found an apartment. I knew this because he had sent me a series of e-mails. I knew the building dated from the turn of the last century, and was gorgeous, and classy, and likely about the most amazing apartment I had so far ever seen. The old woodwork, floors that would creak under our feet. Old Cardinals pennants hanging on the walls of his first personal home.

We drove into downtown Clayton, a mixture of ten-story office buildings and overpriced restaurants. Women in unrevealing skirts stood with jacketless men on street corners, not exactly smiling. The storm that I listened to all night had dropped leaves and small branches from the trees that lined these streets, great bodies of green flirting with squat glass towers. I was always shocked when I returned from LA to find so much color, like some regional détente with nature.

"How are those allergies?" Stuart asked.

"Allergies," I said. "I forgot all about my allergies."

We'd come for housewarming supplies. He parked us between two silver luxury SUVs. The plaque on the wall said: STRAUB'S MARKET: FINE GROCERS SINCE 1901. Whatever sort of place it was back then, what we stepped into was a boutique market where local families kept charge accounts, a spectrum of beige with miniature shopping carts and grated chrome shelves.

Stuart picked a jar of apricot mango wasabi sauce. "I'm guessing things didn't end well with Audrey."

"At some point a guess stops being a guess."

"You look horrible," he said. "What went wrong?"

"Every possible thing went wrong. It was a sequence of mistakes based on various kinds of selfishness. I stand by some of my actions. Other actions I can hardly believe were mine. Remember our plan to travel after graduation? Instead, she's in Europe with Carmel for three weeks and I'm here."

"So this is punishment," he said.

"Yes. Because I am a selfish asshole prick man."

We moved to the meat counter, a thing of local legend. Two goateed men wearing white aprons eyed us suspiciously until Stuart ordered eight flank steaks and four pork loins.

"I think you're going to appreciate some of the work I've been doing. A few recent projects are investment-worthy if I can find the right people."

It was generally assumed Stuart would work for his father, but nobody had the foggiest notion when he'd start. Two months earlier, at school, I'd received an envelope with a business card tucked inside:

Stuart Hurst

Mentation, Ideation, Formulation, and Innovation Specialist
AND
Independent Thought Contractor

"Bringing tomorrow's ideas to the forefront of today's late afternoon."

Mentation as employment, research in its loosest, most wandering sense. No specific hours as such, only the faith that every so often he'd stumble upon a worthwhile thought.

The store's stereo played a Bach fugue. A woman with a green basket over her arm sneezed, and at least three voices blessed her. How many of these women had had face-lifts? It was impossible for me to know. Audrey came from a family of surgeons, which meant she could tell without fail who'd gone under the knife. We'd go on day trips from campus into Hollywood to stroll Melrose and pretend to window-shop.

"Look at her neck," she'd explain in that voice of hers. "Necks don't lie. Also notice she doesn't have earlobes."

I carried as much Budweiser as I could and met Stuart at the checkout lane. Now the old woman in the forest-green apron eyed me suspiciously. Childish features still intact, my face round, nose, I suppose, *buttonlike*, I must have looked a little like every grandson in the entire world, because old women were always finding me charming. This one did not. I handed her my driver's license.

Our total was a little over three hundred dollars. Because he was missing the index finger on his right hand, Stuart's pen grip was always awkward and comical, but now what came out was a fantastic signature, sinuous letters curling into themselves with much flourish. This was new.

The apartment was in the Central West End, an almost-urban area close enough to downtown that half the city was afraid to go there. Lining the highway were commercial developments I'd never seen before. Soon we came to the bridge of the Science Center, where kids on field trips aimed speedometers at traffic. The whole highway moved at a cautious fifty-eight. Once we exited, Stuart made a series of rapid turns and I lost all sense of direction, all I could see were houses and trees, trees *everywhere*, until he came to a stop where a fire truck and several police cruisers blocked the road.

"Well." He flicked his cigarette to the ground. "How's this for something."

I followed a few steps behind. The visuals were powerful— spinning lights, various troops of personnel moving across the

scene, a thin crowd of gawking onlookers. At the center of it all
was a building, its top quarter collapsed by the tree that had fallen
into it. I had been awake for much of the storm that moved
through during the night. There was a solid hour when drops
were massive and the wind a force. And now here was this tree at
this awkward angle, the rubble of fallen brick, a barbarous act of
partial destruction.

I heard shouting and the clunk of boots on pavement. The firemen leaned against their truck and watched. Stuart remained
calm, so I tried to remain calm. I took turns looking at Stuart and
looking at where the tree had fallen through the apartment. His
arms were crossed at his chest.

"Looks like no other apartments were damaged," he said.

"That's the apartment. The e-mail."

"Look close and you can see my red couch in there. See it?
Totally great couch."

Imagine the sound of a tree severing from itself and falling
through a building. Thunderous crack of wood followed soon by
crash of brick and plaster and more wood. At ground level, the
stump and about six feet of splintered tree remained, doomed.
What was this? Surely wind alone couldn't have cracked so massive a trunk down the middle.

"Those firemen look bored as hell," he said.

I looked at the crowd of *onlookers*. Were these walkers who
had just happened upon this disaster? Several were talking into
phones. It would be a hard scene to leave once you stumbled
upon it; a tree falls in the city and select few are there to look.
There would be the natural urge to describe it all to some friend
or family member, dial a random number and share with whoever answered. To describe was to make real; listen to what I'm
seeing. You'll never believe what I saw. I used to say *girlfriend* and
find reassurance, a word to frame that corner of my world.

I overheard the man next to me speaking of a particular fungus. Dutch elm, he said, then again to someone else. Dutch elm.

I shared the fungus theory with Stuart, speaking out of the corner of my mouth as if delivering a grave national secret.

"Well," he said. "Well well well well."

Here was actual trial, and Stuart was handling it like a weathered veteran. Was it really only one year between us? Though I had friends in my class through school, baseball teammates and the normal balance of sundry peers, there was something to having a friend a year older. He was a guide of sorts to whatever was to come in year X + 1, a role I knew he relished. Now he was composed, stoic in the face of immense loss. With this and the signature, I felt honored to be standing so close to him.

"I wonder who you're supposed to tell. The firemen? They'll point you in the right direction, at least. Get the insurance agent out here."

"I got a car full of meat, Potter. Let's go back to the pool house."

We walked back to the car and climbed inside. I adjusted the air-conditioning onto my face and watched the spinning lights until we were around the corner. I didn't know what to say.

"I don't know what to say. Look at you. You're a rock."

Now, backtracking along the route we'd taken earlier, I felt the first bored pangs of recognition. There was the park. The Science Center. Fifty-eight miles per hour.

"I would sure like some response here."

"My apartment has been demolished by a mixed act of nature and insidious vermin. Fine. You want me to talk about it, and I wouldn't mind talking about it, but I am not someone who can complain."

"You can't complain. But even that is a kind of complaint."

"You and I don't live in Cambodia. There aren't land mines in our backyards that could blow off our limbs every time we go out for a jog."

This was my best friend, driving the Ford. *Look at him,* I thought. *Look and absorb and perhaps steal.* It seemed suddenly

very clear that of all the resources I had in the world, all the un-
fairly distributed and crapshoot gifts I'd been blessed with, perhaps Stuart Hurst would prove the most valuable. Because the
basic truth was that I had a decision to make, one I had put off for
as long as I possibly could because I didn't have the proper tools.
Or, rather, I had too many tools and no concept of how to use
them. I needed considerable help.

"I want to contract some thought."

"I know just the guy," Stuart said.

"I owe it to her and I owe it to myself. I have three weeks.
Three weeks to devote to nothing but deciding whether I'm actually in matter of serious fact in love with her. I ask myself all the
time: are you in love with her? And I answer. I say the word and I
believe the word, but then at the same time I *hear* the word, and it
sounds hollow."

"Quick," Stuart said. "Are you in love with Audrey?"

"Yes," I said.

"I see what you mean." He considered this for a mile. "Realize
I have to charge you. We're not playing kickball here. This is what
I do professionally. The more serious I take what I do, the better I
end up doing it."

"Maybe part of the question is answered by the fact that I'm
looking for third-party help," I said. "Maybe that's data for you to
add to the pile."

"Maybe," he said.

"I used to be an emotionally rich young male, Stubes. Now I'm
like, what's the cardboard. Manila."

"This sounds like the sort of thing where I work at my own
pace until I reach a conclusion and then charge you retroactively.
Meaning there will have to be a certain level of trust between us
that I, mentator, am not going to screw you, client. But I will
charge you. Break, sure. Discount, sure. Free lunch, no."

We passed our old middle school, the Ladue fire department,
the Amoco station where I'd once seen two hockey players kick

and tear at each other until the ground was covered in blood and
flannel and khaki. Audrey had questioned what I wanted. We had
entire conversations about what we might each possibly want.
Over time it became clear that what she knew of desire was far
greater than the filaments I had at my disposal. And this, among
so many other things, had led to profound loss of sleep.

"We will of course still throw a party," he said. "Call it a
Welcome Back, Potter party."

I sneezed twice, then let my head fall against the window.

"You expect there to be women at this party? Talkative?"

"Damn yes," he said. "Research."

two

my mother's timing was a thing of minor and inescapable beauty. Two eggs, fried like clockwork into the hollowed middle of two pieces of toast. I came down the stairs into the kitchen and she was there at the stove, angling the frying pan so the meal slid neatly onto a plate. Every single morning, impeccably timed, an act so simple it approached the mystical. She washed and toweled the pan, then returned it beneath the counter, where it waited until the next morning.

I spent a lot of time saying *thank you*.

There felt a certain theatricality in play. I was audience to my mother's ongoing task to prove to herself there were things to be done. I sat on a stool at the counter and watched her move through the kitchen and into the new computer room, pass back through the kitchen on her way to the basement door. Humming some pleasant tune. Or from the living-room couch I could see her outside working in the garden, digging into mud and wiping sweat from her forehead with the topside of her wrist. Other times she would exit stage altogether. Errands conceived from those succinct, colorful notes stuck to the phone and pages of her day calendar. Off to coffee and lunch with her small circle of women friends left over from days of teaching or that bygone era when my family attended church. These were mostly divorced women who I believed relied on my mother as a wholly different sort of character, the compassionate listener who could serve as a hopeful reminder that even in these days of widespread matrimonial ruin, certain marriages could still endure.

The doorbell rang not long after she left. The air outside hung like a curtain, thick with humidity and birdsong and green-yellow greens brilliant in the sun. A delivery woman stood on the porch wearing all brown, box in one hand, signature pad in the other. Her dark face was rich with layers of matte makeup, her hair shiny. I looked from the package, addressed to me, to her brown truck waiting in the street, hazards clicking.

The box was from Audrey. I set it on the kitchen island and pulled a paring knife from the magnetic strip above the spice rack. I walked a few uncertain circles around the island, grim revolutions like a field beast that's stumbled upon another creature's kill. I picked it up, set it down, walked away, returned. I went and sat on the couch and weighed my options. I realized the knife was still in my hand. If I wasn't careful, this package was going to defeat me. So I went and slid the knife through the packing tape and watched the top of the box pop upward. Inside I found purple tissue paper, crinkly hand-torn pieces stuffed to protect a smaller box within. Inside this smaller box I found more tissue paper and a starfish with two of its legs missing. I looked for a note or card and found nothing, though I couldn't help but be impressed by the care Audrey must have devoted to the packing job.

For a brief second I viewed this gesture as something good, even selfless. A gift. But maybe not. Maybe reimbursement of previously extracted generosity. Maybe winking retribution, a nebulous and loaded inside joke. Four years ago I had found this starfish washed onto the jagged black beach rocks at Big Sur, then carried it up the hill to Audrey, lying horizontal on the hiking trail, eyes closed to the afternoon's fleeting bits of sun as it descended into that great blue-gray body of water to our right. I had been searching for something to give to her since we met the night before. I understood neither the origin nor meaning of this desire, but I knew I wanted to watch a gift pass from my hands to hers, and I wanted to see her response. On the way down the hill I'd found a patch of wildflowers and picked a few of varying lengths into what I thought looked like a charming little bouquet. Then I spotted the starfish and dropped the flowers.

Audrey sat up and made an awning over her eyes. With her other hand she reached to take what I was offering.

"What a beautiful gift," she said. And *smiled,* wide, surprised, lovely. "Thank you."

The night before, we'd met while sitting in a circle with others who had signed up for the school's optional Orientation Adventure. She sat at roughly my ten o'clock. Later it became clear that neither of us had wanted or planned to participate in "OA" (two letters proffered with near-cultish adoration, as if the trip's acronymity alone was confirmation of our new school's pure awesomeness and desert of future annual-fund donation) but had each inadvertently signed up in the whirlwind of prematriculation paperwork. Our meeting, then, was the result of an elaborate system of coincidence and what I would come to recognize as monumental institutional forces. Meaning our meeting felt *official* and *deliberate,* but also—and this was our shared view of the equation—resoundingly and cosmically *right.*

Our assigned adventure was piling into two Ford Econoline vans and driving up the coast to pass hastily rolled joints and tepid cannons of white zin around a campfire. We each discreetly made certain to be in the same van.

The sun was beaming and here was this new person, this softly brash Northwesterner with dirty-looking hair, and she was alternately smiling at me and at the starfish.

"Should I treat this like your class ring, or like your varsity jacket?"

I thought about this while the starfish spun inside her fingers. Already I'd begun to long for the reward of her mouth's curl, its opening, the squint of eye.

"There's a good chance I'm just trying to get laid," I admitted. "But I don't think that's all."

Laughter then, and I bore witness to the reward of honesty as the sun lit her cheek as if from inside.

"Don't assume this means you're getting into my pants," she said.

"In that case give it back," I said.

"Never. You gave it to me and it's mine. So just help me up, then back slowly away with that penis of yours."

I had never felt such rich desire to give a girl a gift. In high school there had been ridiculous little trinket bracelets wrapped around teddy-bear paws, pairs of almost weightless earrings that slid around inside their little cardboard boxes. I'd given them because I could tell it was expected by just about everyone and I was highly reverential of the emerging laws of boy–girl activity. But for Audrey, this girl with the small green eyes, I wanted to share everything the world had to share. I would take only what I needed and share the rest. In exchange, she would smile.

Hiking back to camp, we held hands until the path narrowed and we were forced into single file. That night, several hundred yards and also a thousand miles away from the others, we zipped two sleeping bags together and I shared select details about my past, about baseball and the Midwest and my dead brother, Freddy. Then Audrey let me into her pants.

I stood at the kitchen island with the starfish. The box held no evidence of the missing legs, just these two dreadful vacancies where they'd broken from the center. I carried the brittle thing with me to the car, set it in the passenger seat, and drove to Stuart's.

What remained of the Hurst family resided in Ladue Farms. Forbidden: soliciting, trespassing, and shirtless jogging. It was one of many neighborhoods in Ladue marked by one of these wooden or wrought-iron placards hanging quaintly from a painted metal pole. The street was narrow and speed-bumped, overhung by a canopy of oak and sweet gum trees—one that in winter storm would be salted and plowed hours before the city's own. The pool house sat in the deepest corner of the Hurst compound, connected to the main house by a winding umbilical of flat-laid gray stone. Stuart was supine on a lounger by the diving board, wearing a pair of his father's running shorts.

"This shows up today. Shipped I guess before she left for Europe. First and best gift I ever gave her. Last time I saw it there were still five legs."

Stuart took the starfish, smelled it, rubbed it against his cheek, smelled it again, then tossed it into the pool. "Maybe the legs broke off between LA and Portland. You weren't the only one with a long drive."

"I'm to see this as a nonstatement. I'm supposed to watch it sink to the bottom of your pool and think, no big deal. Either that or you're gauging my reaction, making observations."

"Listen to me," he said, shaking the ice around his plastic cup. "You start thinking about this and there's no end. You will be trapped by this gift, paralyzed. You want my advice? On the house? Do not even begin trying to understand what this means."

Stuart spoke in big rounded words that left little room for dissent. I thought of his tree-squashed apartment and felt something like gratitude, for if anything magnified Stuart's wisdom it was proximity to his pool. I also wondered how much of his authority came from having only nine fingers. I did what I could to focus on my immediate surroundings. Here there was food and drink and music and magazines. There were cats, five tabbies that roamed the grounds in a miniature pride belonging to Deanna, Stuart's stepmother, who was of indeterminate age and by all accounts alcoholic. I changed into a swimsuit and took a seat on the diving board. With water up to my ankles, I faced away from Stuart, into the sun, so if I wanted I could look down to where the starfish had come to rest in the deep end.

"She is smart," I said, and let this hover for a moment. "Not to mention beautiful. Not to mention funny, sometimes, when she

chooses to be. Bonus credit awarded to the person who knows
when and when not to be funny. I don't. Plus soft, Stubes, and
hard too, granite when the situation demands. All of this at once.
But did I appreciate her adequately? Of course not. Not until the
second after the second we said goodbye. What's the word to describe the inability to appreciate what you have before it's gone?
Some ancient Germanic term to capture perfectly the nature of
my idiocy. There's a word, there has to be a word."

Stuart walked a lap around the pool, went inside briefly, then
sat down at the deck table. He opened a small Tupperware con-
tainer and dumped a pile of Relaxation onto the frosted glass.
Even missing one finger, my friend was the best roller of
Relaxation I'd ever seen. I assumed this was something he picked
up at Brown, a skill handed down from a brilliant prodigal outcast
son of Sudanese royalty, some moonlit Ivy League passage of
sacred rite. In high school he and I bought five-dollar blunts from
a guy on the basketball team, prerolled with the cheapest
Relaxation you could imagine. The most they ever gave us was a
kind of enhanced headache.

"Here's one," he said. "Take your normal hammer with bright-
orange rubber grip and top-of-the-line head. Heavy iron. Except
the handle itself, in a development I'm sure is my own, is *hollow*.
This allows me to introduce a heavy liquid, say mercury, that will
slide along the chamber of the hollowed-out hammer, providing
an extra kick when the hammer is dropped. K*aboom*."

"The mercury," I said, "provides leverage."

"That's exactly right. The swing downward is augmented by
the momentum of sliding mercury."

"Pretty fine, Stubes. Now can you help me sleep at night?"

"That sounds like personal advice," he said. "I work the technical side, yeses and nos."

A slight hill led from the pool to where the main house stood,
huge and brick, beastly, almost, in its ratio of square footage to in-
habitants. Up there John Hurst lived with his former secretary

among polished hardwood floors and Oriental rugs and plaid wallpaper. After catching him with the secretary—a scenario we agreed was too well trodden to achieve any real heartbreak— Stuart's mom took her divorce settlement and claimed a lake-front home in the Ozarks. He had a sister in DC and a brother in his second year of Peace Corps in Mongolia.

Time here at the pool moved differently, slower or just less evenly than elsewhere. The automatic vacuum probed the depths, every so often spouting into the air when it strayed too close to the surface. I saw Deanna the stepmother's form in a second-floor window of the main house, appearing to gaze out at us for a moment before moving onward. The shade migrated and we stayed at the table, getting at the pile of Relaxation. Deanna appeared and disappeared. Audrey sitting on her parents' living-room floor, bags packed, tearing apart enough pieces of purple tissue paper to fill both of the boxes.

"A job," I said. "At least I could wait tables. Something."

Stuart said, "Let me tell you what happens at restaurants. No matter how hard you resist, your coworkers take over your social life. You can fight it all you like, you can promise you're just going to work there, that this isn't a social thing. But it happens. Drinking at work segues into going out after work. And because you don't know anything about what these new friends do when they're not at work, you find it literally impossible to have a con-versation outside of work that has anything to do with anything other than work. It's one thing when it's just two of you— because it is again literally *impossible* that you're not going to end up dating or at least going home with at least one coworker— but when there's a whole group of you somewhere, then it's even worse, because now the only thing all of you have in common is the restaurant. And at some point the conversation deteriorates into a chorus of personal slander against whatever employees aren't in attendance. Trust me. It will take over your life."

He was a sage. During the next couple hours we went from the table to the deck loungers to the couches inside the pool house. We spoke frequently enough that we never forgot we weren't alone. The television was situated along the far wall, next to the fireplace, and there were two couches, both coffee-brown leather with blankets neatly tossed over their backs, and one love seat. In the free space between the kitchen and the couches was a wooden dining table with four hand-carved chairs. Stuart's bedroom and the bath/changing room were in back. We watched the last half of a Cardinals victory over the Brewers, then went back outside.

The sage walked to the pool's edge and pointed at the water. "Vacuum is having the damnedest time figuring out that starfish."

The insomnia became something I could almost rely on, but not quite. There was the odd night when I slept like a normal human. Usually, though, I'd end up trapping two or three hours of sleep, just enough that I made it through the following day without falling over. There was little point even going through the bedtime motions. I undressed. I went horizontal. I cannot describe the full extent of breathing exercises I employed. I went to the bathroom and masturbated my brains out. Nothing worked. Over and over again I gave up, convinced that the only way I was going to find sleep was by quitting the search. Of course, this was just trying, one step removed.

Several days passed without further word arriving from Audrey. Once or twice I sat in the new office and considered writing, but the lack of anything new to say combined with an image of her in some European Internet café—distracted, shrugging off whatever I managed to put into words, running out into Tuscan sun to explore the countryside by moped, laughing with Carmel about my feeble attempt to rectify, laughing always, Carmel laughing with those lips and teeth—made for a wicked deterrent.

Also: the office looked out onto the garden, where my mother continued with a job I couldn't possibly believe required such abundant continuation.

I spent afternoons sitting at the pool while Stuart worked. Sometimes he paced; other times he buried his face in his palms. He made no mention of the apartment or Dutch elm disease, and I appreciated his continued stoicism. And at night, when cicadas screamed in Dolby Surround, he threw parties. Guests appeared out of darkness to stand around the pool, holding cans of Bud Light. Stuart had become friends with sets of employed couples who lived together with their dogs in two-bedroom houses they rented for less than any reasonable person would expect. I sat within the fruity nimbus of citronella and watched tight shirts stray up women's backs when they bent to test pool water. I saw ponytails threaded through openings in pink Cardinals caps. I saw fingernails painted a sort of nacreous anticolor, all shiny and white-tipped. I tried not to stare.

In the middle of it all, Edsel Denk was diving, and he was really fucking good at it. I watched him run from the basic to the complex, throwing his huge frame into gainers and inwards and front and back flips. Flips with half spins. Edsel was two years older than me, and this was the first I'd seen of him since I left for school. I remembered him as being so tall and so skinny it was hard to say which he was more. But tonight he looked bigger, wider, and the increased size made his presence here at Stuart's pool even more of a violation. He'd also grown a beard. Thick and dark and ragged, it was facial hair of a caliber just pubic enough to suggest the nature of man I knew Edsel to be.

Twice I stood and moved through the party, nodding and smiling at people while still maintaining a close eye on my seat. I caught up with guys I played baseball with, girls I'd taken to homecoming dances, people I wanted to call *remnants* from a past life but to do so implied a current or future life, distinct from the past. Whenever I caught someone scoping my chair at the deck table, I returned to sit at the last possible minute. The third time I did this I saved it from a confusingly old girl-woman who then pulled out the chair next to me. She smiled and asked how I'd been.

"Mainly fine," I said.

She was medium all around and wore makeup that flashed at certain angles in the lambent blue of the pool light. I had no idea who she was. But I sensed a grave struggle between her straightened hair and the humidity, and I applauded her for it. I also found myself liking a small mole that sat central on the girl's right cheek.

"We had AP Bio together," she said. "Didn't we?"

"I'm not sure," I said. "But if so, that means we went to the same high school. Which is a big deal in this town."

"Your name is Potter." Now a smile took shape. "You sat in the lab group two over from me. Potter Mays. You wore big jeans and went out with that junior girl who played tennis."

"Meredith Flackman," I said. "But only until that bearded cocksucker on the diving board stole her from me."

"Oh my God, I remember. *That* was the story about you. Weren't you also really good at soccer?"

"Baseball," I said. "I hit a lot of singles up the middle."

"Jesus, I had such a *weird* crush on you."

I watched Edsel Denk flip his massive frame into the night and remembered the starfish sitting in the bottom of the deep end. I looked back at the girl next to me and in the interest of research I managed to force all Audrey comparisons aside.

"Weird how?" I asked.

"It was the kind of crush that shows up in flashback episodes of sitcoms. When the parents explain to their kids how they met? One of them was usually gaga over someone else. You were the one I had this crush on while I was waiting to meet the other guy, the one who would end up being my husband."

The candle on the table smelled like pears burning inside a tire.

"What are you doing this summer?" she asked.

"Three days a week I volunteer at a not-for-profit women's center. I do counseling work. Grief, trauma, all of these. The other two days I drive down to Jeff City to help run a literacy program at the Missouri State Penitentiary."

"Potter Mays," she said, laying one hand flat and bringing her body over the table, toward my chair. "I thought I had your whole story pegged. Honestly, I'm surprised. I'm impressed."

"And yourself?"

"I paralegal this summer for a friend of my father's, then it's off to Georgetown Law. I can't wait."

I emptied the end of my beer into the bushes. "I'm sorry if I seem disconnected. My mom is going through some pretty serious health issues right now."

"Oh my God. I'm so sorry."

She put her other hand on top of mine and we shared a moment of silence. Her mole cheek was only inches from my face. I hadn't planned on lying, but I refused to be on the short end of this exchange. The last thing I needed was some average woman girl looking at me like a failure. I continued to not lick her cheek.

"Well, if you find yourself wanting to talk, I'm around." She squeezed my hand and left me alone with the candle.

Everyone had gained weight. The men exuded an air of pride, something in their shoulders. A lot of the weight was muscle, but they were also getting fat. They spoke loudly, pointedly, men who understood the importance of active engagement. I saw hairlines in the early stages of recession. Young men who'd been timid and meek in high school had thickened into something else, some small locus of force, a piece in the whole national project.

I decided to find the sage. I pulled my own Cardinals cap low and watched the ground, knowing if I fell into another exchange I'd end up lying again, and this city was too small to lie without extensive planning. Stuart was alone in the pool house, using one of his credit cards to divvy out a small mound of Talkative.

"Brockman's here," I said, sitting. "There's a group huddled out there who keep laughing. He's smoking a cigar and talking about his job in Chicago. What does he do?"

"He sells," Stuart said quickly, "he's in sales."

"What does he sell?"

"I have no idea. Does it matter?"

"I would like it to matter."

"Well, I'm sure he knows what he sells." Stuart looked up. "That's the important thing when you're in sales."

"A product," I said. "He sells a product."

"Or not. Let's not assume."

"People say he's been getting laid like some feral mammal."

"Have you seen his car? He's leasing one of these tiny European coupe things with reflective oversize rims. He picks up dates in his little sex car and takes them out to dinner. He steers the conversation and tips the valet and the women basically fall home with him as if to gravity. His routine could be bottled." Stuart leaned over the square mirror on the coffee table, snorted, and sat immediately up. "Quickly now. Describe the last place you and Audrey had sex."

"Her room. Once all her paintings and photographs and furniture were already packed. Just us, sheets, bed, and alarm clock."

"Was it: A, good; B, okay; C, awkward; or D, something you both knew was a bad idea but felt like had to happen for some sort of closure?"

"I wouldn't say closure. The whole nature of this three-week plan is counterclosure. Awkward, yes. But okay overall. I wouldn't say good."

"Quickly still: list all items of your clothing currently in Audrey's possession."

"In Europe? Or in Portland?"

"Quicker."

"My red hoodie. My blue zip-up hoodie. A bunch of bootie socks. Who knows what else."

"Your socks fit Audrey."

"Sort of," I said.

"This is all very important information, thank you."

I wondered how long Stuart had been in here with the credit card. I sat still and watched him rub his thighs and dart eyes around the room while in the kitchen someone deployed a sequence of words into a cell phone, some foreign code, and outside through the French doors I saw Edsel Denk bounce and lift into the air. Moments later his bearded face emerged from the water slowly, seductively, Marlow or whatever his name is in *Apocalypse Now*. I leaned myself over the mirror and partook.

"Remember the timid Brockman?" Stuart asked. "The one who cried when he got cut from freshman basketball? He drove a beige Corolla."

"I want documentation of the change. Psychological time-lapse."

"Go on interviews," he said. "Find a business that's hiring. Consult. Make money and get laid."

"I could have gone home with a girl from AP Bio. She said something charming about television and I made up a story about my mom dying. Why did I do that?"

"Then you take a guy like Edsel Denk," Stuart said. "You want laid, he's got it down to a perverse science. The anti-Brockman. No money, no dinners, just this evil and stratospheric duende."

"What is he doing here, Stubes? Why is he at your pool?"

"There are two rules for the pool, Potter. No glassware outside and no pissing me off. Edsel comes from time to time because he believes in what's going on here. He is interested in the dynamic, as we all are. I'm not going to exclude him because of his history with women, particularly yours."

"He's an asshole," I said.

"That's accurate, yes. A remarkable asshole."

Outside, people continued to enjoy each other's company. They bummed smokes and flashed smiles and gently leaned into one another as if not from longing but subtle shifts in the earth's tilt. It was all right there, right outside the French doors. Nothing was stopping me from developing a smoking habit. I knew how to smile. And yet all I wanted was to bury myself in the backyard.

"I have to get some sleep."

"That's right." Stuart pulled out his small Baggie, twist-tied and full of white. "Good luck with that."

three

The house, my family's ever-expanding house designed expressly with comfort in mind, remained, for me, a place devoid of comfort. When my father wasn't away on business I made rigorous efforts to avoid being at home with both parents at once. It was when we were three that everything became tightly cautious and liminal: a house caught in that momentary silence between inhale and ex. I was perhaps losing weight, a result of my unwillingness to sit down with them to dinner. Of course they said nothing of this. Unlike Audrey's family, where incidental guilts were traded among siblings and parents like some base form of currency, the more valuable wrongdoings hoarded and treated as investments, our little home's guilt resources had been so thoroughly exhausted by the loss of Freddy that we seemed, perhaps, above it?

Yet there was still the comfort issue. So in an effort to redefine my relationship with the house, I had begun contributing a few basic, menial chores to its upkeep. Each morning I smoothed and realigned the sheets I'd lashed at during the night. I went from room to room, emptying trash baskets into one large bag I placed into a squirrel-proofed metal can in a corner of the garage. I moved among framed photographs with a spray bottle of Windex and a roll of high-quality paper towels. I switched off lights not in use.

And still I could not sleep.

Television was supposed to help. I spread myself out across the couch and searched for some sputtering drama to lull me into unconsciousness. Here were multiracial children discussing breakfast cereal. Here was a demonically gorgeous model molesting a can of light beer. And here was aerial flyby footage of a nexus of buildings surrounded by expansive parking lots. A deep man voice was echoed by a feminine whisper.

> MAN: Prepare yourself for the arrival of the New
>   West County.
> WOMAN: Prepared yet?
> MAN: The Missouri Valley's premier hub of
>   entertainment and emporia, where all
>   shopping unites beneath one luxurious roof.
> WOMAN: A beautiful *beautiful* roof.

Fish-eye shots of fountains spewing from the ground floor toward the ceiling, computer renderings of a crowded food court, all sleek-lined and reflective. Towering palms sprouting from huge clay pots.

> MAN: You have to be there to believe it.
> WOMAN: Be there.
> MAN: Believe it.
> WOMAN: September first. Will you be there?

Upstairs in bed, I listened to things I couldn't see. Air conditioner. Branches against windows. Squirrels in the attic. Soon I heard my mother in the kitchen and recalled that she had her own trouble sleeping when my father was away, and this seemed a nice kind of family tie. I went to the bathroom and drank a glass of water, another, then went back to bed and tried to fall asleep.

At 2:46 I developed an erection, one of these that materialize out of thin air, reversing the natural order of erectile cause and effect—that generate, rather than signify, arousal. Boredom boner. Math class boner. The animal sounds skittered above me and I rolled onto my side.

Two unfamiliar naked bodies zipped into a shared sleeping bag, growing rapidly acquainted. Everyone else could have been on Jupiter. Audrey was from Portland—Oregon, she said, not Maine. I admitted being unaware there even was a Portland, Maine, and in return she admitted she probably couldn't pick Missouri out of a crowd of two. This was honesty, bedrock. She was the baby, with an older brother and sister who shielded her like a secret. An extremely tight family, she said, friendship and safety, yes, very tight indeed. I milked details and hung on words and committed names to memory: brother Brandon in med school and sister Caroline in business school. Obstetrician father Doug and cardiologist mother Marilynne. Audrey couldn't imagine what it must have been like growing up an only child.

"It was . . . What was it? Lonely sometimes. But at the same time you always feel special, like you're the point of everything."

"Ooh. Dangerous," she said, then laughed, and the sound of it I also committed to memory, fearing the chance I might never hear it again.

Sex driven by what I could only call *portent*. Nighttime sky immense and distant, two sleeping bags zipped together, hard earth surely somewhere below us though we no longer had any knowledge of or use for it, she ran fingers across my hairline. Curled into my shoulder and, in that bedtime voice I came to love, then tremble beneath, then eventually react to with nothing but confusion, added, "Can't believe I just did it with a stranger."

"Yeah," I whispered back, "did it."

I stood from bed and put on shorts and shoes, a T-shirt to keep the mosquitoes off my chest. Downstairs, I thought briefly of my mother back there, alone and restless in her own bed. Except now I realized my father wasn't out of town. To avoid even momentary consideration of this development, I rushed through the front door, leaving it unlocked, wondering if I should have put on socks.

I walked in the middle of the street, moving clockwise around the neighborhood's loop. The pavement beneath my feet was smooth and black and recently tarred. My plan was to pound memory out of my head, beat it senseless and move on.

For me the cheating might have germinated in something as simple as tradition, the oldest and most habitual example of human weakness, our mundane inability to find happiness inside what we have. But never for a second did I feel consciously unhappy, so my own explanation felt more complicated than these and was further compounded by disgust for the very redundancy of the whole thing.

And whatever scant sense this made remained the best I could possibly do. Headlights gave me a carnival shadow. A station wagon passed me on the left.

This was the break between sophomore and junior years. We had spent much of the previous vacations making various trips east and west, more camping and more driving, guest rooms in parents' homes, two hands reaching over voids to pull the other across. Some of this was fear, yes, acknowledged out loud by us both. The normal caution of two people who have found something very right and dread the catastrophe of its loss. The normal doubts of our love's fortitude in the face of the normal selfish impulses. So it was perhaps as a test of strength that we had each semi-passively developed a separate agenda for this second summer. I'd given in to the idea of an INTERNSHIP, a word I ran into everywhere, something meaty and real with a PR firm that required a tie and taught me the value of coffee. I was certain this was a good idea. Her own plan, involving Spokane, Washington, and work as an ecological watchdog, felt just as certain, and the thought after two effortless years was that distance meant trial, and trial meant strength, and strength meant, among other things, health. And so: we would be apart.

About midway through the summer, I ran into a girl at Stuart's pool whom I remembered from a neighboring high school, a girl taller and blonder than Audrey who drank like a sink drain and wore this blood-red minimal tank top thing with one tiny strap that kept falling off her shoulder. Audrey was too pretty for me; everyone I spoke to agreed with me on this. In defense I always thought of myself as the smarter one, even in the face of staggering counterevidence. This blond girl was not pretty. But she was attending Denison, or maybe DePauw or it could have been Kenyon, and all other factors equal, nothing brings two people together like a shared sense of missing out.

"Football games with cheerleaders," she said. "A short balding guy waving a huge flag."

"Rabid bands of fraternity guys burning couches after a big win," I said. "Or loss. Either way. Guys who leap at any opportunity to ignite something big and inert."

"Or dating," she said, and sipped from my beer. "There's no dating at a small school. It's either you're with this person, or you're not with him. *With*. Like welded onto."

Audrey had begun speaking vaguely about a nascent interest in health, basically of all sorts, and there was apparently more cancer in Spokane than there should have been. Before and after what happened with the blonde, Audrey and I spoke on the phone roughly every three days, and no conversation felt long enough.

During these I found words and made sure to believe them before I spoke: "Places on my body I didn't realize were linked to emotions. My elbow, I think of you and my elbow hurts."

"I like this." Audrey's voice *warm* through the cool plastic of phone. "Keep going."

"There is a paradox here. Because the only way to offset the pain of missing you is to think of you even more. Your image is the only thing capable of easing the pain of your image. I think of the breakfast we had at that little airport diner after you kept me up all night. Your hair up in a bandanna, only one earring."

"Your fault up all night. *Your* fault only one earring. How could I sleep after that? How could I let you sleep after doing that with me?"

"We are in a state of total sexual exhaustion. You are sitting at the table stirring your coffee. The planes are to my left. You lift the coffee with both hands to blow across its surface, I see the two rings on your right hand, and your lips pinch into a shape like an animal home or cave opening. And I watch closely while you watch me, and you blow out, and I imagine crawling in and exploring. Then you do the wink and I nearly die."

"Potter, tell me again you love me."

"I love you," I said.

"You don't have to say it every time I ask."

"I know that," I said.

"Tell me again," she said, and I did.

But look. There I am on the couch of Stuart's pool house, and here is the admittedly not beautiful blond girl in the red tank. She has the shoulders and neck and body of all women. She is another woman. People are going home and she is leaning, pressing a hand into the leather cushion and saying:

"You probably shouldn't sleep on this couch."

"My skin," I explained. "It sticks every time I roll over."

"What you should probably do is drive me home. I'm staying in my parents' basement. You should see it. My mom just had it redone like an apartment down there."

I parked two driveways down from her house. We ducked through a basement door into a room dark as punctuation, with the dank smell of sustained moisture, and all I could think was *BE QUIET,* like as long as we didn't make a sound everything would be just fine. We stumbled onto her bed and went straight for the middles, no respect for nicety. On my way back to the car I stopped, curled, and puked violently into the hedge, which I suppose lent a taste of realism.

Having completed one loop around my parents' neighborhood, I began a second. I was going to walk until I'd barely make it up the steps to my room, drag my sorry frame up there, and fall immediately asleep. Squirrels or no, eventually insomnia had to yield to exhaustion. I walked faster.

A month later we were back at school, together in Audrey's room. The internship was over and people in Spokane continued to have cancer. How hard would it be to pretend nothing had changed?

"Tell me something," she said, threading arms through a shirt.

I ran a hand up her thigh and spoke truthfully. "I missed you so much there was a texture to it. I could palpate and feel myself missing you." I reached up and lifted her shirt.

Little pieces of my running shoes reflected the streetlamps, and this, for some reason, made me walk even faster.

I had never known true guilt, never known even a diluted version to hold up to what I felt once I was back at school. And the experience of guilt was more worrisome than the fear of the guilt's origin coming to light, was worse for its utter complexity and richness of feeling and certain sort of beauty. This would become occasion for great internal turmoil, that the guilt felt richer even than what I called love. But of course if not for the love the guilt wouldn't be guilt, it would be only a sense of achievement, however minor.

But the real *poetry* of it all was housed in the fact that Audrey, too, had cheated that summer. With a man named Jim. She allowed Jim to stick his dirty hippie penis into her precious and private vagina. Jim who continued to exist in my mind, as I walked without growing tired, as a thick, tall, curly-haired beaver man in broken-down sandals and a perpetual three-day beard.

We passed months at school before anything became known. Into October. I awoke those mornings in her flowered sheets, angled into her vacated half of the bed. She would be at class or out jogging or really wherever, and my eyes would come into focus on the things that defined her: the raggedy bear without a nose or ears; framed pictures of her with brother and sister, the dock of

some lake, pictures of her parents in their youth, pictures of the
five of them, their own little private army, on Christmas morning; her clothes scattered madly across everything at all.
Computer up there on her desk. Windows open.

On the third lap I switched from brisk walk to slow jog. A man
in a bathrobe hustled from his house to a Mercedes in the driveway, rummaged by dome light through the front seat, then
turned and sprinted back inside. The house's automatic lights
stayed on for a few moments, a footprint in wet sand. I kept jogging.

Somewhere is a doctorate thesis waiting to be written on how
many times a given person can confront an open e-mail in-box
before personal ethics and respect for privacy defer to animal cu-
riosity. Or to suspicion born from guilt. Plus, if I wanted to check
my own e-mail while at Audrey's, on the chance that say a *class-
mate* or *professor had written me*, it meant I had to first sign out of
hers. And hers was open. There. Still naked, I moved from bed to
her desk chair, and there they were: a series of messages from *out-
doorjim71*. Cool sweat, the sweat of panic as I scrolled down the
page. In ten minutes I had read them all, roughly twenty messages from Jim. Who tested soil pH and loved the earth mother.
Who spoke of the nights around the fire and the guitar he played
for her. Who *wrote songs for her*. Hippie asshole Jim, who claimed
to love and cherish my Audrey in ways that far eclipsed the
amount of time they'd spent together.

I still still wasn't wasn't tired.

Audrey sits cross-legged on top of the bed I made after discov-
ering the reality of this Jim hippie fuck. I stand by the door.

"Love? He *loves* you? Two months in the forest and this guy
tosses around *love* like some what, like Frisbee? Some glowstick?"

"This is my computer. These, all of these, are *my* messages."

"You are an evil, evil woman."

"Potter? Did you see what I wrote back? Nothing! Because that's
what it meant, all of it. I swear to you, I *swear* it on everything I

have. My family, Potter. My life. I don't know why. Please don't make me say why or how or what. I'm sorry, lover. I'm sorry. I'm sorry."

I open her door and scream into the hallway, "Evil!"

Shapeless colors behind shut eyes, rage. Slammed the door twice and stared. She sat still, legs crossed, breathing through her nose. Same spot in the middle of the bed, she hadn't moved. Oh, she waved a hand and shook her head, her face twisted into some highly specific version of grief tempered by dismay at my invasion of privacy. The pressure at the base of my throat, rage, my esophagus massaging a swallowed mouse, and I could imagine my own face's exact mixture, rage castrated by immoral symmetry, and all I wanted was for the world to be angry, purely and simply.

And so I told her.

"You FUCK," she yelled, and *now* she stood and pointed and repeated her charge for some time. I began slamming her door again. Soon she dropped the *you,* leaving only a series of *fuck*s ringing over the sound of the door.

"You!" I reminded her. "You! You!"

Before I could begin a fourth lap I was stopped by a series of white arcs drawn in the neighbors' yard, dozens of unfurled white banners. They came from nowhere and trailed across house and grass, up into and through trees. I inched forward and saw dark figures moving efficiently through the lawn, launching rolls of toilet paper into the air, waiting, then launching them again. I admired their stealth. When my friends and I had done this, noise had always been our downfall. We could never suppress the hubbub of mischief and adolescent nerves. These kids were silent. Determined. The prank had evolved, grown more severe, and I was relieved to see it in such capable hands.

At some point that night at school, when we were too tired to go on, all the *fuck* and *you*s changed to *sorry.* It made sense; the fight was doomed from the start, constrained and defeated by its own parameters. We screamed and screamed, then crumpled on the bed like two dirty tissues. For a while, neither of us was willing to make a move. Then I touched a single finger to one of her toes.

"I am," I said. "I *am* sorry."

"Now what?" she asked. "What's left? Who's the asshole?"

"Come here. Just here."

"No. No. You come here," she said. "You come closer."

One of the teenagers spotted me and communicated with the others in a signal I didn't catch, but slowly the rolls of toilet paper came to rest. There were only four of them, four boys, though with their efficiency it had seemed twice as many. They exchanged nervous looks and it occurred to me that they'd come here because of the youngest Hoyne, the neighbor daughter who by now must have been in high school. I approached the closest kid and saw a face equal parts wholesome rebellion and magnificent fear. For a second I seriously considered punching him, to see if the other three would rush to his aid and beat me enough that I'd finally get some rest. The kid breathed loudly through a mouth ruled by braces. I reached out and we engaged in a prolonged handshake, long enough that by its end rolls of toilet paper flew again, leaving hygienic white trails that scaled trees and striped across the yard. I crossed back to my parents' driveway and sat with my back against a tire of the 4Runner, hoping the kids would keep going through the night.

The lack of worthwhile rest began to complicate my interactions with the world. At times I delved into a fugue state and corners went fuzzy, objects floated by with no apparent destination. I grew suspicious of just about everything, including the queasy awareness that somebody knew me well enough to forecast within seconds when I'd want to eat breakfast. I began instituting little tests of my mother's timing. One morning I stalled upstairs

after brushing my teeth. This was no problem for her. The following morning I essentially sprinted from my bed to the
kitchen, only to find her at the stove, angling the frying pan,
toast-eggs sliding onto a plate. She was unflappable.

I waited until she was outside in her garden, then began
searching through the cabinets below the phone. I moved my
search outward, eventually going through every cabinet in the
kitchen. I wanted the Yellow Pages, and this much was good: to
want. Frustrated, I moved to the new computer room. And there
it was on the desk, displayed as if the Yellow Pages were the
whole purpose for building the new room. I split it open and
turned to *temporary employment,* picked the largest ad, then called
a small one next to it.

"We accept walk-ins any day of the week," the woman explained. "We're here 'til five."

"You mean today? I expected some sort of wait. Maybe I
should make an appointment for later in the week."

"Walk-in only. Thank you for choosing ProTemps."

I dug through a still-unpacked duffel to find my olive-green
pants, a wrinkled white shirt, and the cleaner of the two ties I
owned. I found my dress shoes and a pair of black socks from my
father's dresser. It took six tries to get the tie right.

Stuart phoned during my drive. "What is the worst injury either of you sustained in the presence of the other?"

"I broke a finger one night. Tripped over a bush."

"Broken finger. Good. Afterward, did she care for you: A, ten-
derly; B, fairly; C, politely; or D, rudely?"

"She said I was an idiot for trying to steal a security golf cart.
Then I don't know. B? Which one was B?"

"Very good, Poot. That's all I need for now."

A woman behind glass slid me a clipboard with a pen attached
by twine. I dropped it, picked it up, and took a seat between a
teenage Latino kid with slick hair and a thirty-something black
woman in purple stockings. The fourth of us was a young white

girl, no older than me. She bit at her lip in concentration, pen in one hand while the other gently rocked a baby carrier in the next seat. I turned in the forms and was given a second clipboard, along with a small, solar-powered calculator. This was a rudimentary problem set of arithmetic and basic geometry I sped through without the help of the calculator. Clipped behind that was an alphabetization quiz. I worked rapidly, impatient to secure some sort of labor. I was ushered into a back room where I sat at a computer and typed a passage as quickly and accurately as I could, something about a woman named Sandra and sales projections. I was sent back into the waiting room. I found huge satisfaction in this evaluation; the whole sequence of movement and tasks was just what I needed. After a short wait, I was led through a door, down a short hallway, and shown into an even smaller room with one desk, a ficus, and two framed pictures hanging on colorless walls. The first showed a long bone-white beach, electric-blue ocean rippling onto the shore, *Acapulco!!* bright red in the sky. The other was puppies crawling out of a picnic basket in a field.

A short beefy man with a very big nose stood behind the desk and gestured for me to sit. I crossed my legs professorially and interlocked my fingers over my knee. I could feel my face bright with accomplishment. The nameplate on his desk said *Alex Doggerty*.

"Potter Mays."

"Here I am," I said.

"Well, great. Let's get right at it, shall we? I've got your test scores here, Mr. Mays. Tell me, what sort of work were you looking for?"

"I'm not sure," I said. "That's why I came here."

"Good, Potter. We're glad you did. No need to panic whatsoever. At ProTemps we pride ourselves on the ability to find work for everyone, from the highest skilled down to those we call 'legs' or 'hands.' So you have nothing to worry about. Now before we begin, is there any chance at all that you might have, accidentally or on purpose, either way, any chance that you shall we say embellished your educational background?"

"None chance," I said, and he made a note, looked at me, and made another note.

"Okay then. That's terrific. Let's have a look." He opened and spun the file so I could read it. "We'll begin with the math. Not your strongest suit, but I'm sure you knew that by now. Incorrect answers are marked in red."

The paper looked like it had been mauled. Nearly every problem was marked incorrect, blood-red lines scrawled from top to bottom. And worse, upon further review they actually were incorrect. Long division, multiplication, simple subtraction; I had failed awesomely.

"Also, there are a few hiccups with the alphabetization," he said, and I'll give him this much, the word *alphabetization* caused him no trouble at all. "Here you've got Peterson in front of Parvenik? And here, on the one-through-ten sequencing. You put the four next to Kennison, the five next to Jacobs, and the six next to Harris."

The puppies in the grass tussled with their gleeful little puppy snouts. I was almost sure Alex's tie was a clip-on. He tapped his pen on the desk and held a steady grin.

"But typing, my goodness. Seventy words per. That's something, I should say. Something." His voice went flat.

"I wrote," I said, "a lot of papers in college."

"Ah yes. Of course." Holding his pen like some brand-new and intimidating piece of technology, he scribbled a note on the pad of paper in front of him. "We're going to find you work, Mr. Mays. You might not believe it now, but I promise. And though basic knowledge of arithmetic and the alphabet is crucial to most office work we staff, that doesn't mean we won't succeed in placing you in a just great job. So keep that head up, alright, hoss?"

I remembered something.

"I believe *hoss*, Alex, came into usage as a bastardization of horse."

"That's great!" He stood and extended a hand. "Thank you for choosing ProTemps. We'll be in touch just as soon as something comes up."

I shook as firmly as I could, then turned and carefully left his office. I walked with both hands out in front of me, completely distrustful of my spatial relationship to earthly objects. The baby was staring and the secretary was quite possibly laughing as I sped through the office, back out into the spiteful glare of an impossible and disastrous summer day.

four

Several days later I came home to find a second package waiting on the kitchen island. White box, flat and rectangular, sent from abroad. *Par avion.* I shook it and listened. I set it down and glared at it. My mother entered through the side door, her hands caked with dark brown earth and face like birthday candle flame, a shade of red stretching well beyond this single moment.

"Sonny boy. That came for you today."

She went to the sink to wash her hands. My mother's feelings for Audrey were less than clear. The natural wish to see her only son made happy set against the stealthy undercurrents of rivalry, and the protective factor, the inevitable distrust. With my father it was perfectly simple: he liked Audrey. Adored her. That first dinner together, all the questions he had prepared for her, and how his face alit at every question she offered back. From that first visit between freshman and sophomore years, Audrey was exceedingly good at this. She knew to ask about the additions to the house and to ask about law, funnel what she knew of public health into a series of questions about first Richard's legal practice, then about *SLH!* once he took over as director. And she knew enough to never ever ask about Freddy.

I watched my mother use the small brush to get underneath her nails. Now she handed me a steak knife and stood on the other side of the island. She could, if she so chose, stand there

forever. I cut through one end of the box and removed a single
rectangular object encased in bubble wrap.

"A picture," she said.

Dammit, she was right. A picture of the two of them outside
a beautiful European chateau on top of a hill above this green-
yellow tableau of trees and hills and fields and far far in the background the gray pinprick of a farmhouse. The whole scene
illuminated through Jesus Christ cloud break, just so nicely beautiful it might have been painted. The picture was set in a hand-
carved frame of some dark ancient wood, intricate squiggles and
beautiful tiny flowers. I examined closely the setting, the margins
between chateau and sky, looking for signs of forgery or en-
hancement. But the colors were real. Scenery: real. Girls: beautiful. And one of them: bisexual.

My mother found her reading glasses. "Who is that with
Audrey?"

"Carmel," I said.

"She's very pretty," she said.

"Yes," I said. "And a robot."

Before Audrey and Carmel's friendship, I knew Carmel as
everyone else knew her, the gorgeous and lithe girl from Long
Island, olive-skinned and enchantingly standoffish. She spent that
first year running through boy-men, obliterating them. I saw
three of my personal friends fall by her hand, crumble into pathetic heaps and then take months and more to claw their way
upright. Women, once her interest in women became known,
fared no better. She was not wicked and she was not cruel. She
was not governed by malice. All she was was immune to what
anyone might call humanity. She was a robot.

The photograph's subject was more the terrain than the girls,
but the delicacy by which they'd been set toward the bottom
right corner was worrisome. For someone had taken this picture,
some person with whom I was now irrevocably linked, the photo-
taker a surrogate me, and I surrogate him. Or her. Or him.

Audrey's other friendships remained loose affairs with little given or taken. She had her family at home and me in her bed. By the spring of sophomore year, Carmel had become the third. For a time I had to remind myself that Audrey having a friend this close was a good thing. But there was something almost promising about this variety of selfishness. Clutching at her like a boy in a sandbox unwilling to share his favorite toy, I demonstrated my love. Add to this the manner in which we moved on from the cheating, confident, recklessly confident, and were made *stronger for the experience*. Mounting evidence that this, Us, was to be celebrated. Later, once things between us were descending into something not very good at all, I would think back to my reluctance to accept her nascent friendship with tousle-haired Carmel, razor-blue-eyed robot, and wonder what I might have seen then, briefly, before my eyes fell shut in the peace of alleged love.

"Well, it's a thoughtful gift," my mother said, and went into her bathroom to shower. I continued to examine the picture, searching for either a flaw or message within the shapes. Ten minutes later she came back to the kitchen and began rummaging through the freezer for pieces of things to turn into that night's meal. I was still looking at the picture.

"There's plenty of food, son, if you'd like to eat at home tonight?"

"Yeah. Think I might."

I took a seat at the kitchen counter and watched her move from stove to fridge to cabinets, opening the oven to check on the chicken. Carla's cooking was simple but rewarding, the sort that succeeded by sheer repetition and basic heartiness. Thawed boneless chicken breasts in simple sauce. Croissants that burst from within cardboard tubing when she unpeeled the wrapper. These meals contributed to my sense of our wealth as a bit junior-varsityish. It was also partially geographical—we were privy to neither that snobbish entitlement of the Northeast's aristocracy nor the whimsical grandeur of California's recent rich. Nor did our wealth have the history and blemish of the South's. Like St. Louis itself, we had our heels planted fast in the soil of the middle ground.

Not that my father had ever failed to work as hard as he possibly could for his salary. He was the director of *St. Louis Hooray!*, a publicly funded consulting project conceived to revitalize, invigorate, and elevate the city of St. Louis back onto the national stage—what amounted to nothing short of a metropolitan makeover. Before that he'd spent thirty years at the law firm of Cave-Bryant-Newman, which would have been Cave-Bryant-Newman-Mays had he not asked to remain silent in his partnership. He took a junior position with the firm immediately out of law school and, with steady and dutiful grit, ascended. Under the aegis of former Missouri Senator John L. Dunleavy, *SLH!* selected my father as their founding director for his deep local roots and unfaltering dedication to the city's future. Born in South City to German parents, skin and soul toughened by the rigor of immigrant life in Middle America and the early loss of his father to cardiac arrest, Richard's story was one of real trial and actual hardship, a protracted struggle to MAKE ENDS MEET. He won scholarships to the University of Missouri and Washington University Law School. His mother succumbed to breast cancer within a week of his passing the bar, at which point he watched two younger brothers depart for coastal pastures, one to Boston, the other to Charleston. Through it all, Richard Mays remained. He'd never worked a job out of state and had dedicated himself to the city he loved deeply. Enough to win widespread local respect, even a certain kind of regional fame.

General consensus was that I looked more like my mother.

She maneuvered through her kitchen with almost musical precision, reaching here for this while balancing this over that. Eventually I stood and began opening my own sequence of drawers and cupboards and set out three place settings around the circular glass table in the dining room. I straightened napkins and

made sure the spoon was outside the knife. The house was filling
with the fragrance and sounds of mealtime, vegetable odor, the
clatter of pots, creak of oven door.

My father entered through the side door wearing a gray suit.
Briefcase leaned against wall just inside the new computer room.
Son high-fived, wife kissed on cheek. Tie loosened in a two-step
pull—down, *down*—as habitual as his steps across carpet.

Next the wife, with her own acquired and polished habit: "Day
go well?"

"The day was fine, actually. The meeting with the mayor." A
moment's pause as he seemed to process that I was in the
kitchen. "Three of us tonight? Should I open wine? I should."

The father disappears into master bedroom to Mister Rogers
his shoes, hang the jacket, rack the tie. He moves toward comfort, decompression, release of less permanent cords of tension.
Goes to basement, emerges with bottle, joins wife and only child
in kitchen. Pleasant meal at home with the family.

I filled glasses of water from the tap and carried them to the
table. For a few moments I examined my reflection in the
smudgeless glass, and when I looked up they were upon me, closing inward, bearing serving dishes of chicken and vegetables as
we triangulated ourselves around the circular table. My father
spoke his quiet grace, which I applauded for its elemental role in
the grand ritual, a nicely official starting point. *Amen.*

"I had lunch with Nancy Hoyne today." Carla spoke while
dumping what was surely excessive salt onto her plate. "I didn't
realize Jesse was in town for a few weeks before he heads back to
Northwestern."

I nodded with a full mouth, unsure to whom her comment
was directed. Richard and the Honorable Derrick Hoyne, neighbor, had a history that dated back to high school wrestling. Nancy
was one of my mother's few still-married friends. Their son,
Jesse, was an outrageous prick and engaged to a former J. Crew
or some such model, some cute, small-faced New Englander.

Then there was the daughter, a blond pigtailed little girl I'd always glared at out of totally unfair association with her brother.

"Nancy and I both wish your father and Derrick could get over their little disagreement."

"That's what happens, Potter, when you're a judge and sit in that chair all day. How can you be wrong when your chair is so high? Look at their tiny heads down there. They look like ants."

My mother reached again for the salt. I tried to keep track of the things that were being said. Much of what could have been their own private conversation was being channeled through me. I watched my dad take a bite of his chicken. I watched his jaw muscles work. But this feeling of remove allowed me to perceive them in a certain way, a setting-apart of the mother and father so I could more fully honor them, commandment numero five. My mother spoke and I watched her wait for my father's response. Incredibly, our first meal all together since my return, the First Supper, and at some point I would have to offer a contribution of my own. I thought to describe my trip to ProTemps or discuss the sounds from the attic I heard in bed. Or baseball, because there was always baseball, a sport that was perhaps invented by a father in search of something to discuss with his son.

Audrey's fluency in the language of gesture: the way she leaned into a response, closing in like an insect to nectar, eye contact and gentle movements of the head and shoulders, the way she sent cards and handwrote letters and called distant cousins on birthdays, the scarf she learned how to knit to give Carmel. And now the starfish undisturbed in the deep end of Stuart's pool and the photograph of Carmel at the foot of the stairs. Gestures of infinite meanings, codes for which I lacked any key.

"You know, Dad, I realized today I have no idea what's going on with *SLH!*"

But my timing was off, and now he had to hurry to finish chewing.

"Let me ask you a hypothetical, Potter. Imagine you have a job that pays between fifty and seventy-five thousand dollars a year. You are a successful young professional. But your job is not your life. You still enjoy meeting friends at a bar, going to ball games. You are either married or a bachelor."

"So in this fantasy I don't live entirely off the charity of my parents, you're saying."

What I saw on his face might have been a very very subdued and reluctant smile.

"I know for a fact," Carla said, "that whatever you end up doing, you're going to be great at it. What*ever* it is. Could be *any*-thing."

I couldn't believe how much salt. I thought about warning her, but which was salt—heart attack? Or blood pressure? Surely this was my father's responsibility.

"The hope," he said, "is that young people of considerable trend impact will choose to live in an urban environment. This is what we learned from Denver. It comes down to lofts—young adults with disposable income. What a term. Disposable. Right now we're exploring options. Widening sidewalks for outdoor café seating. Planting trees and creating incentives for urban groceries and restaurants. We're considering cobblestoning one or two key streets."

My mother was watching me listen to my father. I instinctively reached for the asparagus. She passed the salt.

"We have a city stacked with empty buildings. There are dozens. Old paper plants, button factories. What we've begun doing is looking at the city from the outside, as a prospective customer or resident. Is it kind of sad to have to sell the city to its own residents? Yes it is kind of sad. But it's also crucial, because if we continue to let downtown," he paused, "*slide,* then the inner rings of suburbia become threatened, and the movement continues forever outward, to the fringes."

A lot of this sounded familiar.

"These people out there don't understand why their tax dollars should be funneled back downtown. The city is where they go to see baseball, and then they leave. But nobody *has* to leave. Leaving can be undone." Here he set down his fork and began gesturing with his hands, flat, gliding motions over his plate. "The goal is a mixed-use, pedestrian-friendly neighborhood. Downtown doesn't have to die. We're going to pump that place so full of life people aren't going to know what to do about it. There will be people and life on every corner, there will be people bumping into one another. There will be life brimming from the streets, everyone watching each other live. People will wave and say hello. It will not die. It will *not*."

The table was quiet. I tried to focus on knife in fowl, fowl in sauce, fowl and sauce coming on fork toward mouth.

"What's really neat is the level of control," Carla explained. "With a loft you can say where you want the walls. Imagine that: *wall here, please. Bathroom over here, if you don't mind*. One catalog I saw offered six different models of sliding glass doors."

I was eating and having a conversation with my parents, under whose roof I was once again living. They'd been married for thirty-some-odd years. Their anniversary, like all anniversaries, was in the summer. Look at the posture, the nonverbal cues, notice the tone of words. Consider the ramifications these variables imply. Take extensive notes.

There was an entire family of squirrels living in the attic. I heard them up there, a cluttered, domestic scampering directly above my head. A family of squirrels, each one with its funny little character traits. Mom clad in apron, dad in bowler hat, little vest, daughter squeaking on tiny little squirrel cell phone, son pushing around on miniature skateboard.

Sadly, this was all I had. Because if days were tough, these sleepless nights were a kind of Audrey multimedia carnival. I saw our past charted graphically, four years' worth of colored bars

and slices of pie. I saw emotions as historical artifacts, their gene-
sis and evolution, eventual conflict and abatement. Initially I'd
fallen for the farthest reaches of her extremities—tips of fingers,
those half spheres of gentle skin behind forever unpainted nails—
then worked my way inward. By the time I made it beyond her
calves and forearms, thighs and shoulders, and reached her center, it was clear she felt the same. She ran fingers over my childish
frame and smiled.

You try to sleep, then try not to try to sleep, then try not to try
to remember what you're trying. You sweat and rage and fume
over the fact of your sweating, raging, fuming.

The incidentals came at me from all angles and with shocking
resolution. A particular trip to the Ralphs on Indian Hill when
Audrey stopped among the vegetables and reached down and
wrapped her fingers around a rubber-banded bundle of asparagus and brought it up to her ear, listened, laid it right back down.
As if trying to get a sense of where the asparagus was coming
from. The trip to the twenty-four-hour Toys "R" Us by the outlet
malls in Rancho Cucamonga when, during a frowned-upon race
through the aisles on little pink girl bikes, I stopped briefly to
check out a reissue of Optimus Prime, then had to pedal furiously to catch up to her. It was the pedaling furiously I remembered, how hard I had to work.

And oh Jesus that *noise*. Even when the squirrels were at rest
there was another sound, this awful like *tap* or *pat* from somewhere up there with the squirrels, in apparently the busiest goddamn attic this side of the Mississippi. Sex everywhere we could
manage it, exploring campus nooks and crannies. Put your foot
here. Hold this. The study lounge of her dormitory, carpeted.
Later that week we lay naked in bed, fan blowing, Audrey pressing a finger against the twin rug burns on my knees. Pain and joy.
Memories arrived with perfect lucidity and a fondness that
worked like some inverse torture. Sharing a table in the library,
studying, she reached across and pushed my copy of *Franny and*

Zooey to the floor. I retaliated with her *City of Quartz*. One by one until all of our books stacked into a beautiful interdisciplinary pile. Our ridiculous laughter.

Like some kind of godshit squirrel *carnival* up there. I went to the hallway closet that accessed the attic. Tossed winter coats and slid boxes of Christmas decorations into the hall. I lowered the ladder and stared up into the black black black above. Scared. There was a light switch, but it was upstairs in the middle of that darkness, which now seemed absolutely idiotic. Squirrels, I thought, squirrels *bite* and carry *disease*. Everyone knows this. I was wearing boxer shorts and nothing else. I climbed the ladder and stood with my shoulders and head through the trapdoor, listening for signs of squirrels. Nothing. Minutes passed, and I climbed the last few rungs until I was fully and completely in the attic.

From the inside, darkness isn't as dark. My eyes adjusted quickly to the light from the only window. Boxes were stacked in awkward piles that looked like they might fall at any moment. Here was the only room in the house untouched by my mother's decoration, the structure in its raw state. Planks for floor, walls and ceiling of poofy insulation. This was my family's attic, an explosion of data. I wondered what could possibly be inside all the boxes. I inhaled and panned from one wall to the other and back again.

There was somebody sitting on a box. A person. He was shirtless and shoeless, wearing a bathing suit and water wings. He was sopping wet and dripping onto the floor. And he was feeding squirrels.

"If you're going to stare like that this isn't going to work do you understand."

Low and steady, his voice sounded like someone translating words into English that had just recently been translated into some other language, from English. I nodded several times in succession.

"I'm worried about you," he said. "You used to be so smart and composed and now look at you you're a mess. These furry guys will spend all night long with you if you're holding food look see how they're waiting for me they will wait all night."

I moved a step toward him. The attic smelled like trapped breath. Freddy was in perfectly adequate shape, not fat and not skinny. He looked to have ten pounds on me, no more. But what distinguished him as a character was the authority with which he sat on that box and fed the squirrels. He had a motorcyclist's ease about him, a formal serenity that gave the impression of someone who knew precisely what was what. I took him seriously—this despite the bright orange water wings around his arms.

"I have advice to give you if you want it I don't know if it will help," he said.

"You're Freddy," I said idiotically.

There was no doubt that this was my dead brother, grown. Age twenty-seven, a spitting image of my father. He sat on a box with his elbows pressed against his thighs, bent forward, holding what looked like a dinner roll. Five squirrels waited motionless at his feet.

"I've been waiting to give you advice and now you're finally here."

"Do you mind if I sit?"

"Sit if you want but please don't stare it's not polite to stare."

I sat a few boxes over, and for the next several minutes that was it. I sat on the box and he fed the squirrels and I had a brother. I tried to steal glances in directions I hoped he wouldn't notice. *Older brother,* mine. I looked at his bare wet feet and followed his legs up to his knees and elbows, gliding over the water wings to his forearms and hands.

"I'm being serious if you insist on staring I'll have to leave I mean it."

"Sorry," I said, and looked to the floorboards.

"I expected you would come up here sooner that was the

whole point of the squirrels you know but instead you stayed down there and suffered why didn't you just come up to see?"

"I was hoping they'd go away on their own," I said.

His hands and fingers were thin and pruny, *waiflike*. The squirrels scurried when he broke a piece of bread from the roll and dropped it to them. The drip off his wet shorts was a steady pulse of taps, taps.

"You don't want to stay up here all night so I guess I could give you the advice now if you want but really I mean it's not very good don't get your hopes up."

"I need advice badly," I said. "Please give me advice."

"Okay." He threw the rest of the dinner roll to the squirrels. "First don't smoke because it will kill you quicker than you could ever imagine."

I watched the squirrels watching him and felt him watching me.

"Alright," I said. "Good."

"Second don't take Richard or Carla for granted because they are amazing parents and before you know it they will be dead."

"But I don't take them for granted," I said.

"You're lying you don't appreciate all you do is watch. One of the things that happens when you die is you can tell who's lying and who's not or maybe it's not like this for everyone who dies but it is for me so stop lying and stop watching and start appreciating. Love alright listen love is the issue with them Potter because they love you so much they ache and tremble sometimes because all they've ever wanted was to make this love real to you."

I nodded and looked at Freddy's wet feet.

"Also you I mean *you* Potter should love whomever you can love and love them with your whole complete body throw everything you have into it because there is nothing else that matters."

How was it so simple when he said it? Words layered like scripture over the rhythm of falling water. The older brother from beyond the grave explains the fantastically contrived cult of human emotion in fifty words or less. Simplicity, the *tap tap* of falling water, Freddy sitting in utter, if damp, peace. While I was sick at heart.

I realized that despite his warnings and despite my attempts to honor his wishes, I was staring. First I was staring at him, at the ghostly shiny droplets of water that covered his body. As I stared, the drops began to dry, and I found myself staring more and more through him, past him, at the cardboard boxes of who knew what part of our family history. Freddy, offended by my staring, was gone, gone away with his water wings and advice, leaving behind only a small puddle.

"Shit," I said.

Silence like a cinder block in the middle of a square room. The squirrels watched me, up on their haunches, beady little eyes and mouths aimed into my chest before skittering off into their dark corners.

five

Childhood. My mother's fingernails would brush against my back, light as cork. Break the news of a new day. She scratched long soft lines and my eyes would open and she was there, beaming. Morning, *sonny boy.* How many mornings did she open the shades and then leave, and minutes later call up the stairs to make sure I was getting ready for school? Thousands, more.

Standing in a great green expanse of city park, my father, our dedication to the pursuit of Catch. His glove from high school, supremely brown, *mitt,* he called it, ancient term, stained with years of oil and use. These memories are percussive and word-less. Catch. An occasional apology when my throw sailed out of reach. A knuckleball that defied physics and expectation, unimaginable fatherhood hands. I remember the first halves of car rides home, then the garage door crawling open as I woke with seat belt pressed into my cheek.

Someone must already have noted: memory weighs more at night.

I woke to my mother standing by my bed, clutching the phone.

I sat up quickly. "What's wrong?"

"Wrong? Oh."

What followed was a loaded moment of her looking down at me, either baffled by the question or torn whether or not to answer.

"Is Dad okay?"

She nodded. There was mud packed beneath her fingernails and beads of sweat lining the top of her forehead. The alarm clock said 6:30 in the morning and she had been gardening. I could hear my father in the kitchen. She glanced at the phone to confirm that her hand was covering the mouthpiece.

"Mom?"

"There's a man on the phone for you. I should have asked his name."

I smiled. She smiled. Then she left.

"Hello?"

"Mr. Mays. Exciting news to share."

"I don't know who you are," I said.

"Alex, from ProTemps. This morning I received a request for a set of legs at the Pine Ridge Water Company."

How early, exactly, did everyone else in the world begin their day?

"It's six-thirty."

"Yes it is! Now, Potter, you're to show up at Pine Ridge Water Co's main offices in the Hanley Industrial Park and report to a Ms. Deborah short Debbie Dinkles, who has assured me that the position is not mentally taxing. Dress is casual, allowing for movement. Any questions?"

None. I knew: where to go, when, what to wear, and who to find. I dressed in shorts and running shoes. Breakfast was of course ready in the kitchen.

"I think I just got a job."

The parents locked eyes in some private moment of confirmation. Carla went to open the refrigerator and look inside. The newspaper sat folded open next to my father's breakfast. He was nodding.

"I'm glad to hear it. Good for you."

It didn't appear that my mother was looking for anything in particular, just standing upright in the open door, wet with early-morning sweat.

"What did you find?" he asked.

"No clue." I dipped toast into runny egg yolk. "Something at the Pine Ridge Water Company."

"Good for you. I'm glad to hear it."

It was a minute before my mother shut the refrigerator and stepped away with the makings for three miniature sandwiches, which she handed to me by the front door with a small smile and a series of blinks. Thank you.

At Pine Ridge, I was surprised to find myself ushered into the small office of Debbie Dinkles, president of the company, where I sat and listened attentively. I kept my hands folded in my lap and maintained eye contact. Debbie was a thin, anxious woman who hotched around as she spoke, rearranging papers on the desk and constantly adjusting her chair. Pine Ridge delivered five-gallon bottles of water in three grades, Purified, Natural Spring, and Premium. They had a crew of drivers to handle daily delivery routes, but they needed someone to pick up the extra orders they expected as a response to their Summer Special promotion. Three complimentary bottles along with a free month of cooler rental: a trial offer that expired after a month, at which point normal billing would commence automatically. I would potentially drive a van, installing coolers and bottles for new customers.

"The question is," she said, pushing a bowl of M&M's across the desk, "can I trust you? Are you a reliable and hard worker?"

"I believe so, Debbie." I reached for a handful of candy. "Of course, to be totally honest I can't say for sure. I know my father is the single hardest worker I've ever seen. Work is to him what breath is to me. So it would stand to reason that I'd be both reliable. And hard."

"Father." She looked to a file in front of her, which I hoped wasn't the file from ProTemps. "I wondered when they sent this over. I thought, *Mays. I wonder if he's Richard's son?*"

I nodded.

"Richard Mays! The Small Local Business Initiatives. And I can see it in the nose. Of course."

"Dad's great," I said, reaching for the M&M's.

"Then I'll make a copy of your driver's license, okay, and we'll get hopping."

Outside her office, I was given a deep-green parody of a Polo shirt with the company's logo embroidered on the left breast. I met Dennis Looper, a pockmarked delivery manager in his upper forties with anemic gray hair running laterally across his head. He took me along for a day's work and made me follow our progress on a road map in my lap. He showed me how to carry bottles so your hand doesn't fall off. My hand almost fell off. He espoused copious opinions on race, gender, the endemic idiocy of the world. He gave me step-by-step instructions for filling out the invoice, which part you give to the customer, which you keep to file back at the office. He showed me how to calculate sales tax. I was quite obviously an idiot.

And the other drivers, I was pretty sure, hated me. When the day was through, Dennis sat me down in the Pine Ridge lunchroom. Gradually they arrived, middle-age white males trained to operate heavy machinery, skin-hardened men who had license to drive forklifts and four-axle trucks. The drivers worked slowly through their day's paperwork at the wobbly table in the Pine Ridge lunchroom, sharing tired accounts of children and ex-wives, VFW bars and ball games. Adhering to body language I hoped illustrated nonjudgmental interest, I quietly listened to this runoff from a world I'd never known. Insurance premiums were on the rise. A wife's shit-worthless brother kept asking to borrow money. About the crew who worked the warehouse I heard *nigger* and *chocolate,* terms uttered quietly, semi-illicitly. Words my exclusive West Coast liberal arts school would react to with a series of candlelight vigils, silent nighttime marches, and solemn classrooms.

I wasn't sure why I was still there.

When Dennis began speaking to me, I realized he'd waited for the room to fill so he could make a production of it. Smiling, he said he didn't care whose son I was, Jesus H. Christ Himself's for all he cared, first time I showed up late I'd be fired. Grown men with wrinkled faces chuckled and watched. I nodded slowly. He said if I didn't think, if I even thought to have the thought that I couldn't handle all the lifting, then how's about I save us both the trouble and step aside now. The drivers crossed thick arms and leaned back in folding chairs. They murmured and laughed conspiratorially and I felt a new wave of sweat emerge from a million tiny holes. Dennis promised the job would be nine times harder than anything he imagined a still-baby-pudged boy like myself had ever been called upon to do. He said college diploma be damned, you waste my time I'll find a way to take it back from you. *Boy.*

Look hard enough into eyes and you can see through them, glimpse the machinery operating these faces, the classical distaste for untested youth. The squint of judgment, the vacant gaze of absolute indifference, the steely eyes of those gauging privilege. The child sits among men, quivering.

"I don't plan on letting anyone down."

"Then I suggest you pull that ass back here at eight o'clock tomorrow A.M. Prompt."

At home, I found a new package sitting at the foot of the table inside the front door. White and rectangular, no bigger than a shoebox, with one top corner covered in postage and international ink stamps. *Poste Italiane.*

No, no, I would not let this one beat me. This inanimate *box*. Upstairs I set it on the bed while I peeled drenched cotton from my frame. I carried it into the bathroom, closed the toilet lid, and placed the box on top. Then a shower, shock of cold water on

filthy-hot skin, the slowly achieved equilibrium. I dried with a
very soft and very large towel.

I was still naked when I opened the box. I stood in front of the
sink and cut the tape with a nail clipper, then probed inside with a
finger. Counted two objects, smooth and cool and rock solid.
Spheres. There was a note also, which I set aside while I let the
balls roll around my palm and clack together. There was a re-
demptive, simple beauty to these balls—a peacefulness I could
appreciate after a full day of adult labor. They arrested and
calmed.

With the other hand I opened the letter:

> Potter—
>
> I don't believe I know anything right now, but some-
> thing is making me think this trip should be longer. So
> we extended our train passes and shaved our heads.
> Carmel's looks like a peanut. I hope you're well. I
> hope you're well. I hope you're well.
>
> > Loves,
> > Audrey

I checked the postmark. Nine days. For nine days Audrey knew
she wasn't coming back on schedule while I carried ignorantly
on. I dropped the note into the toilet. I opened the window and
threw the balls into the neighbor's backyard. I flushed the toilet.
Then I got dressed and drove to Stuart's pool, where I drank and
drank and then slept with my green shirt as a pillow. The next
morning I woke up, put the shirt on, and drove to my first ever
day of professional work.

Pine Ridge Water abided by no real system of inventory, neither
for bottles nor coolers, so I erred on the side of abundance. I

pulled bottles from great four-by-three-by-four metal racks and wheeled them to the van on a splintering dolly. Loaded one at a time, forty pounds each, gripping around the neck and pinching. I leaned and pushed shut the rusty door, climbed behind the wheel, and reversed out of the warehouse.

The van was old and white and windowless. And *creepy*. Only a Pine Ridge door magnet distinguished it from the gazillion cable and plumbing and child-molesting vans like it. With just one exterior mirror, cracked badly, the van gave little more than a vague idea what was behind me at any time. But it did move, and this was key.

In North City neighborhoods famous for criminal desperation, low-pressure fire hydrants sprayed sad arcs of water while unimpressed children sat on nearby stoops, clenching bright Popsicles that melted over their hands. I'd never used this word, *stoop*, but these couldn't have been anything other. Roughly every third building's windows were boarded, shattered, or simply gone. I scanned the few addresses I could find and smiled at the kids. The green polo and rusted van and the cooler I carried all functioned as camouflage. Behind an open door I saw five grown men in folding chairs, cardboard scattered across the floor. One more man than fans: two rectangular box fans resting in window frames while a standing fan occupied the room's corner, oscillating in stuttered bursts, the fourth shaking as it spun overhead.

"Damn if it isn't about time."

One of the men stood and introduced himself as *Carl, fella who's been calling over and over again*. I smiled. The others laughed and then coughed from laughing too hard. Carl said he didn't care where I put the cooler, as long as it worked. Warm air circulated through the room. They continued to laugh and I threw in a sleeve of paper cups, then thought what the hell and added two Premium bottles, gratis. Harmless gift. The old men clapped and whooped and laughed and coughed.

Other deliveries were as brief as setting bottles on a porch, collecting empty bottles, and tossing them into the back of the van. Mine was an antiroute of sorts, half drawn from the MUST DO stack of complaints in the office, half in response to the Summer Special. Into the kitchen nooks of houses bigger and colder than museums of modern art, switching out bottles while housewives looked through Lands' End catalogs. Audrey now hairless, Audrey now at the hands of the robot with her emotionless finalities, her ones and zeros. Meanwhile, my daily routine was to become one of penetration into these homes dense with history, displayed like exhibits for a highly specific and private audience, which suddenly and mysteriously was me. The water guy. Potter Mays.

I was the first back to the warehouse and rushed through my paperwork with the immediacy of a man pursued. Back home I found a small collection of luxury sedans and medium SUVs parked in front of my house. My father was on a trip to Detroit for a convention on the Decline of the American City. I could hear my mother's company as I went immediately upstairs from the front door, a chorus of loaded laughter echoing through the house. I took my time showering before returning downstairs. I stood at the border between kitchen and living room, clinging to this small bit of separation. The room was full of divorced women drinking white wine. Six of them plus my mother over by the window, all smiling now at my appearance. I sensed that these women all knew something I didn't, a secret gained through the emergence from the wreck of failed marriage. I remembered that this was supposed to be a book club, and I began to worry for my mother, slumming it with these divorcées. What kind of influence was this? Quiet comparisons going on across the room, inquiries into my life, my plans.

"Yes," I answered. "Still with the same girl."

Later I sat with Stuart at the pool's deck table, the candle's orange flame glowing into an otherwise silver dusk. I was admiring the abrasions on my hands, the blisters-turned-open-wounds. I watched my friend lean forward to light a cigarette from the candle, then held one of my hands up for him to see. He squinted and nodded approvingly.

"I have to like what you've done about work. I'm impressed, Poot."

"Mostly I needed a steady reason to get out of the house. There's something afoot in that home, something weird."

"Let's linger a second on these hands of yours," he said. "How did you and Audrey treat the holding-hands question?"

"We disagreed," I said.

Our respective heights were such that to hold hands while walking, I would have to effect a slight shrug, or lean just a little bit away from her, in order for our hands to meet. I had on several occasions tried to explain this to her.

"Then how about standing still?" she countered. "It would I guess kill you to take my hand once in a while just to say hello."

And I said, side by side? Standing still and holding hands as if overlooking some gorgeous view?

"It's not some mystery or riddle, Potter. You know how much I like it."

But over time I began to suspect it wasn't about *liking* at all. For Audrey, holding hands represented a sort of proof, and I sometimes took exception to this ongoing need to prove what should otherwise be assumed.

But that was *love*, she told me. That's what I didn't understand about proof.

"You think it's some like chore. When really it's supposed to be a joy. That's love: proving over and over. Lovers hold hands because they want to. If it feels like work, then it's not proof."

And one morning, I remembered, she woke me with an elaboration on this point and spoke of an isolated beach she imagined, a trite piece of Caribbean fantasy. She must have been awake for a while. In her fantasy we woke up each morning and had our sweaty sex in the bamboo hut, or lean-to, or however she saw it.

Then we would gather our things and walk to the beach, holding hands the whole way.

"And then you go fishing while I sit down with needles and yarn, because I love you, and I want to knit you a cap."

"Knit cap," I said, rolling over. "On the beach."

"Shut! Up! Look. I sit down in the sand and make something for the man I love. Anything. And I watch you go down to the rocks and stand over the water with your *spear,* and this is how the morning goes. I knit and you fish. And then at some point I hear you scream out in joy, and I look to see you smiling at me, holding up the spear with our breakfast on it. And you are smiling hugely and bursting and overcome with joy."

"So in this fantasy I'm the hunter and you're the domesticator. Meanwhile, you're about to have a minor in women's *studies.*"

"It's our beach, Potter. It's all ours and there's no one there but us. No eyes no nothing, just us. Nobody is watching and we hold hands because we want to. No other reason. We made the view, it's ours, and we hold hands because from where we're standing, the world *is* a beautiful view. Do you see?"

Stuart left briefly and returned with two more beers. I held the cold can between my injured hands. The labor was good, he had said so himself. No need to rehash these details of our past, or of Audrey's postponed return, the metallic balls. I opened the beer and sat there with my friend, quietly, resting after a day of work.

My brain would simply not complete the steps required to imagine Audrey bald.

How silly I'd been before this job to think I knew what it meant to sweat. I threw myself into my new labor, driving and lifting and working. And *sweating.* Driving brought minor relief, but with no air conditioner, the sweat was constant. To accompany the tinny sound of radio through one blown speaker, I found myself reading road signs out loud in my normal speaking voice. I

passed beneath billboards with huge radio call letters and an al-
luring catchphrase. A lamppost banner said, *Hooray™ Downtown:
Progress—Fun—Character.* I wore a backwards Cardinals hat stained
with a mountain range of sweat. I sweated a *V* onto my green
shirt, the kind of sweat I had previously associated with tennis
pros and middle-age pickup basketball.

Sprawl—say the word slowly and it begins to make sense.
Sspraaawwwwll.

The current goal was Oakville, on the very southern edge of
St. Louis County, which bore all the signposts of regional development. Empty lots cordoned off and marked for construction,
immense corner gas stations facing each other across the street,
brilliantly colored and glistening new. This was my father's
competition; downtown's offspring growing into its own self-
sustaining world, the implicit patricide. All these shiny, colorful
places to consume set among aboveground pools, granite quar-
ries, baseball diamonds, and go-kart tracks. I saw my turnoff as I
passed it and threw all of my weight onto the brakes, sending a
vanload of hollow plastic bottles tumbling. Cars honked half-
heartedly, geese on quaaludes.

There were kids playing tag in the yard on my right, lunging
and sprinting after one another like sparring hyenas. Houses here
were low and wide and brick, with cramped yards and garages
full of hardware and bed frames and garden hoses. I saw stubby
driveways and zoysia, plastic sunflowers that would spin if there
were a breeze. I idled, scanning faded mailboxes and front doors.
The invoice read: *T. Worpley, 1427 Waldwick.* I saw 1419, 1425,
then 1431. I turned the van around, then backtracked even slower
than I came. I stepped out of the van. I had until recently considered myself an intelligent young man.

Leading from the sidewalk through a swath of dead grass was
a dusty brown rut barely distinguishable from the yard. At the
end was a small white building, not much bigger than a garage. I
lifted a cooler from the van and carried it awkwardly along the

path. Nailed into wooden siding, paint chipped away in long horizontal strips, were the bronze numbers 427. I climbed two concrete steps onto a small wooden porch. Behind a screen door the
house was a cave. I craned my neck to wipe a temple with an already drenched shirtsleeve, then knocked. Echoes of television
garble leaked from inside. A chip of paint came loose under my
fingernail. I knocked again. On the third knock a kid, maybe
eleven or twelve, appeared behind the screen door.

"You're from the company?" He spoke carefully—candy and
strangers. "You brought the free water?"

"I am. And I did."

The boy held open the screen. Inside, windows were drawn
and lamps were off, the TV the only source of light. The house
was a phenomenal mess. An overturned floor lamp rested along
one wall, a detached closet door against another. The couch in
front of the TV was threadbare and saggy. There were unwashed
bowls and plates stacked at the foot of the sofa, Underoos draped
flaccidly across the back of a chair, a scene of sustained neglect. It
looked like I imagined a frat house would look if everyone became really interested in soda.

"Over here."

In the kitchen a stack of dishes sat in and around the sink. The
contents of open boxes of cereal spilled across a counter sticky
with residue unknown. A refrigerator sat silently in one corner,
door missing and shelves barren.

"It doesn't work anymore. Dad knows a guy that gets fridges
real cheap. The cooler should go over there. Then you're supposed to bring three bottles for free."

I set the cooler down in the corner and uncoiled the power
cord. I crouched and looked for an outlet. There was grime
amassed in the joint where the wall met the floor, dirt thoroughly
integrated into the structure itself. The kid stood in the middle of
the kitchen, wide-eyed and quiet.

I told him the cooler would work without power, but if he
wanted the water cold, it would have to be plugged in. His hair

was blondish and eye-length, typical boy. He squinted and pinched tight the left half of his mouth while slowly lifting his weight onto his toes, lowering, then lifting again.

"Hey. Dad's got an orange extension cord in the shed."

I stood and wiped hands on my shorts. I thought of my father's old workbench in the garage, the two towers of miniature drawers standing side by side, finger-sliding drawers full with variously sized instruments of boyhood wonder. The kid looked at me.

"That cord sounds like just the thing," I said.

As he disappeared through a back door, I turned to make my way back to the van for bottles. In the living room I stopped to watch a cartoon with a frenzy of flashing lights and flying dinosaurs zooming madly across the screen, clashing with bright stars of impact, pure magnetic chaos. Enthralling. The dinosaurs wore earpieces and spoke into wrist communicators. One of them had an English accent, one was brown and clearly voiced by a black man, and they kept repeating each other's names so we all knew what to yell when our parents took us shopping.

I turned to find a silhouette of a figure filling the front door. At first I was so absorbed into the realm of cartoon I had a hard time believing the figure was real. Then he stepped work boots into the living room, great heavy booming tired steps.

"Hell is this."

"Pine Ridge Water. Mr. Worpley? I've got you guys signed up for the Summer Special."

I held out a hand he did not take. Instead, he exhaled deeply and shook his head.

"You got the wrong place, kid."

"It's free, Dad." The boy had reappeared behind me, holding a bundled extension cord. "That's what's special about it."

The father moved into his home. He flicked his bright orange cap onto the sofa and passed me without a look. The reek of sustained toil, a more permanent and pungent version of the smell I showered away each evening.

"Calling something free don't mean a single solitary thing. Ask this guy here in green," he said. "Ask him if it's really free. Ask him what kind of fools go around handing out free water. Go on. I'm sure he'll explain everything."

I remained frozen. And when the kid didn't answer or even look at me, the father stepped into the kitchen. After a moment, the kid turned and followed. I did not.

"But remember how Mom made me drink a glass every night before bed? Even if I thought it made me get up and have to pee, she would go like, *here,* and push it into my face."

"That's right. And now you sleep all night and take your pee in the morning. Instead of waking me up in the middle of the night."

I found myself closer to the front door. The young boy stood with cord in hand, staring at either the floor or the clothing on the floor. I heard the father in the kitchen and once again wiped my brow with a shirtsleeve.

"But they got an ad in the paper says free. They got a Summer Special."

I was standing at the door, one hand on the screen.

"Someone says free, Ian, don't you believe it. Got that? No such thing." The kid went silent. The father appeared in the doorway and pointed at me. "I think it's time you removed yourself from my house."

Then I was outside, motion, scrambling into the driver's seat. I felt the van struggle to life and pulled away. I opened a sixteen-ounce sport-top bottle and drained it in one long sip. It wasn't until I was back on the highway that I thought of the cooler sitting unplugged in that kitchen, humming in the corner, waiting patiently for a bottle.

six

there was no reward, as such, for hard work. One afternoon I finished my deliveries in what must have been some sort of land speed record, because Debbie Dinkles was shocked to find me in the lunchroom. She immediately found five more invoices and sent me back into the sweltering afternoon. I learned that day to place a ceiling on my productivity, and from then on when I finished my deliveries early, I did what came naturally—drove to the pool house.

I parked the van in the Hurst cul de sac and followed the walkway into the backyard. Stuart sat on the pool's deck with one foot pulled up against the other leg's thigh. A girl lay facedown on a lounger near the diving board, the strings of her bikini top untied and hanging on either side. Leaves, everywhere, did *not* rustle in summer's complete stillness.

"If you figure a way to run cars on sweat, my undercarriage alone would bring in a small fortune."

"Nice, Poot."

I went inside for a beer, then sat at the deck table and watched my friend stretch. He switched legs and leaned.

"I realized that in order for me to get the most out of my mentation, which is after all my whole purpose for waking up every day, I should maximize harmony between my mind and body."

"I rely on you to not be fruity," I said.

"Read your Putnam," he said. "The mind is nothing without the body. Read your Searle."

"Different mind–body issue," I said.

"Questions for you. One. Would you, if times and ennui were to get bad enough, would you further consider the option of attending law school?"

"Law school is the escape hatch," I said. "The rip cord. I will absolutely not go to law school."

"Good. Considering, next, all of the options you have in the morning, how do you decide which shoes to wear for the day?"

"It's interesting. I find myself caring more about shoes than any other item of clothing. But why? They're so far away from my head, everything about them is base. My shoes are either white, black, or brown. I keep my options limited to minimize the stress of decision."

Stuart stood and waved his arms in circles. His interest in limbering up made me suddenly aware of my own inflexibility, compounded by repeated heavy and awkward lifting.

"Three. When you think of the transition from day to night, do you see the day giving way to night as if exhausted? As if the sun's main job, to provide light for this world, at some point becomes a responsibility too burdensome for the day to bear? And so each evening the sun and its daytime grant themselves respite and yield to night?"

"I do, actually." This was in fact remarkably accurate.

"And Audrey, is her perception of night, unlike yours, one in which night penetrates day like ink drops in water, a gentle but thorough dissolution of darkness spreading itself across the day? Wherein night is the aggressor, the force to overtake and erase the day?"

"I don't know."

"Of course not," he said. "This has been helpful. I am going to stretch my hamstrings now. If you think of anything to add, please speak directly into my asshole."

I stood and began a walk around the pool. I slowed as I neared the girl. Her hair was brown and straight, pulled to one side of her neck. The undersides of her feet were white with prune and pool-deck dust. She was that nice middle weight, slim but still curved, the sort of body they were beginning to show more frequently on television so we'd all think how refreshing it is to see someone *normal* for once. Stuart sat at the deck table, sprinkling bits of Relaxation onto two overlapping papers.

"Who's the young lady?"

"Late last night I went shopping for cake mix and found her wandering the aisles in bare feet with the most pleasantly detached look in her eyes. I felt a profound obligation toward meeting her. I said good evening, how are you tonight. She said nothing. I didn't take it personally. Then, when I'm outside getting into my car, she climbs in the passenger door and fastens her seat belt. Hi there. Her name is Marianne and she's from Cuba, Missouri." He ran his tongue lightly across the joint and set it on the table. "She left town three months ago to come to the big city. I get the feeling she's come to find a man. She admitted up front that her mother never taught her to cook. Couldn't make an omelet if you put a gun to her head. But baking, she says, baking is her domain."

"I'd love a piece of that cake if there's any left."

"The cake didn't come together. We were up all night talking. It was frankly astounding how easy it all was. We spoke like this was our fourth lifetime together. Do you know Cuba? About an hour southwest of here, down 44 toward Rolla. Parents are literal farmers of the American heartland. I dozed off around eight, then woke at noon to find her lying out here. I told her that stepmother Deanna might get jealous and handed her a swimsuit. I think she's planning on staying and I don't think I mind. She has a farmish ease about her that rubs off on the whole poolside. Don't you feel calm? I for one feel calm."

I thought of our OA circle that first night, our group of children on the cusp of institution. I had a feeling then, even before school did something to me, a feeling of our cute little circle as gateway, a momentary figuration of bodies that pointed outward (upward?) to bigger circles, a series of expanding circles that began precisely then and would terminate eight semesters later. An experience to be bookended, a single happening that would also be a thousand. Nameless figure, female and with shoulders at my ten o'clock, to whom I would soon hand over everything. And then gradually thieve back.

Stuart held the joint between his lips and patted his shorts for a lighter. I watched the topless girl rise from the lounger, breasts exposed and bouncing a little with each step toward the table. Various articles over the years had named the Schnucks supermarket on Clayton Road a *Top 5 Local Spot to Meet Singles*. The girl pulled out a chair and nodded at me as if from beneath a Stetson. When he passed the joint, the girl received it in her open palm, so quaintly wrong a gesture I immediately liked her. She took a shallow pull and closed her eyes. The sacred red and white Budweiser cans sweat condensation. I allowed myself quick glances at her breasts. In a vacuum, such indulgences of the body seemed vain and flauntingly arrogant. But something about this girl's demeanor, her generously plain face and peacefully closed eyes, made it okay. Stuart's past relationships were brief codependencies with gorgeous but hideous New York daughters linked to inheritances in the range of his own. Here was a girl bred within the ethos of our middle land, reared among field and stream and earnestness. Others wore nudity like some costume, but not her. I looked at Stuart, then back to her, and had to give them credit for such brazen disregard for the regime of time.

But my watch said it was time to go back to the warehouse. I had to empty the empties from the van, break down cardboard boxes and fill out paperwork, return home to shower away the job's evidence, and prepare for the night's Cardinals game.

"I am too much in the sun. What about tonight? I hope you don't mind driving."

"I enjoy driving," Stuart said to the topless brunette.

"To the game, I mean. A sea of red. Beer delivered from the brewery to the stadium through a system of subterranean pipes."

"That's right, yes, game tonight." Now some gear clicked and he turned to me, and there was his crook-toothed smile. "I've got to go pick something up and I'll come get you. Oh Jesus are you going to love this."

Walking backward with tired, swollen arms spread outward, I watched the two of them battle for the joint, the Missouri girl's eyes focused on my friend.

There were caterers wearing tuxedos moving through the kitchen. I sat at the counter and thought of Freddy in the attic and his top-down vantage. Because I assumed Freddy had X-ray vision, and that sometimes he watched us with judgment in his eyes, sometimes shaking his head at the preposterous fancies of the living. My mother waded among the tuxedos, overseeing and occasionally salting a dish.

When my father came home the circus reached a new level of absurdity, the caterers suddenly torn between who to fear and respect. My mother still essentially running things, my father changed from work shirt and tie to entertaining shirt and tie. Then he returned to stand by the counter and speak to me, so ambivalent to the inconvenience this created for everyone scurrying around the kitchen that I felt immensely proud to be the man's son.

"How's your back doing?" he asked. "Sore? I'll bet it is. You'd expect as much, a good and sore back to remind you of the day."

My back ached enough that it was starting to affect the way I saw the world. And I was beginning to wonder if this nebulous *maturation* everyone spoke of, capital Growing capital Up, was really nothing more than the psyche's lunge to catch up with a deteriorating body.

"Not too sore," I said.

"I envy you. Getting out there into the day and building a little sweat. Have I ever told you about my first job?"

"I forget."

"I shoveled horse crap for about fifty cents an hour." He reached for a stuffed mushroom cap. "Basically been shoveling it ever since."

My mother said, "Richard."

"Who's dinner tonight?" I asked.

"An assortment. Dan Wennings and his wife. The tallest of Senator Dunleavy's daughters and her new husband, who I believe is attached to the D.A.'s office. Who else? Hard to say without counting chairs. Various old colleagues of mine and other politicians. I'm sure we'll discuss the progress with *Hooray!* They're watching me always. Tonight we have an informal meal that is officially not on any record. Strictly social as I nudge you with my elbow. Are we having salmon, Carla? About two out of three of these dinners are salmon."

I heard Stuart's honk outside. My mother assured me she would tuck a plate away for me if I was hungry later. I thanked her and said good luck with the people. She said something to my father I didn't catch, and the caterers cleared a path for me through the kitchen. He followed and caught me as I opened the front door.

"You know, among the things these people tonight can do is get us some good tickets to a game. What do you say? I'll get Dan's tickets, Dan Wennings. You and your old dad. When was the last time we went to a game? Years, at least."

"Anytime. You pick a game and I'll go," I said, and we both raised eyebrows and nodded.

The car waiting in the driveway was not the old Explorer or Stuart's father's car or any of the other cars they owned, which were many, but a garish and outrageous Volkswagen Beetle, painted in that fluorescent that eyes gravitated to but nobody ever really wanted to see. There was yellow and orange and purple, along with red shapes wrapped diagonally around the domed hood and roof and across the door. Letters, red letters.

I squinted. "Does this say . . . St. Louis Tan Company?"

"I have been given a car for the summer. To drive. For free."

We pulled onto the highway and made our way downtown. I watched people consider our rolling advertisement, look and squint to decipher the nature of our product. I looked into the exterior mirror and saw myself bordered by neon and tried not to think of skateboarding and BASE jumping.

"A car has been given to the wealthiest person I know."

"We are witnessing an evolution in the universe of promotion. What a glorious time to be alive."

"I'm counting your family's cars. I'm up to seven."

"This right here is a cog of our very gears, a rolling manifestation of all we stand for. This ironically German automobile."

Stuart had spent his four years at Brown plowing through continental philosophy. His bachelor's thesis applied Hegel's notion of *Aufhebung* to the lyrics of House of Pain's "Jump Around." Professors called his attempt ambitious, brave, and endearingly ridiculous. In an e-mail he detailed to me a serious consideration of pursuing a PhD until he awoke one morning with his copy of *Zettel* open on his lap, its pages the unfortunate recipients of his first ever wet dream, at the age of twenty-two. After that he stopped reading German philosophy.

"I appreciate the nonchalance of the letters," I said, "as if they just *fell* onto the car."

"Fifteen franchises in the greater metropolitan area, all open until two A.M., seven days a week. And they are blowing up in West County."

"Tell me who tans at two A.M."

Stuart's grin expanded. "The masses."

Traffic grew thick as we approached the stadium, cars packed tight amid a flurry of red-shirted fans making their way en masse from the less expensive lots. Men and women in orange vests waved orange flags. Park here. This many dollars. Stuart turned into the parking area closest to Busch Stadium and handed the girl a Diamond Preferred parking ticket. Out of the car, we were absorbed into the crowd. Stuart shouldered his way through and nobody seemed to mind. A saxophonist played "When the Saints Go Marching In," and peanut vendors shouted into the dank evening. I was happy to follow his lead, through the gates of our giant concrete stadium, down beer-soaked steps to the field-box level, all the way to the concession line.

"I want to discuss the answer to your problem."

"There's really no need to rush," I said. "Audrey has delayed her return, so the element of hurry is gone."

Stuart appeared to consider this development. "Good. This will give us time for a second phase. Wherein you spend concentrated time around and learning from Edsel Denk."

That beard dripping as the massive beast man emerged from the pool, the cocksucker returns to the diving board. The plunge and the emergence. A beard like the pelt of some forest mammal stuck to his chin. Displaced Appalachian woodsman.

"No thank you. Pretty confident I'm not up for phase two."

"Right now I need you to trust me, Poot. Think about where you are in this process. Is it fair to say you're a wreck?"

We stepped forward as the line grew shorter. A father and son moved from the counter to the condiment table.

"You are a wreck. We both know it. The evidence is right in front of us. Everything you thought you believed about this girl is no longer believable. You may still love her. Or you may not. You may have never loved her to begin with. Unfortunately, you no longer have authority to say, because you're too entangled within the question. What you need to do is move outside yourself. Trust me when I say I appreciate the importance of this decision. Could possibly be the most important decision a man can make."

A bald man behind the counter operated two taps at once.

"Which is why you're going to spend time with Edsel Denk."

"Wait. No. Naive as it was, fine, naive and silly, but there was a definite period when I truly thought I was going to marry Meredith Flackman. She was my first love. Until that asshole came along and *stole* her, Stubes. Theft of a lover."

"Consider it a social internship. Anthropology, if you want. I'm going to in fact order you to do so. Follow him around and observe. He has seen things you and I have not. Partake in his behavior, maybe. Say what you want about Edsel, call him misogynist and label him asshole, but his is the nature of man in the world. The qualities he embodies are those of manhood, swollen brawn and brute force. You likely won't like the experience, but it will definitely be good for you."

We had reached the counter. I waited for Stuart to tell the woman what we'd be having. I sure as hell wasn't going to step forward and take charge of a single thing.

"Beers," Stuart said. "Will be on you tonight."

The cashier glared. "I'm gonna have to see some ID."

seven

W hat a mysterious array of forms and sounds emerge from dark silent solitude. I stacked three cardboard boxes against the only window to block the streetlight, then sat and waited. Against the uniform blackness of deep attic corners I saw patches of darker darkness, amorphous and phantasmal but in the end still lacking the definition and presence of true specter. I had a place to spread out, a short line of boxes slid together to approximate some kind of mattress. I'd begun coming up here when sleep in my bed proved unfeasible, which I could now safely conclude was not the fault of the squirrels that had disappeared altogether. I lay across the boxes and let my sight be drawn into the attic's gloomiest recesses, drifting into and out of shallow sleep. Even without Freddy, there was a therapeutic timelessness up here, my clever stack of boxes voiding the effect of sunrise. Still, I kept my cell phone in my pocket, alarm set, just in case I did sleep heavily. Increasingly, my job had become something I relied on, and I feared the potential calamity of losing it.

Summer was gathering force. I spent the better part of a day in Illinois at a series of small churches Dennis the bigot refused to visit, out of racial concerns. I added bottles to each delivery, and thus the list of people in the region who thought me

generous grew by the day. On my way back into town I hit grid-
lock on the bridge and stuttered forward with my eyes locked
on the Arch's legs as they appeared to close, briefly become
one, then open. Thick wet warm air swirled like convection
through the van, the smell all semi exhaust and hops. Soon the
heat would be too much, and people would venture outside only
when absolutely necessary, birds singing to no one but themselves. My forearms were thickening into something like extremely low-gauge wire, tumid and strained from the repeated
labor of lift.

Right now I was at the point in the system when I left downtown and went back to retrieve the cooler I'd left at the
Worpleys'. But of course since there was no inventory at Pine
Ridge, or official review, this was just an excuse, my own little
contrivance, of which I was eminently aware.

I parked the van by the sidewalk and walked the dirt path,
stopped short where bits of cement detritus littered the dusty
yard. Like the first time, a mélange of high-pitched screams and
crashes streamed from the television and out of the home.
Something was going to happen here. Either the skinny son or
world-weary father would come to the door. I knocked on the
frame of the loosely shut screen door, wiped my brow, and
waited.

It was the son who answered. He held one hand against the
door, not pushing, just touching the screen.

"Hello," I said. "I was here about a week ago."

"Yeah, I remember. You brought the cooler and then ran away
like a girl when my dad got home. It was funny."

"The thing is that I need to get that cooler back."

"Figures."

The kid turned and left me standing on the porch. I let myself
inside, where all the same feelings from the last visit were reiter-
ated. The young Worpley's feet crackled as he walked, the slappy-
click of bare steps across a licked-lollipop linoleum floor. The old

fridge had been replaced by another old one with a door. The cooler was in the corner, emitting the faintest buzz as it tried its best to do its job. A bold orange extension cord trailed out the kitchen's back door like some sort of pathetic tail.

"Go on and take it if you have to."

"You plugged it in," I said.

"Dad said I could use the cord until he needs it."

I thought about taking the boy instead of the cooler. Leave it standing with no bottle and throw him over my shoulder. Carry him to the van and tear the lone side-view mirror from the passenger door so he wouldn't have to look back, and then go.

"My name's Potter."

The boy stared at the floor. "I'm Ian."

A dog somewhere began barking, and soon at least two other dogs were barking back at it. A woman's voice screamed for them to shut the hell up, and they did. The cooler hummed in the corner.

"Where's your dad?"

"He works every day but Wednesday. He works for the city. On the roads."

"And you're here alone the rest of the time?"

"Sometimes he gets to work the jackhammer. And not one of those wimpy little fifty-pound things but the eighty-pound ones. He says you can feel your teeth jiggle."

"What are your thoughts about being alone for so long?"

"It's only seventy-four days, then school starts back up."

I dropped to a knee and separated the orange plug from the black end coming out of the cooler. The motor wound down in an extended sigh. In its absence, the silence in the kitchen felt far more audible than the idle hum there before.

"Dad says most people don't get how heavy eighty pounds is. You know what my dad says is the heaviest thing an adult ever carries? A regular adult?"

"Tell me."

"A gallon of milk," Ian said.

"You want to guess how much a gallon of water weighs?"

"I don't know how to do that," he said. "I can't guess in water."

I waddled the cooler away from the wall so I could get at its handle. The coolers themselves weighed less than a bottle, but their weight was distributed so unevenly there was really no best way to carry them. The longer you worked with things, the better you became at handling their specific system of challenges. The calluses on my hands proved my body's proclivity to make its job easier. But I hadn't been exposed to enough poor children alone with nothing but cartoons and darkness to get them through the day.

"Eight pounds," I said. "Eight per gallon."

"I didn't know that."

"And milk probably weighs a little more, because of its density."

Ian shut his eyes and whispered, "Density."

Something was wrong. My character was not supposed to be here. I realized if I didn't get out of there with all possible diligence, there was going to be failure. Something was sure to crash, the system would fracture, and everything in this kid's already shitty plane would go even further to shit. I picked up the cooler and began the walk to the door. I heard the kid's footsteps behind me and started walking faster. Halfway through the living room, I stepped on some floorborne object and dropped the cooler to the ground. Of course. The kid stood behind me and watched. I bent and picked up an inexpensive baseball mitt. Tucked inside was a brown-green baseball, scraped with the marks of street use.

"If you're gonna take the cooler we should at least play some catch." He was wearing swimming trunks and a peach T-shirt with fluorescent designs puffy-painted in bright yellow. "Fair's supposed to be fair."

"We need another glove," I said.

"Yeah, I *know*. Me and Dad both got one at Glove Night. It was a long time ago. The guy at the gate gave me a glove just for coming. Free except for paying for the game. I got one and so did Dad, 'cause he found one sitting outside the bathroom. It's in the closet somewhere."

I opened the closet and found two winter coats, both turquoise, hanging among a dozen empty hangers. The floor was a pile of assorted balls and skates and hockey sticks. The other glove was on a shelf above the hangers, stuck between board games and the wall. In the front yard we stood only a few paces apart and tossed lazy overhands that arced and fell into basket catches. Gradually, we spread farther apart and began throwing with more velocity. There was catharsis: the movement to reel in Ian's throw, eye–hand coordination, the quick rescue of ragged ball from glove, spun with intuition into throwing hand so that index and middle fingers crossed the fraying seams. And finally the pendulum drop to the waist before rising behind my head. Release with follow-through. There was artistry somewhere within this sequence of muscle memory; too long dormant, awakened now by this filthy poor little kid and a pair of complimentary pleather gloves.

After a while our throws crossed the length of the yard. I was shocked by the strength of his tiny little arm. Arms like this were reserved for corn-fed little machine boys who went to summer camps with Louisville bags and sliding pants and sweatbands, who wore protective cups even before they knew why. I stood backed against the old porch and Ian was near the van. Back, forth. Each throw and catch was a link to the continuum of baseball procedure and lore. There was tradition here.

One of Ian's throws bounced short, but before it did I watched it change from a short throw to a blooped single knocked out to me in left field, and I saw a runner circling third, his coach maniacally waving home the potential tying run. I charged and scooped just as I was supposed to, crow-hopped, and fired.

Ian screamed *JESUS* and fell to the ground. The ball hit the van with a hollow *crunk* and rebounded back into the yard. Ian glared at me from his knees. My shoulder twinged with pain as I made my way slowly to the ball.

"Ow," I said.

"Oh, poor you," Ian said. "You could have killed me, but your arm hurts so I guess that's more important."

"Yeah, sorry about that. I got a little carried away on the last one."

"I think you literally could have killed me." Ian looked at his palms, then looked up the street. "My dad'll be home soon. Give me your glove."

"That was a mistake," I said. "I'm sorry. Let's throw a little more. A few short ones to keep a good thing going."

"I'm going inside. Give it. Give it here."

I handed him the glove. He stuck it in his armpit and began walking back to the house. I was sure something more was expected of me.

"I wasn't trying to hurt you."

He kept walking and said, "It's fine."

"Hey, you're not following through enough," I yelled, and saw him stop and turn around. "You're short-arming it a little. Your motion, it's good and natural but a little bit off. Nothing that can't be fixed, but if you let it go on you might run into trouble later."

"You threw that ball really hard," he said.

"I know. And I'm sorry. Look, maybe I could come back sometime. Check on your motion."

"I guess, as long as you promise to never do that again."

"I promise," I said. "I do."

"I'm saying *ever*. You coulda took off my head, you know. *Pop.* Me on the ground bleeding from my neck because my head is gone. Blood all over the place. I saw a show once about this guy who accidentally killed a kid with his car. You'd go to jail for like ever. Nobody cares if it's an accident or anything."

I drove away wishing I had a baseball of my own to hold and spin. Pinch between thumb and middle fingers, send it spinning upward with a snap, catch without looking. Repeating as needed.

eight

i walked through the pool-house door to find an even larger version of Edsel Denk fingering a deck of cards at the table. His neck looked like a very hardworking straw. When our eyes met I thought of that children's song where the other day (the other day) I saw a bear (I saw a bear) and the bear sees me and then something happens I forget what. Except here was a thuggish beast lacking a bear's anthropomorphic cuteness, more ogre than bear. While Edsel continued to shuffle the deck, I stood very very still and located my primary exits. He wore a ribbed tank top, a visor from the Bellagio casino, and God only knew what under the table. His beard was thick and uniform and a frankly awesome accessory to an already imposing face. Sweat moved from my right armpit downward.

"Potty boom botty."

I turned to see one of Stuart's hands shoot upward from the couch. I moved quickly past the table to join him. My friend was horizontal with one arm hanging lazy to the floor, watching baseball.

"Game's on," he said.

I rubbed my still-sore shoulder and, even though I knew the answer, asked when was the last time Stuart had thrown a baseball.

"Years," he said. "I watch and cheer and wear lots of red. I am a supporter. I avoid any form of play that might detract from this role."

We watched the Cardinals struggle against the Rockies, whose leadoff hitter was walked, opening the door to a series of base hits, then a homer, then a walk, a pitching change, a walk, a wild pitch, and a base-clearing double. The runs piled up against us. Stuart reached for the remote and turned off the volume. I found myself drifting into and out of brief but madly satisfying naps before awaking to Edsel's voice rolling as if downhill from the table.

"Believe me when I say you ain't seen baseball until you've seen it played in other countries. They've taken our game and made it into something else. The Thai people have a version of baseball to make your head spin. It's fast over there. Fast and wicked." I hadn't recalled his voice being so rough.

Stuart had caught me up on the basics of Edsel's life after high school, how he attended the University of Missouri and sold lots and lots of drugs. How after graduation he took his drug money and embarked on a two-year journey: first to New York, where he shuffled among various friends slash clients from college, filthed about the Lower East Side and failed resoundingly at stand-up comedy, then to Southeast Asia, where he grew the beard and took digital photos of Angkor Wat, rode elephants in Chiang Rai, hired multiple prostitutes in Bangkok. Stuart swore that something profound had happened to Edsel while abroad, an Eastern shift in the way he understood the universe. How upon his return he began lifting weights with regularity, how he started *growing*. The cards sat in two stacks on the table in front of him, horrified, I imagined, at the prospect of returning to his hands.

"Wiry little gookers slapping singles and running like hell. Playing for hours on the beach with a bat made out of driftwood."

Stuart stepped in front of me and went to the kitchen for his Tupperware, then joined Edsel at the table. I watched our scrappy leadoff hitter lace a double into the right-field corner and get thrown out at third.

"Tiny men push around carts stacked with mountains of insects. Old Buddhist men with wrinkled faces shiny with sweat. You look down an alleyway and you see rows of the carts all lined up. Some carts got wheels, others just sit there. At night the lights shine on the carts and the bugs look like donuts if you don't know any better. And I'll tell you something about these wrinkled little brown men, they love to see a white man struggle with a grasshopper. They smile and stare into your eyes and wait for you to retch. Happy bastards."

"Did you retch?" I asked.

"Shit no I ain't retch."

Joint hanging from one corner of his mouth, Stuart caught my eye and twisted the other into something sly and knowing. Behold the ogre, and bask. Edsel's accent was that of a cross-legged whittler sitting somewhere up near Twain's Hannibal, so thoroughly aligned with the beard that even if it was affected there was no point objecting.

"The women got their own carts. They mix whatever the boatmen caught that morning with simple noodles. Talking about old women who look like they never had teeth to begin with. They smile and chatter away in their bird language, then nod and ask for a dollar fifty. Daughters charge ten times that in the massage parlor around the corner. And another thing—the Thai don't use chopsticks. I don't know who's behind that myth, but fact is those bastards love a fork."

A buzzing encircled my head, a high-pitched wail like a tiny lobster dropped into a thimble of boiling water. I watched a mosquito land on and dig himself into my forearm. Couldn't believe his drive and desire to dig into my skin. Her. Stuart stood up to answer his cell phone. A finger onto the skeeter left an oval of my blood on my skin, dead skeeter on my finger.

I watched Stuart's mouth, I saw laughter and facial expressions, I saw him lean against the counter; then he hung up.

"I do believe tonight's the night," he said. "So far she has refused to sleep with me, a refusal I greet with thorough respect.

We have made it to genital fondling, naked tumbling on the bed, but no sex. I admire her for this. I think I even admire her parents for this. Ed, she insists on meeting you. Insists. Poot, she says you're fine."

With its added length of beard, Edsel's nod was a force. Such affirmation.

"What does that mean, I'm fine? Fine how?"

"She says she already knows whatever it is she needs to know about you."

"That's absurd. This is the girl with the breasts?"

"The beautiful breasts, yes." Stuart closed the Tupperware and took it away. "Perfect breasts are among her long list of total or near perfections. You two met the other day."

"We didn't share a single syllable," I said. "You never introduced us."

Edsel stopped shuffling. "You always like this?"

"Sometimes you imagine things, Poot. But doesn't matter because she says she gets it. You're fine. Now I need to prepare myself for what's to come. You two enjoy your dinner."

Then Stuart was gone, back into the bedroom, and I was left at the table with the ogre with the playing cards, and on TV the Cards losing and defeat silently mounting, the central air churning, and somewhere in Europe Audrey was laughing and laughing and moving and bald and laughing and twirling. I couldn't tell who was supposed to make the first move. Edsel was older and much bigger. I was the one with the car.

"I guess I should drive."

"Then lessgo."

The sky was gray-blue-green and lower than usual. A group of rabbits sat like dander in the big patch of yard between the pool house and the driveway. I half expected the ogre to lunge for one of them, a ferocious and not necessarily graceful show of predatory will.

Once we reached the driveway he stopped moving and raised one arm, pointing at the ad.

"Eventually Stuart's going to let me behind the wheel of that thing."

"I don't know. I think there's a system in place."

"System or not, he'll get bored. You guys are always getting bored."

I took us westward, away from the river and the Arch, into the very depths of the county. The ogre next to me bit his fingernails, his thick sausage fingers disappearing into the forest of his beard. And this man, I thought, procures for himself women in abundance. I wondered what Stuart had told Edsel about this proposed internship. I eased the gas pedal, the speedometer revolved clockwise, seventy, then eighty, passing and merging and flowing deeper into the current westward leg of an ancient American dream. I felt sleazy by association, and it wasn't entirely bad.

I exited on Manchester Boulevard and continued west. Five miles later, Edsel grunted, "There."

Yes. I signaled and turned into a sprawling parking lot divided by stand-alone restaurants and landscaped partitions. Supermarket, discount shoe outlet, big and tall clothing store, DMV, another shoe outlet, and baked sub sandwich shop. Twenty-screen cinema. People sat outside each of the four floating restaurants, waiting to be told their table was ready. There was Crazy Sticks, California Cocina, Bighorn Steakhouse, and Beneath the Sea.

"I know a tiny girl who bartends at one of these places. Forget which one. Short girl, tits like this."

"People make a point of coming here," I said. "It's a destination."

At California Cocina we were handed a translucent black disc that would buzz and glow when our table was ready.

"Emily," Edsel said. "Keep your eyes out for a short girl with hairy arms."

Eventually a skinny brunette led us to a small booth squished between two larger booths, each filled with a chewing sipping talking family. I focused my attention squarely on Edsel. He occupied his half of the booth with aplomb both physical and psychological, the remorseless ogre, and I began to think that perhaps Stuart had been right, that perhaps here was someone whose stark deviance from whatever flimsy morals I possessed could serve as education. I watched him read the menu, eyes narrow and intent.

I said, "How do these places manage to feel both crowded and empty at the same time?"

"Pesto chicken pizza. Grilled tilapia in mango salsa. I wonder what they offer that's encrusted."

He liked it here. Hence that aplomb, the palpable contentment oozing from his side of the booth. In a setting so rife with flaws—and it was, surely, just look—he either didn't see them or didn't care about them. How this contentment was related to physical stature, I wasn't sure. But the ogre could have been anywhere and it wouldn't have made a difference. And I had to wonder if this approach—this ambivalent comfort and brute ogre stoicism—was one of, perhaps, *love*? Wasn't Casanova's conflict one of loving too widely? Love not unlike sprawl, far-reaching and nondiscriminatory. Or Don Juan? The hostess made another pass by our table, smiling like a child's toy.

"Let's order," he said. "Sooner we order, sooner we can get on with this."

"This. On with this."

He set the menu down. "The slaughter, Potter. The destruction of every little she-girl we can get our hands on. Isn't that what we're here for? Stuart said you were looking to get laid."

I left the booth and maneuvered into the back of the restaurant. If I happened upon a restroom I would use it. I stopped at the giant fish tank and watched helpless little fish swim into and quickly back out of miniature castles. There were eyes everywhere. I turned and found a father and mother glaring up at me from their booth. When I found myself back at the booth I sat down, relieved to see the menus had been taken away.

"I ordered you fajitas because I figure even you probably like fajitas. The surprise is gonna be chicken or beef."

Edsel broke off a section of bread pole and shoved it into the hole in his beard. I would have given damn near anything to grow a beard like the ogre's. He had become a monstrous individual, and the divergence of this monstrosity from the present of middle-American kinfolk should have been stark. The bearded ogre among scores of timid men, women, and children. Instead, somehow, he managed to fit into the picture, to slide himself into their realm. And to thrive.

"You pick up very heavy weights over and over again," I said. "And you do it for women. That's the motivating factor."

"Let me explain something very simple about this world, this shithole of ours. Whatever they say about the universe, our puny little globe is only getting smaller. The bigger I become, the more of this world I get to claim as my own." Here the food was set in front of us. Edsel added, "Which is the whole damn point."

We ate without discussion and stood once the ogre declared the restaurant devoid of prospects. Outside, there was a brief moment of aimlessness before Edsel led us determinedly toward another of the restaurants, presumably in search of Emily the short bartender. I appreciated the return to movement, the sense of journey. Our paths momentarily diverged in the parking lot and we spoke over car roofs.

"You go in there to burn things off," I said. "So there's got to be some level of catharsis. You go into this smelly old South City gym and direct yourself inward, testing the limits of your body. It's got to be at least somewhat about discipline, controlled masochism."

"Simple math. I get bigger, world gets smaller."

At Crazy Sticks we ordered beers and sat at the bar, facing outward. Here, too, the clientele was dominated by families. And no Emily. Edsel appeared undaunted, silent and faithful for what the near future would hold. I was less sure.

"Then why not just get fat? If volume is the thing, why not just eat yourself into fatness? Think about the water displacement of a fat man lowering into a tub. If it's size you want."

"Fat men lack confidence. Lookit this guy here, blue shirt. Lookit his shoulders. Fat slouch."

"And you need confidence," I said. "For women."

"For the slaughter," he said, standing.

Nor did Emily the bartender appear during our beer at Bighorn Steakhouse. We drank in silence until I asked what he thought Stuart had meant about Marianne, how she wanted to meet him but not me.

"Don't know or really care. Is she beautiful, this girl?"

"Maybe beautiful inside," I said.

"And this is really bothering you, is it?"

"A little. Yes."

"Must be exhausting as hell."

"So confidence is everything," I said.

"Wrong. Confidence is something, alright, but without technique it's nothing. Lessgo."

In the car he grunted directions to a place he knew, somewhere he promised would be fruitful. I remained resoundingly unsure how I would react if confronted by a legitimately available woman. We continued quietly westward, straying deeper into the county along roads that became residential, following curves alongside enormous new-construction houses. Then back into a commercial district, car dealerships and fast-food chains and bright colorful signage. He directed me into a strip mall and I parked facing something called the Baja Beach Club. What followed would prove to be his longest and most horrifying lesson.

"Forget the specifics of women. Sooner you stop differentiating, the sooner you realize that the women are not the point. A man's got to start somewhere. There's one thing I learned in Thailand it's that the world is full of people waiting to be overpowered. Passive smiling Buddhists or bored married women or barely legal teenage girls. You get wrapped up in differences, but the point is there isn't any difference because the techniques are the same across the board. The point is the techniques, learning the behaviors people expect. Intimidation. Physical mastery of your surroundings. False flattery as a technique, showering praise when you know praise is what someone wants. People crave praise, they feed off it. Using silence and dead air to create an awkward situation that you secretly control. There's one thing I learned it's that people fear silence, forces them to say something they don't always mean. Pounce on this. Slaughter them. The technique of the wince, using your body to react to something said. Bigger body, bigger wince. You wince so they begin to doubt whatever they just said. These things work, these gestures. You get them to agree to something big, then add little things onto that something. Nibbling away. God bless the nibble. Create false deadlines. Say take it or leave it. You gotta learn the gestures and learn how people react. After that it's simple as matching the gesture to the situation. Easy as anything in the whole world."

"I don't like anything you just said."

"Yeah, see, you ain't gonna like it."

We got out of the car and began walking toward the Baja Beach Club.

"Are you gay?"

"No," I said.

This was man. A particularly brutal example of man, for sure, but exemplary nonetheless. The men in the hostels in Europe, the backpackers walking a few steps behind Audrey and Carmel. American? Care for a drink? Listening to their stories, cocking their heads to project interest. Gestures for Audrey, the things I'd stopped having to do. Men trained in the arts.

"Hold on. Why is everyone so young? What is this place?"

"Technically legal is the same as totally legal. Don't think about specifics."

We were close enough now to read the sign that said *18 and overs ONLY*. I knew of such clubs out here, with an indoor sand volleyball court and the rhythmic pump of bass, hair gel gleaming in the strobes programmed to match up with that song about wanting to fuck you like an animal. Jäger shots spilled while being

passed from adults to children, wall decorations that glowed fluorescent in prevailing black light. I stopped walking.

"Edsel. Don't go in there. These are children, tiny little people.
Look at their legs, look how small. Look at the zits on the guys. I
can't go in there. Be serious."

"You're either coming or you're not. Don't make a single difference to me."

End of lesson one. I watched him move into the middle of the
line, an enormous body among a collection of small frames in
jeans that rode low and tight. The ogre surrounded by tube tops
and plastic hoop earrings. I returned to my car and drove back
into my father's city.

The Hoyne daughter was next door, shooting lazy jump shots
at the basket bolted above her parents' garage. She shot and
missed and followed the stray ball as it dribbled into the lawn,
pulling from a cigarette as she walked. She hit a few and missed
several more. I had memories of this little girl running insane circles through a front-yard sprinkler, cackling and spinning. Now it
occurred to me that she had seen me pull into the driveway and
had likely noticed that I hadn't left the car in what felt like at least
three or four hours, and she was probably at this moment trying
to recall the Five Simple Steps to Reporting a Sexual Deviant
memorized for health class. I opened my car door just as she
lobbed a shot that was short and left enough to bounce off the
rim and into the grass separating the two driveways. She ended
up following the ball, facing me as I pushed the door shut.

"You fall asleep in there?" Her hair was straight, feathered at
the end so it just reached her bare shoulders.

"I was looking for something," I said.

"You should have tried turning on the light."

"Except the thing I was looking for, that wouldn't have
helped."

"Oh Lord. You're home from college now and all deep."

"I am a very complex person. This is true. I am rife with
depth."

"Outstanding. May I offer you a smoke?"

The girl stepped over the ball and continued toward me. I pressed a button on my key and there was the flatulent honk of alarm.

"Word around our house is it's good for your parents to have you home," she said.

"They keep telling me that."

She lit a cigarette in her mouth and passed it over. "Where'd you go?"

"A tiny school near Los Angeles I promise you've never heard of."

"Loss Angle-less. Wow. I bet you've got a story about running into someone famous at a place you totally wouldn't expect, like the dentist. Because we always assume people like that either don't go to the dentist because their teeth are too famous for cavities or they have their own private dentist on the set. Which are both completely wrong, I'm finding out."

"If it weren't for the burritos I'd say bomb the whole place."

The girl laughed and put her thumbs in the belt loops of her jeans. I took a shallow drag and tried desperately not to cough.

"I've got plans to go west also. My dad says Stanford, and I say Berkeley, so I guess it'll come down to my SATs. They want me to take one of those classes, but there's something gross about paying for some number."

"I agree completely."

I wiped a palm on my thigh and tapped ash from the cigarette in a manner I hoped looked cool and practiced.

"I should go inside. I'm only out here because my parents banned cigarettes from the house last week. They're afraid all the smoke is cutting into our cat's life expectancy. Hey, come say hi next time you see me. Neighbors and all."

"I'll do that."

"Righteous."

I smoked the rest of the cigarette and watched her walk back toward her house, kicking the ball as she went. Just before reaching the garage, she turned.

"How'd you do on the verbal?" she yelled.

"Not bad. I was an English major. So."

"English majors get the chicks, right? Isn't that what they say?"

Inside my home, I opened the fridge, removed the plastic carton of chicken salad, doused its contents with pepper, found a fork, and stepped into the living room. My father was spread out on the couch, watching baseball highlights. I fell into the recliner.

"Your mom asked that if I was still up when you got home to please tell you good night. So good night."

"Good old Mom."

"Cubs won. Houston won. Cincinnati won."

"What's that make us, six back?"

"Seven." He sat up. "Noticed you talking to the little girl next door."

I saw past my father through the curtains to where I'd been standing minutes earlier.

"I can never remember her name," I said.

"Ophelia," he said. "Or is it Lolita."

I laughed, just a single shot of air from my mouth and nose, but it was wonderful. I remembered that he was a funny man sometimes, when he wasn't so engulfed in the struggle to keep this city alive. I suddenly felt guilty for where I'd been with Edsel, out cavorting in the farthest reaches of sprawl when I should have been supporting downtown.

"There's wine left if you want. In fact, why don't you bring me the bottle. I could use a little more." My father stretched his hand straight out in front of him, looked at the watch that had slipped around to the underside of his wrist. "No. Never mind."

The two of us sat in the glow of the TV. My father was gathering steam to go to bed. Soon this man would stand and I'd hear the sequence of creaks and pops from his bones, wispy exhalation through big nostrils. I found myself wishing he would stay.

"Names. I ask and people tell and I listen, I'm sure I listen, but then it's never there."

"I'm exactly the same way," he said.

"You request info, you receive info, and yet for some reason you don't retain info?"

"Why ask for info if you don't want it?" he said. "Whose time are we wasting? Everyone's is whose. Everyone's time."

"It's our fault," I said.

"Certainly not theirs," he said.

And yet still he stood up. Bones popped and he picked up his empty wineglass and he breathed heavily as he turned the corner around the couch.

"Hey," I said. "We going to a game sometime soon?"

"I would love to go to a game," he said. "Pick a game and check with your mother if I'm in town. Or check with Sherry. Sherry probably over Mom. My schedule changes."

He stood over the couch for a good minute, and I could only imagine what sort of torture his thoughts might have been, how this schedule weighed on him, owing so many things to so many different other people. His *wife*, my father had a wife to think about and care for, not to mention a *child* for whom he had to provide. Not to mention the union itself, *marriage*, institution. And then the whole entire city, the city itself relying on his success. And how much love? How could one man contain so much love for such copious others?

"Good night, sport."

After a while, I stood from the TV and walked stiffly through the living room to the basement door, then descended. I found the boxes I'd hauled across the country and had to tear open several before locating the right one. Then I went upstairs to lie in bed naked on top of the covers, one arm at my side, the other holding the book I suddenly wanted very much to read. William Strunk Jr. and E. B. White's *The Elements of Style*.

I listened for squirrels but heard nothing.

july

one

her family never liked me. This was a message passed with little subtlety. The surgeon father and med-school brother glared at me with delirious conviction: this young man does *not* deserve our Audrey. Even before the cheating, the screaming and slamming. At dinner during the first Portland visit, I was sure med-school elbowed me in passing. The business-school sister pretended I was either too small or too dumb to address. It didn't take long to realize that general disinterest and prevailing rudeness were symptoms of an issue more basic than whether or not they cared for me personally. The problem was my love. Whether the decision was communal or something each came to alone, none of them bought that I was in love with Audrey. They decided quickly and unanimously that my claim to love was insincere. And thus why bother? Why even pretend civility? It made sense. Of the four, only the cardiologist mother spoke to me as a wholly rational and worthwhile human being. Given the same data, she interpreted my alleged nonlove as a signal of inherent weakness, an unfixable character flaw, and thereby found reason to pity and speak softly to me with tender condescension I had no trouble gathering she enjoyed.

"Families worry," Audrey said. "They need to believe that I'm in good hands."

She took my hand and pressed it to her mouth and made clear that her faith in me was deep and unqualified.

"You love me. I know. If they don't know now, they will eventually. Just you be Potter and I'll be Audrey. Like normal. They'll see. They have to see. They're not idiots."

Before I left this first visit, they stood together once more in a line so I could observe their considerable force. Gathering to see me off, aligned as if to say, *In the permanent reality of our family, this, too, we know, will pass.* Littered waste cleared off their lawn. And on the way to the airport Audrey avoided excuses, because you don't have to excuse family, and we spoke predictably of missing and longing and the number of days before we'd see each other again.

The second Portland visit occurred winter of junior year, post Jim and the blonde in the basement. And this time I explicitly focused on the impression I made. I cleared the table and washed dishes and poured the med-school brother wine. I brushed the small of Audrey's back in passing, leaned and whispered into her ear in full view of the parents. She crept into the guest bedroom and we made silent love, then lay staring at the ceiling.

"Stop worrying about them," she said. "Just be Potter. I'll be Audrey."

Trembling at the sound of her voice, I recognized the girl at my side, epicenter of my world, was capable of mass demolition. That she could disappear, or die, or declare this whole thing over. At any given second she could crush, kill, destroy, with a word. Twin bed, musty guest room, hostile environs: where I came to understand just how much of love was based on fear.

And still the family didn't buy it. This time no phalanx, hardly even a goodbye. Airport drive, I squeezed Audrey's hand and told her I loved her more today than any day before. She nodded and said, I know.

During the third visit that following July, only Marilynne the cardiologist was home. The other three were on various trips of their own. I prepared fresh salmon and lentils from a recipe I'd

memorized and we talked of our final year of school and the up-
coming presidential election. After dinner the women turned in
early, leaving me alone in the TV den of their massive doctor
house. I had never seen such thorough photographic record of a
family's history. Here were Brandon, Caroline, and preadolescent
Audrey floating off some lake dock. Here was Marilynne with
children at a formal affair. A thousand smiles passed between
family. How could these people have been wrong about me?
They were surgeons and ambitious young adults sharing a nature
of familial love I had never known. They were not idiots. And this
was troubling.

Our parents would finally meet at commencement, a few
loaded and awkward moments while Aud and I stood tight-lipped
in gowns and dress shoes. Overlapping fields à la those of mag-
nets, the forces here what your boy's problem is and what we find
lacking in your girl. Silent. Masked. I wanted to fucking explode.

Nor would she even really look at me in their presence.
Because by then Audrey's defection was nearly total, to the surgeons' theory and consequently to Carmel's heartless ones and
zeros. No more forgiveness, no maybe, no benefits of any doubt.
This boy does *not* love our Audrey. Never mind that her parents'
opinion might have created its own eventual outcome, as
prophecy so frequently can. Never mind that we were still Potter
and Audrey, still two halves of some whole, something, this injured limping organism of our private creation. No longer did or
could or would I provide the proof she needed. Never mind that
pain itself could be her proof, if she would only step back and
look. Look! Never mind any of it. For she was off—off to colorful
Europe with binary Carmel, leave this sprawling gray region behind.

It was a noon-ten first pitch against the Cubs and we had the
French doors open so we could watch from outside. I sat at the
deck table, glazed and getting glazeder in the heat, picking at

some nature of crust on my T-shirt. Stuart was in the kitchen, pouring a blender of margarita into pastel plastic cups. There was little mystery how the afternoon would progress. Edsel would appear sometime soon, somehow, then Matt and Becky would show up and maybe Eric and Melissa, other couples with their dogs. Couples in St. Louis usually have dogs and are usually engaged. In the kitchen, Stuart stuck a finger into his ear and jiggled it. Saturday.

At some point the Saturday thing had begun. There were people in the pool, people on all sides of me, people in the kitchen, talk of sports and whine of blender. Now the ogre was throwing horseshoes in the grass. I leaned back in my chair and watched pregame footage of batting practice. The center fielder shagged a lazy pop fly.

"We lose another series to these fucks and I'm gonna fucking barf all over the place."

This was Eric.

Melissa his fiancée said, "It's the Cubs, honey. Fuck the Cubs."

It was this rivalry, Cards–Cubs, at once fierce and passive, that most bookmarked our city in the national arena. Chicago's proximity made for near splits at either ballpark, the stands like some insipidly cordial Crip–Blood mixer. Richard had raised me to both despise and pity the Cubs, though it always felt to me that a true rivalry required at least some venom and ire. But people believed in it, and that, finally, was what mattered.

Matt tossed a tennis ball his yellow Lab ignored. Becky turned a glossy page of her women's magazine. A girl I'd never seen before, Kathy, visiting from Indianapolis, stared gloomily at the middle of the table. Melissa discussed with Becky the plan to join a new gym. Kathy continued to stare through the table and said she hadn't worked out since she and her boyfriend broke up, a breakup that was apparently behind her visit here.

Becky said, "Because, you guys, the other day at the Galleria I was buying a shirt for this thing and I kept literally running into this big fat woman. And I mean it wasn't even her fault. The stores are tiny. The *Post* ran a thing today with the plans for the New West County. The stores are way way bigger."

The girls wore flip-flops and kept their hair up in jubilant ponytails. They went for hour-long elbows-out walks because you only get one set of knees.

Stuart said, "A kid I knew at Brown is devoting his summer to visiting every major-league ballpark."

"The fuck for?" Eric said.

Sometimes I imagined pissing on Eric's face.

"My thought is he believes it will keep him alive longer." Stuart raised his hands and gestured. "Checking them off of his list."

"He should practice yoga," Melissa said.

"Consider the raw vigor of a professional baseball game," Stuart said. "Twenty-eight stadiums in one summer, bypassing two in Canada. You average, what, twenty-some thousand people per game? We're looking at serious life exposure."

I watched shirtless Edsel throw four horseshoes, then make his way over to our table. There was something always vaguely threatening about the slowness with which he'd approach. The predator bearing calmly down.

Stuart finished the Relaxation with one grand pull. "Going to a ballpark on game day is like putting death on hold while you click over to see who's on the other line. Once the summer's over and he's seen the parks, I'm going to sit down with him and have a nice long talk. See if he feels more alive. My guess is yes."

Eric said, "You want to feel alive? Contribute. Put on a pair of slacks and go to work."

And I thought, *Just because you and your future wife say* fuck *back and forth, it doesn't mean I have to respect you.* I watched the ogre squeeze the tennis ball in his palm. Every now and then he caught my eye and twisted his face into some rictus of I couldn't tell what because of the beard: joy, pain, mockery, repulsion.

"Contribute," Eric said. "Save the nonsense for retirement."

I lit a cigarette and held it between my lips. Grasping the wrought-iron chair, I turned my torso severely to the right, stretching my sore back. Matt and Eric had moved to floating recliners, their distended stomachs baking like flesh muffins in the summer heat. For a moment they appeared not as peers but as decaying matter, two assortments of biological dross wasting in the sun, slowly and relentlessly advancing toward death. I put out the cigarette and stood.

"I think I'll go for a drive."

Stuart walked with me. "Marianne will be here soon. I've gone over my list and I believe Matt, Eric, and Edsel are the only three remaining male friends she hasn't met. I am abiding by her wishes to the fullest of my ability. Whatever middle-Missourian ritual this is, I want to honor it. I've begun revealing things to her that I never intended on revealing to anyone. Deeply held beliefs, shameful admissions of misconduct. The goal is an unprecedented version of nakedness. Physical nudity was almost immediate with us. The curtain was yanked back and she shrugged her shoulders, said *of course*. What's the naked human form to a girl who woke at dawn to milk cows? But this, Potter, this is something bigger. We say *emotionally naked*, but it's always metaphorical. She's aiming to eliminate the metaphor. She's a genius, I'm beginning to believe."

We reached the driveway.

"Have you slept with her yet?"

"I'm no longer divulging such details. Marianne and I are moving toward a sort of sanctity amongst ourselves. Where are you going?"

"Away," I said.

I climbed into the 4Runner and commenced a series of turns before merging into highway traffic. Once off the highway, I followed a UPS truck for a while, then a Cadillac that approached and executed turns with much deliberation.

The heart devoted elsewhere confers little attention to the world that surrounds it.

I was back in Oakville without any real sense of why I'd come, other than to suppose I must have wanted to. Once again children played in the yard at the corner of Yeager and Waldwick, the same hyena children careening off invisible walls and knocking into one another like footage you see of religious fanatics. Ian was sitting on the porch with something in front of him. I got out of my car and made my way up the path.

"I'm building a building," he said. Frown. Pause. "That sounds stupid. Where's your van?"

"It's Saturday."

"Yeah duh. That's why there were cartoons on all morning."

"I don't work Saturdays."

Out of nowhere I remembered the exhilaration of stopping at a McDonald's with a Playland, all those wonderful plastic balls, the Hamburglar burger fort with a ladder entrance. Happy Meals.

"My dad works on Saturday," Ian said. "On Saturdays Mom used to let me cook my own waffles so she could sleep in."

In his little hands was an erector set that looked circa 1960s, old enough to be worth something maybe. All chipped metal and straight lines. For me it had been Lincoln Logs and Legos and then Capsela. This was old and metal and rigid, unforgiving, from a time long before my own. Had toys returned to some golden era without my knowing it?

"What kind of building?" I asked.

"I think a courthouse or a shopping mall. Something important. My dad brought this home for me yesterday. You can help if you want. Here. Put this piece on the top. Feels good."

And it did feel good, oddly therapeutic. I attached a second piece onto the first. Ian nodded.

"My dad likes me to have things to do when he's at work, because he doesn't want me to be one of those kids raised by TV."

A cartoony soundtrack came from inside the dark house, the jingles and crashes and raccoon voices of characters I didn't recognize. I remembered the Snorks—just Smurfs that lived

underwater. Gummi Bears, bouncing here and there and...
Good Lord, how I used to *adore* Saturday morning cartoons.

The boy had stopped building and was looking at me. "How
come you're here?"

"Just to say hello."

This was sufficient. Ian nodded and returned to the building. I
watched his face distort in concentration, then straighten when a
piece fit the way he wanted. As soon as one piece was attached he
reached for another. I looked through the open front door at the
squalor inside. The little hands that reached for another building
piece were browned with dust and covered in boyhood abrasions,
tipped with the black of fingernail grime. And not a single care in
this kid's countenance. Just the repeated nod: approval, compre-
hension, confirmation.

"Enjoy this," I said. "More, enjoy how much you enjoy this.
This might be hard, but that's my advice. Right now everything
for you is singular."

"I don't know what that means."

"Look. You're sitting on the porch, playing with this erector
set. And you enjoy it, right? Sure you do. It's simple. What I'm
saying is, don't take this simplicity for granted. Enjoy it."

"Are you smart?"

"I mean. Technically."

"How do you know?" he asked.

I brought my fingertips together in a chin-level steeple, like
maybe the physical posturing of thought would aid the real thing.
I could hear the hyena children at their ongoing game of tag on
the corner.

"It's not always easy," I said. "There are gray regions."

"Dad says if you can't say something smart you should just do
everyone a favor and shut up. What's your last name?"

"Mays," I said. "Like Willie."

"Willie who?"

"Willie Mays, the old ballplayer. Twenty-something-time all-star. Six-hundred-and-something career home runs. Lifetime average somewhere north of three hundred."

"Was he white or black?"

"It doesn't matter. He made that catch you always see in deep center field. Sprinting toward the wall and catching over his shoulder. Then firing sidearm back to the infield."

"Oh yeah. Black."

I picked up one of the pieces and snapped it onto the building's side. Then another, and then several more. Soon Ian moved away from the building and let me take over.

"How old are you?"

"Twenty-two."

"Wait here."

He got up and carried the unfinished building inside, then returned with the cheap baseball gloves and ball. Once we moved into position, I made sure this time to ground myself in the immediate surroundings so I wouldn't lose composure. My feet scuffed through the dirt of the lawn as I stepped for Ian's throws. After a few catches, I dropped the glove to the burned ground. I wanted to feel the ecstatic slap of old ball against bare palm. I caught left-handed, one-handed. Ian shook his head and threw harder. Simple old ball, simple bare palm. Each sting was a little gift, amazing.

We stepped toward each other as the catch wound down. I asked if he liked ice cream.

"See, that's a stupid question."

"Yes. And we could get some. I feel like ice cream, I'm saying, and you could come with me. If you want."

Ian held the ball. He looked at his house and then the ground. "I'm going to need some shoes."

Ian fastened his seat belt without being told to. He ran a hand over the dashboard and fiddled with the electronic windows. He dipped his seat back and brought it back up. He turned the air conditioner on high. I'd never been more sensitive to the silly opulence of my car.

I said, "The difference between frozen custard and ice cream is you don't put custard in a cone. And it has more butter, or cream, I think. Or eggs. Ted Drewes is custard."

"Is that where we're going? Awesome. I haven't been to Ted Drewes since I was a kid."

"What are you, eleven? Twelve?"

"I'm going into fifth grade, which is almost junior high. I like to round up."

There is a sort of history you can reach for and touch, the official chapters. Since the early forties, a shingle-roofed white house in the South County region of St. Louis has stood as the city's premier source of frozen custard. Forever averse to franchising, Ted Drewes endured populace migrations, regional development, countless diet crazes. In summer, herds of people amass in amorphous queues outside the stand's three service windows. Parents wait and study the hand-painted menu while children spastically circle their legs, chasing and fleeing. I parked between two SUVs that made mine look like a Matchbox toy and followed Ian to the back of the lines.

"Shit," he said.

At what age do kids start to cuss?

"Pardon?"

"That girl. Shit. Shit."

I wanted to hear him say *fuck, asshole, bitch, bastard*. He stepped around so that my body hid him from the girl. He ducked his head and his hair hung over his eyes. I looked at the girl, who was too busy with her parents to notice Ian.

"Who is she?"

"She used to live up the street from me until last year her parents got rich and moved to those big houses over by school. We used to go to the woods by the creek. We had two chairs. Then she moved and took her chair, and I stopped going there because what fun is one chair in the woods."

"Do you still talk to her?"

"Are you crazy? No way. She won't even talk to my friend

Tyler, and Tyler was all she could say when we'd go to the creek. Tyler is so cute I'm gonna marry him and have his kids, Tyler this and that and Tyler everything else. She called him Ty-Ty."

Ian stared mainly at the ground, stealing occasional furtive glances at the girl.

"She probably misses you too," I said. "Don't get wrapped up in the mythos of the female. I can't tell you how much it would have helped if someone would have explained this to me."

"Are you serious?"

"I'm trying to destroy the mystique before you commit to it."

"Do you even have a girlfriend?"

"Yes," I said. "Do you know your order? You should decide what you want before we get to the window."

Ian asked for an elaborate mixture of cinnamon custard and apple chunks and pie crust, cinnamon powder and a viscous brown topping. He was explicit, clear with his order. I, on the other hand, had no idea. The girl behind the counter tapped her nails on the counter. I asked for plain.

"We don't got plain. You mean vanilla."

We sat on the hood of the car my parents bought for me and spooned frozen dessert into our mouths. I heard a woman yell to get Lindsay's shoes from the backseat. Two teenagers on what looked like a date passed by, laughing. Children scurried about while Ian methodically worked through his custard.

"My girlfriend left for Europe," I said. "It was supposed to last three weeks but now I have no idea when she'll be back."

"My mom left."

I thought about this for a second and spooned more dessert into my mouth. Yogurt had plain. There was also vanilla, but it was a flavor.

"I say girlfriend only out of habit, by the way."

"How do you know if she is or not?" he asked.

"I think it has to do with the way two people talk to each other."

"Maybe you have a picture of her in your wallet? That's another way to tell."

I didn't think I did, but I found one wedged behind my driver's license from a hike we took one spring at Lake Tahoe. Corners torn, colors slightly faded, Audrey with a boot up on a stump, leaning over to tie her laces. I had gone *psst* and taken the picture before she looked all the way up, so her eyes were focused on a spot just below the camera. Ian took it and held it at arm's length in front of him.

"She's pointy," he said.

"Pointy."

"Well, she's not fuzzy."

I thought about this. "I suppose if those are the two options, then no. She's not fuzzy."

I glanced down at Audrey's picture. Those green eyes, tiny circular fields of grass, and the subtle galaxy of freckle just below. Her hair up, I loved it up, exposing that seamless path from chin to ear, elliptical curve of neck. Here they were, Exhibits A through like F, immortalized in handy carry-along dimensions.

"Dad says I have to stop talking about Mom. That talking about her won't bring her back so why bother."

I was not qualified for this. One at a time the enormous SUVs on either side of my own backed out of their spots, immediately replaced by more enormous SUVs. Ian held the paper cup of custard in one hand, little plastic spoon in the other. Tiny spoon. He'd grabbed one of the mini taster spoons from somewhere, potentially the ground.

"It's not your fault," I said.

"Never *said* it was my fault. I know it's not my fault."

A parade of silent moments while we finished the custard. Surely there was more I should have said. Families arrived and departed: white families dressed in every color of the spectrum. A van, a lot like mine from work except with windows, parked nearby, *Hope Eternal Church* painted across its side.

Ian said, "It's not permanent. It's just right now we don't know when she'll come back. But not knowing when, I mean, doesn't mean it won't happen. Sometimes I forget when a TV show comes on and when it does I'm like, oh yeah! This show."

My custard had melted into a pool of off-white goo. Ian scraped the last bits of apple syrup from the bottom of his cup. I threw both cups away and we got into my car.

"Shit! Why are the seats so hot?"

"That's the downside of leather."

We drove back to Waldwick Drive listening to one of St. Louis's four classic-rock stations, songs filling what would otherwise have been a nauseating silence. Time was running out. I racked my brain for a fact, some niblet of wisdom to share with this kid whose mother had disappeared. One hundred twenty thousand dollars spent on my education—I should have had facts to spare, wheelbarrows full of excess knowledge.

"I never met a problem frozen custard couldn't fix."

I heard the kid's laughter like a bag of popcorn, lighter than you expect. He laughed through the better part of the instrumental intro to Boston's "Foreplay/Longtime," then stopped abruptly and told me I was crazy.

When we pulled up to the end of the dirt path to his short house with peeling paint, Ian pushed open his door and hopped to the ground.

"I can hit too," he said.

"Good. Hitting is important."

"I have a line-drive swing. I go with the pitch. I pull the ball, I go the other way. I don't have a power swing."

"The second you start to overswing, you know what you're going to have?"

"Yeah."

"A handful of pop-outs. Power comes from technique. Good. I'm glad to hear that."

He had closed the door and was standing now on the running-board step, elbows on the window. Time passed. I wasn't sure what was supposed to happen.

"So next time you go to a batting cage, maybe you could come by here and I'll go with you."

I was shocked and elated that he would see me again. There was the cage out Highway 44 with the go-kart track, another one by the water slides. The indoor place out by Westport Plaza. Reigning over all of these was the clear king of area batting facilities, Tower Tee.

"Alright. It's a plan."

I sat at the stop sign on the corner, waiting for a break in traffic. I looked over and saw the hyena kids at rest, sitting in a loose circle, watching me. I held a hand out the window, a sort of wave, and they stared back, completely still.

two

I ate one night I came home to find a figure alone in the darkness. It was my mother, seated with legs folded beneath her so they disappeared within her purple robe. With no legs and her arms close to her side, she looked like a chess piece set there on the couch.

"Mom? Jesus. I almost peed myself."

"Oh, I'm sorry, honey. Normally when I can't sleep I sit in the living room, but I wanted to see you come in."

"I thought this was the living room."

"This? No, this is the family room. The living room has the fireplace."

"Are you sure?"

She held the mug centered at chest level and stared in a way that I kind of wanted to drop to the floor.

"Why, yes, I'm sure. This is the family room."

I was almost positive she was wrong, and I felt a certain warmth for this dash of parental fallibility. The light on the answering machine blinked tiny red dashes.

"What keeps you up so late?"

"Thirty-five years of snoring from your father. You'd think by now, wouldn't you? You'd think one would adjust. But still, here I am."

She shrugged and brought the mug up to her mouth with both hands. I slipped off my shoes and walked past her into the kitchen. She looked even stranger from behind, just shoulders and head. I tried to recall if her head had always been so *round*. I unwrapped a slice of American cheese and sat down in my father's recliner.

"Dairy," I said.

My mom sipped from her mug. "Are you enjoying being home?"

"Yes."

"Are you going to leave?"

"Mom."

"When the snoring got this bad I used to think about sleeping upstairs in the guest bedroom. Just go up there for the night. I held out because I didn't want to hurt your father's feelings. Then one night, this was recent, within the past few months, I went up there. And do you know what? Something about the vents, maybe because the guest bedroom is on top of our room, and the vents? Anyway, the point is that he's even louder upstairs. I know it sounds impossible."

"It's bizarre," I said, "because I don't hear any of it. And trust me I've been awake."

"No. It doesn't make it over to your room. I'm glad it doesn't bother you."

By now my eyes had adjusted to the lighting and I felt bad about my initial shock at finding her here. And upon further review I decided she was right about the living room. Of course she was. This was more her home than anyone's.

"You've slept in my room?"

"No I have not."

"Let me ask you something, Mom. Do you ever hear anything up in the attic?"

Her hands and mug went from chest to lap. "The attic?"

"I'm just wondering. Any sounds at all."

"Is this about the squirrels?"

"Different than squirrels."

"How different?"

"Just different."

"No," she said, raising the mug. "There's nothing in the attic."

For several minutes neither of us was willing to speak or leave or do anything besides sit there.

"At least stay through the fall, honey. I know how much you love our falls in the Midwest."

"Mom."

"You were always saying on the phone how much you missed the seasons. There was that funny thing you said about smog doesn't count as a season."

"You mailed me that box of leaves," I said. "I loved that."

"You and your father will rake the yard," she said. "Do you know what that would mean to your father? To rake leaves next to you, side by side?"

"These allergies," I said.

"Christmastime around here is so special. All the energy, all the trees hung with lights, the decorations at the Botanical Garden. It's going to be beautiful."

A pause lingered.

"And who can resist the spring? I don't have to tell you how nice our springtime is. All the green, the yards. The bulbs sprouting through the softening ground. The whole city blooms. Color everywhere."

"I don't have any idea what's going to happen."

"The other day, Potter, just the other day I had the oddest memory of your childhood. Right in the middle of lunch. Someone was saying something about some group of people down in the wine country, and then all of a sudden for some reason I remembered when you were first learning to speak. I was trying to teach you colors, but all you wanted to talk about was yellow. You loved yellow. I think you liked the softness of it.

Gentle yellow. Only two colors mattered: yellow and not yellow. Except you pronounced it *yayo*. I'd point to something and you'd say *yayo* or *not yayo*. I held up a banana. *Yayo*. Outside in the grass. *Not yayo*."

As we sat in icy dark, the vents exhaling freezing streams that collided somewhere overhead, then settled downward, I pictured a world in which all things were so wonderfully reducible. By this point I was positive my mother had seen Freddy. The jurisdiction she held over this household, her deep knowledge of its most recessed nooks and crannies, she must have.

"That message on the machine is from Audrey," she said.

"What? She called here?"

"About fifteen minutes ago. I thought maybe the ringing would wake up your father so I sort of let it go until the machine picked up."

In addition to trying very very hard not to leap over the couch to get at the machine, I was also working to come up with an explanation for why Audrey would call my home over my cell phone. I pictured her clutching an international phone card, bent over the alien shape of some pale gray or blue phone terminal, handset resting horizontally in that European manner, poking the elaborate sequence of card number, country code, area code, and the final seven digits. She was sad, perhaps. Longing for some connection with a household, the anchor of home. Was she crying as she dialed? She might have been crying. Or laughing, Carmel's fingers tickling her bald head.

"She's in Germany," my mother said.

It was amazing what this tiny bit of knowledge did for me. Germany, a smallish country, roughly, I approximated, the size of a middle-American state? I could now pinpoint her in a region. This was a problem for us, my habit of not exactly needing, per se, but very much appreciating knowledge of her location. She couldn't stand when I left her messages with *not sure where you are, but I'm ...* or some such passive query. And part of me was pleased that my little habit angered her. It showed that the finer points of our communication mattered, that our words counted in some larger sense. I stood and crossed the room to the little stand where we kept the answering machine.

"Here. I'll give you some privacy."

"It's fine," I said. "I mean you've already heard it."

She settled back into the couch, relieved and heavy, and I wondered if maybe there was something besides milk in her mug.

> *Hello, Mayses, it's Audrey calling from Heidelberg, this wonderful little German town on this wonderful German river. We're near the Black Forest. Or wait, maybe we're in the Black Forest? Carmel has a family friend at the university, so last night we had this meal, oh my God this meal, and I drank ale from the horn of some creature, some horned beast. What else? There's a castle up on this hill we're about to hike to. Oh man, card's running out. But Potter! People here say there are faeries in the woods around the castle, actual real live faeries that will grant you wishes if you catch. Oh the lady is saying there's no more time. Anyway, Carmel bought this net? Shut up lady! Okay so I hope everything is*

End of message. I replayed it once more, then pressed delete and went back to my father's chair. I stared at my toes inside my socks. Carla sipped her mug and held it just below her chin. Never had I so thoroughly appreciated my family's penchant for conversational minimalism. What could my mother think of this girl? *Faeries* said it all. What was there for her to ask? To answer? No, we opted for silence because it was what we knew best. And now something must have been altered or made somehow special, some new layer of noiselessness left behind by Audrey's voice, because only now did I hear the faint nasally rips of my father echoing from back in the bedroom.

"Sounds like a walrus dying," I said.

Carla leaned back so she could unfold her legs. She stood and stretched arms over her head with the mug hanging from one finger. Then she approached me in my father's chair, leaned forward, and kissed my forehead.

"I love you so much sometimes I wonder if it's even fair."

When I awoke, still in my father's chair, the first razors of dawn were slicing through darkness outside and everything looked a color right smack between yellow and not yellow. I heard the first cries of early-rising birds and the metallic, ratchet-like snores sounding from the master bedroom, where I imagined my exhausted mother lying, eyes open, staring at the ceiling above.

It was almost time to go deliver the city's bottled water.

I worked. I went and loaded and drove and unloaded and reloaded and drove and punched my time card and came home. I showered. Each day I considered writing something to Audrey, and each day I did not.

I sat on the front porch sipping a beer, listening to the come-and-go drone of cicadas. One house over, the Hoyne daughter emerged from the front door and began the walk to a silver Jetta parked in the street. I followed her blond hair against the background of prevailing green, like some halo accompanying her frame, and her name came to me: Zoe. She drove the twenty yards to the front of my house, then sat there with her left arm hanging out the window. She didn't look at me. And there was something about her arm, a nonchalance, call it a poetic carelessness, hanging there, hand patting the beat to whatever music she had on. I finished my beer at what I pretended was my own pace, then set the bottle down and approached her car in deliberate steps, stretching my forearms as I went. She wasn't wearing any makeup.

"You should get in."

"Into the car, you mean. Where you headed?"

"Anywhere. I had to get out of my house. Mom is on the phone with my brother because something's wrong, or his version of wrong, so she had to console. My mother consoles loudly." She smiled, and something I kept inside ceased to exist. "Come on."

"Tonight's a big night. The mother's got some kind of roast going in the oven."

"How about you just get in the car."

A woman in a minivan passed by and waved, while a squirrel sat motionless on the power line directly overhead, nibbling at something in its paws, watching us all. I walked around the car and got into the front seat. The music was old, staticky reggae. The interior was littered with the normal bits of teen-girl livelihood. Magazines full of bad advice. Those cheerleading shoes with the removable plastic-triangle colors. Things I wanted to call trinkets. I was pleased to see a standard transmission. I pulled a cigarette from the pack in the emergency-brake divot and examined the song list from one of the blank CD cases scattered around the front seats. I put the cigarette back. We still hadn't moved.

"I'll admit a small amount of relief that even your brother needs consolation."

"He's probably eight times more pathetic than you'd ever imagine." She picked up the pack of cigarettes. "He calls with weekly law school updates on his class rank. And Christ help us if it ever falls below three."

"How long have you been a smoker?"

"Been a smoker?" she said. "Oh God. I've never thought of myself that way. I started in sixth grade to make sure none of my friends would disown me."

I formulated a plan to avoid any and all references to age, grade, or temporality in general. Which I knew was impossible since this immaculate girl was a full six years younger than me,

meaning right now the ratios of age disparity over personal age
(6/22 and 6/16) were too significant to shrug away. I had already
run through the usual extension of relativity: at my thirty, she'd
be twenty-four, and so on. But these thoughts worked regressively
as well: the deeply disturbing image of a six-year-old me like some
wolf, fangs dripping drool onto the newborn girl below.

"Are you aware that the songs on these CDs are horrible? This
is a concern my generation has about your generation. This
comes from a complete certainty that our own music was crap,
and therefore yours must be even crapper."

"You can't judge someone based on something given them as a
gift," she said. "A gift only speaks of the person giving it."

"I remember one Christmas being given two different Jane
Goodall biographies," I said. "The ape woman."

"And what's this generation nonsense?"

"Are we still sitting here?" I said. "I was sure we'd begun moving by now."

Zoe laughed and pulled us away from the curb. I could see this
little girl at her fortieth birthday party, taking the number in
stride, stepping over it like some sidewalk crack.

"The boys I know seem to think a mix CD is this like ultraper-
fect present. And I'm supposed to gush thanks and think of them
every time I play it. Since they require upward of five entire minutes to make."

"There was a time when a mix tape meant a lot of clicking
noises. Holding your finger above the pause and record buttons
of the tape deck. My God. You don't remember any of this."

"Old man sitting next to me," she said. "Dear old man in
my car."

I felt her downshift into a curve and accelerate out in second
gear. The kids who'd thrown toilet paper at her house might have
had no other option. They were only doing what they could to
keep up. I clutched the rubberized handle above the window so I
wouldn't have to think about where to put my hands.

"Where are you taking me?"

"You and I are going for a drive because we're neighbors. Stop being suspicious."

My legs were crossed tightly enough to hold water. She had one hand on the gearshift, the other draped over the steering wheel. Hair ponytailed neatly. I wiped a palm on my thigh.

"Left," I said.

"Well then."

The evening was cool enough that we didn't need the air conditioner. The odor of barbecue hovered thick and smoky everywhere we went. Grilled MEAT. Zoe ejected the CD and tossed it into the backseat. I chose a case from the floor mat and quickly scanned its song list. Once again I was appalled. What nature of person would combine these songs? I slid the disk into the player and went to track four.

"Go right," I said.

"I like this one," she said. "Who is this?"

"Johnny Cash, one of a select few men who could get away with doing Taco Bell commercials. Apparently one of your suitors has good taste. I say pick him."

"I'm not *picking* any of them. These CDs don't represent a catalog of potential mates. They give them to me. Sometimes I listen."

There were very few cars on the road with us, and those we passed seemed energized in a way I wasn't used to. They were more determined in their goinghood, drivers eager, I guessed, to get home and cook meat. Summer nights like this can be counted on fingers in St. Louis, they are the exception to the rule of mug and weight.

"I got my license from the DMV in that strip mall over there," I said.

"I don't think that branch exists anymore. It's been closed for a few years."

"I'd be happier if we didn't think about that."

"You're really not all that old, you know. Also I wish you'd realize how little it matters."

I replayed the Johnny Cash song and said, "Turn into here."

It was a small parking lot for a small public park, empty but for a dark blue station wagon tucked alone in the back corner. At one end of the lot was a group of picnic tables beneath a kind of wallless barn. Beyond were baseball diamonds and soccer fields. To our right was the reason I'd brought us here, the Rocket Slide. Zoe parked us facing the playground area, and for a moment we sat in silence, taking it in. There was the red, white, and blue spire painted to look like a rocket, the system of ladders and bridges that spiraled around it, the three slides and unsteady wooden bridge and jungle gym components at its base. The swings and other attractions were off to the side, several gravelly steps from the heart of the Rocket Slide.

"Beautiful," she said.

"My parents used to bring me every week. For a long time this slide was the single scariest thing in my life. The rest of the park I loved, but that main slide, so steep and final. Pure childhood mortification."

"I can't believe I've never been here."

We got out of the car and approached slowly, stepping heavily through fine, crayon-brown gravel. I felt my feet sink and drag as Zoe and I split from each other. I ducked through a short archway into the base of the main tower and climbed the lower rungs of a narrow ladder, cautious with my head and elbows. I was far too big, but I kept going. She went to the opposite end of the thing, away from the rocket portion of the slide. I heard echoes of her bouncing loudly across the bridge. I reached the top of the ladder and stared down the long, skinny, steel walkway, flanked by an enfilade of whitewashed chain-link. Just above was the biggest of the slides. Soon Zoe was crouched next to me.

"Each slide has its own character," I said. "The really short one is more for ascent than anything, a ramp. The mid-level one off to the side of that ladder that just bruised the hell out of my knee is where kids begin. See the gentle bumps? Perfect for your novice slider. Once you mastered that one, you'd move up to this one here, which is really the focal point of this place."

Next to us was the dark mouth of the curving, partially covered slide. Cicadas went *skee-her, skee-her* beneath or beside the sound of Zoe's little breath.

"I'm embarrassed to say how long it took me to get the nerve to go down this thing. I had no problem with the medium one, which is actually steeper and faster than this one. I think it was the darkness that scared me. The tunnel curves around the pole so you have no idea where you're going once you're in. Jesus, it used to scare me."

"There's definitely a metaphor there. Scared of the dark future." She patted my elbow.

"You're not allowed to patronize me."

"Oh no. I'm with you on the scariness thing. If the hot older neighbor is scared, I'm petrified."

She looked at me, her eyes a blue like Stuart's lighted pool at midnight, then swung herself neatly into the tunnel. I followed close behind, but lost momentum before I reached the bottom. She laughed and made her way toward the swings while I squirmed down the last few feet of slide and followed.

Once she was seated on the swing, her smile turned immense.

"I love to swing. Love it."

I nodded and took the swing next to her. The simple fact, though, was that I was a very bad swinger. I had never successfully worked out the physics of it, and this made me mad. It was gravity, after all, and yet I was hopeless.

"In fact I can't think of a single thing to compete with the reckless joy of swinging," she said, and suddenly it was as if she had entered a new plane of existence. Two quick steps and she was going like kitchen fire, soon eclipsing three and nine o'clock while I plodded slowly along like an old pet. Her chain slackened as she reached an apex, then stretched taut with downward acceleration.

"I don't understand how you're so much better than me."

"You're trying too hard," she said. "Or not enough."

Her hair streamed behind, paused, then collapsed around her face. And again. I felt that semi-aquatic form of small astonishment that comes during the early stages of a new relationship, when every small lesson of a person's wonder turns the air between you more viscous. I hopped from the swing for a better view of the miraculous swinging angel, taking a seat in the gravel. The sweep and arc of her movement, the leaning, how her body's shifts worked in perfect concert with natural law—these her gifts to the world. She went on for quite some time before riding one upswing to its peak and leaving the swing behind, briefly flying, then landing back in the gravelly earth with its rules and constraints. She joined me in the gravel.

"How's the studying?" I asked.

"Words, words, words. I like *natation*. The act or skill of swimming. My mom says she'll pay you to tutor me. She and your mom have already discussed it. Wheels are turning."

As cars passed by, we heard bits of stereo against the underlying and constant cicada buzz. Just south of the Rocket Slide, Hanley Road changed to Springer Road where it entered into Webster County and became more residential and curvy and tree-lined. Roads did this in St. Louis, spontaneously switched names without warning. Zoe smacked a mosquito that landed on her arm, then showed it to me on her palm, bloodless.

"*Ebullience* will be on there. I personally guarantee."

"Oh, I *like* that," she said. "Eb-boo-lee-ents. Another one, please."

"*Marasmus*. A wasting of the body associated with insufficient intake of food."

"See, this deserves pay. You could be on the clock right now." She threw a handful of gravel at my legs.

"I don't have any sort of teaching certification," I said. "There could be surprise inspections. Who knows what sort of trouble I'd be in."

After a few minutes she said, "I think there are insects living in this gravel," and we drove back home.

three

the noise that woke me was thunderous and singular, contained to a small region just above my head. In the otherwise black of middle night, big green hexagon numbers glared tauntingly from my bedside clock. Now I heard a drastically different sound, small and softer. Sounded almost like the chirp of a bird but muffled, with a note of restraint. Sounded like a bird in the attic.

I opened the closet and moved Christmas decorations and winter coats into the hallway. I climbed the ladder into an attic I hardly recognized. Everything was brighter. It seemed that the top box of the stack I'd constructed in front of the window had fallen, and now light poured in from the streetlight outside and I saw more of this room than I had in weeks. I could see distinct shapes where I was used to blackness, including what appeared to be a bird perched atop a box near the window. And Freddy, except this time he was wearing only a Speedo and no water wings.

"The box I had to move the box to let in light it was too dark up here."

I had promised myself if I ever saw him again I wouldn't look, a promise just self-defeating enough I thought maybe I had a chance. Our last meeting had been cut short, and fault was entirely my own. A valuable lesson learned: *do not look*. I took a seat on my makeshift bed and watched the bird sitting by the window, its head antsy and curious.

"If you stare I have to go away."

"I promise to not stare."

"Going away is the closest I feel to pain not pain exactly but it feels odd and so please do not this time don't stare."

"Promise."

"Are you willing to cross your heart and hope to die?"

I had a feeling that this line, this artifact joke left over from his life as a five year old, was a test. And now my urge to look was compounded by a fresh and crushing understanding that my brother Freddy had at one point been a *human being*. This ghost swimsuit Freddy was once a person, with flesh and hair and bones. Freddy the son and Freddy the brother, who really only wanted to retrieve his ball. A little person who wore *shoes*. How in the world had I gone twenty-two years without thinking of Freddy's feet?

"It's a cardinal too did you notice that part probably yes you did because you seem to notice everything."

My stomach went tight. I folded at the waist and rocked gently back and forth, clenching. When the feeling subsided, I sat back up on the box and looked to the bird in the window. It had the tri-angular beak and distinct head plumage, chest puffed out in round contention.

"I thought you would appreciate that since baseball and how important baseball is to you."

"Thank you, Freddy."

"It's too bad we never got to play catch later you were good at it when you played your arm could have been stronger and some-times you swung too hard with two strikes but overall you were a real addition to the team."

I had thought myself well equipped to meet Freddy again; I had devoted hours to solitary rehearsal up here. I had questions planned and conversations plotted. Now all I could think of was a scene in the apartment kitchen, me the infant strapped into my high chair, babbling and waving hands as my mother stands at the counter, head craned around to the table where Freddy sits and waits for lunch. Carla asks what he would like on the sandwich and Freddy says *cheese and mayonnaise, please*. I babble incoherently and wave my hands. Family of four, father at the office. She turns to the table and sets a plate in front of him, and he looks into her eyes and says *thanks, Mom*. I babble louder and pound hands against my high chair. Freddy finishes the sandwich and goes outside to play with his ball. Carla says *be careful, sonny boy*. I whine for another spoonful of formula.

"I've been waiting to hear your voice," I said.

"It's hard to talk to you because you don't listen to anything I say."

"But I do. I'm sitting here hanging on every word."

"Then why didn't you do what I said? It was so easy Potter appreciate Mom and Dad simple appreciate them and let yourself love someone and don't smoke stupid dumb killer cigarettes and you ignored all of it."

"I'm working on the love part," I said, and accidentally ran my eyes across his form. "I'm going back over memories like an old film reel. I have all day in that van to review. Stuart was supposed to help, but he's forgotten. But I'll get there. It's either love or it's not."

"Calling something love saying the word does not make it love because words you know this part you learned at school words come apart they are empty signifiers these words."

Freddy, glossy and frail and very much deceased, bent down and examined one of the boxes. For the moment he was occupied and I allowed myself a sustained look. When he stood I quickly dropped my eyes.

"Love is motion Potter love is forward movement but you said yourself the memory reel backward it's all backward with you. You are stuck back there because Potter you don't let yourself move forward your eyes get stuck on things and people."

The bird by the window turned to give me a full profile. My gaze went to the shadows on the attic's floor, which I followed over to the small puddles forming around Freddy's pale feet.

"That's the reason you can't look at me it's your eyes your eyes are like teeth like shark teeth they are starving. Eyes can show love but there is no love in teeth. Your shark eyes make me have to go away."

"I understand," I said. "And I think it's an issue of resentment. I think part of me resents you for leaving me alone."

"I'm here I'm right here."

"Either I resent you or I resent myself, or maybe I resent Richard and Carla. I'm trying to figure it out."

"But there's no difference no difference we're the *same* because Dad is the same and Mom is the same we're all the same thing. This is what it means to be a family to have everyone separate but the same."

An idea came to me. Such joy did I take in this idea that it left almost no room to be pleased with myself for coming up with it. I knew enough about myself to know it was only a matter of time until I disobeyed and looked at Freddy. As long as I could see, I would look. This could only work if I was somehow made blind. I stood and moved toward the window.

"Where are you going what are you doing?"

"If there's light in here, I'm going to look," I said. The cardinal cleared off to another corner of the attic. I bent to pick up the fallen box. "I'm a visual learner. It's that simple. Hold on a second. Once it's dark we'll be fine. I won't be tempted to look."

"Leave my box there don't move it."

"Cardboard boxes are designed to be moved," I said, lifting.

I hefted the box on top of the other and shimmied it back against the window, sealing out the streetlight. I turned and faced back into the attic.

"Freddy?"

I struggled to adjust to the modicum of remaining light. After a minute I was able to pick out the shapes of boxes and the trapdoor and ladder downstairs. Freddy, of course, was gone. I laid myself across the box mattress and heard the bird flitter through some unseen ceiling aperture back into the night.

I stood in the warehouse, watching the company's black workers run the bottling machine. Purified water, drawn from the city's wells and treated with some combination of chemicals and filters, got red caps. Turquoise was Natural Spring, from a spring somewhere in southern Missouri. Blue caps were saved for Premium, drawn from an exclusive, highbrow spring in rural Arkansas. Cheap, better, best. But the more I looked, the more it seemed all the waters were coming from the same giant drum. I was likely missing something simple and easily explained. But what an infinitely abusable system: the arbitrary assignment of quality and value based on color. These basic long-standing assumptions I held about goods and services and the way things worked—threatened every time Marshall pulled a lever to fill the bottles, which slid to Eddie waiting at the end of the belt. No check, no balance. One big drum. Eddie grabbed soft plastic caps from the boxes at his feet and hammered them onto a bottle. Bottles collected into racks arranged by color. *Worth.*

The van, though, was real. All the rust and all the stink surrounded me as I waited in highway traffic that made no sense and seemed to come out of nowhere. Two lanes thinned to one, and the left-turn signal of the car in front of me pulsed endlessly. But there was nowhere to turn. I began a series of maneuvers to alert the car's driver of his signal. I turned on my own blinker and let it go for a minute. I waved my left hand out the window. I tried to honk, but the only sound that came of it was that of fist pounding dead steering-wheel vinyl. A total breakdown of communication. The signal blinked.

Audrey always had difficulty reconciling the titanic danger of driving with the laissez-faireness with which most people approached it. Whereas otherwise her life was defined by a sort of

reckless assertion, which I loved, behind the wheel she went tur-
tle. The caution she exhibited at every corner or hillcrest, every
highway on-ramp. Driving as if acceleration itself was to blame
for the modern world's many crises.

"Green," I would say with forced patience, which isn't anything like real patience. "Aud. Green light."

"What's our hurry here exactly? Must you snap?"

Riding shotgun, I was implicated and therefore guilty to the
force gathering behind us, the fully justified rile. Horns and the
squeal of tires as drivers cut around us, then back into our lane.
Glaring on the way by or slowing briefly to our pace and gesturing, yelling.

"It's just there's a contract in play. We all agree that when the
light changes, we'll move forward. By not moving forward—"

"Am *too* moving."

"By inching forward like this you violate the contract. Which
explains the honking. And this guy with the finger."

"Oh hurryhurry big hurry. We're, what, slaves to a lightbulb?"

And for the lightbulb comment I would fall back into love with
her as we accumulated speed, only of course to stop at another
light a few blocks down the road, be surrounded again by the
same cars and fingers and the same eyes. Whole thing all over
again.

I finished the day's deliveries by one-thirty and went directly to
Stuart's. I stepped over a cat and made my way around the house.
There was one body at the pool, a female person in a lounge
chair. Marianne. This was becoming serious, and I felt myself
inch toward some psychic sort of edge. Who was this farm girl?
What really was she doing here, really? She waved to me, and the
well-known guidelines said I was supposed to wave back and continue my approach. Then I realized it wasn't Marianne sitting by
the pool waving but Deanna, Stuart's stepmother. I unlatched the
fence and walked toward the pool.

"Can you believe it? Sometimes even little old me is allowed to
use my own goddamn pool."

There were two plastic cups and a crowded ashtray on the table next to her chair. The top to her swimsuit hung loosely and covered her in a way that seemed coincidental. She wore dark sunglasses, big black circles like two coasters hiding most of her face. There was no way to know if she was looking at me or the house or nothing at all.

"And now, which one are you?"

"Potter Mays," I said. "We've met before."

"That might could be, Potter Mays. You the one who just finished school?"

"They gave me a rolled-up piece of paper and everything."

"Well well. That makes you how old?"

"Twenty-four. I took two years off halfway through school so I could travel around. Just you know. Be."

She dropped her glasses down her nose. I stood near her feet. She appraised, then smiled, showing an unnaturally bright set of perfect teeth.

"Bull*shit* you did. You're no more twenty-four than I am sober."

Deanna was a tall woman with long legs stretched and crossed at the ankle. I wanted to age her in the early region of forties, but with second wives it was sometimes hard to know. She'd been John Hurst's secretary for six years when he told Stuart's mother they were no longer husband and wife. Twenty-some-odd years of marriage, an unspeakable betrayal. So there was a villainous sheen to the woman, a covering of something like dust from the marital demolition she was so central to. This combined well with the boastful air she conveyed. Two years ago I'd reacted to the news of the divorce with a mixture of undefined awe and reluctant envy. Allegiances shattered, commandments broken—it was a scandal compelling on several levels. But that they'd gone so far as to marry somehow saddened and thickened the farce. I considered asking how many words she could type per minute.

"He's not here, I take it."

"Him and that country girl drove off an hour ago. Can't say

where they went. But if you're planning on staying I'm going to insist you make me a drink. Gin, splash of tonic, and about five ice cubes."

I went inside and pulled a plastic cup from the cupboard. What was it about second wives? X years his junior. X years younger than wife the first. Without these bases of comparison they would float agelessly among us. Maybe it was the adjective alone, *second*. All this word implied. The same way ours was a *college* romance, encapsulated within a very small and jagged-edged universe. Outside of that universe we were without adjective, floating in the ether. Gin and tonic happened to be Audrey's drink of choice. It was also Carmel's. In fact it was Carmel's drink first, decried with rigid authority. Boop bop gin. Beep blip tonic. I stirred the drink and walked back outside.

"There's a doll. Damn if it isn't hotter than all hell."

I saw the slightly exhausted sag of her upper arms, the prominence of veins on legs bent and pinched at the knee, the patient weariness in the corners of her mouth. *Gravity.* But still she lacked the markings of a serious caregiver. Stuart's real mother was a small and gentle woman, the sort of mother who's made ecstatic each time one of her children surpasses her in height. Teaching her family to share and listen and care for those with fewer resources, which for the Hursts was everyone; her work was to offset the various corruptions embedded within the world of limitless capital.

I asked if I would offend her with a personal question, and she said, "Oh *please.*"

"Why didn't you ever have children of your own?"

"A certain mechanic I loved once told me I lacked the shocks and struts to be a good parent. No, I have never been keen on children. How about you. Kids?"

"Just myself."

She took a long sip, then swirled the ice with a finger. I asked what she thought of Marianne and she licked the finger.

"Where in the hell is your drink?"

"Stuart believes she's a genius," I said.

"Oh, he does, does he. Well, she might be. Though I wonder if he's thinking of the right kind of genius. Got a tendency to miss things from time to time. Misinterpret. There ever was a boy who got wrapped up in his own legend, it's our Stewey. Of course I never said that. Who am I to judge the prince of this land."

"I'm not sure I know what you mean."

"Sit down, Potter Mays. You're in my sun. That's better. What I mean is, Stuart Hurst, Esquire, fancies himself the center of a very specific world. Am I right? Heir to a throne he doesn't much want. Am I right?" She set down her drink and dropped her lounge chair two clicks toward flat. "Lends him an air of authority. He's got this kind of resistance about him, though everyone alive knows it's a matter of time alone until he goes working for his daddy."

"I guess. Sure."

"Sure you're sure. Now. What is it brings you to the prince?"

I looked at Deanna and felt a gust of exclusion blown in from some foreign land I was too young and stupid to even visit. I felt like a dog might feel, staring at a horse. We were the same shape, roughly, but the differences in scale and skills were immense.

"Just a quaint, selfish concern. Nothing important."

"Some girl, I bet. Some dumb girl doing dumb things got you worried might be the goddamn end of the universe. And by now we're old friends, Potter Mays. Friends share."

Here was a woman who'd persisted long enough as a secretary that she eventually usurped her boss's master bedroom. Before, she had loved at least one mechanic. But what else? What jobs, what varied lives with what array of others? She had been run through a system, her own sequence of boxes checked or left empty. She emerged older, scathed, and was rewarded with astounding wealth, empty days of cat-watching and gin. By all standards, she'd won. Deanna Hurst had beaten them all.

"There's a girl," I said.

"Sure is."

"It's an issue of love. After four years together we've reached a kind of chasm. Who was chasm? Hegel? Point is, I either step into this chasm or turn and walk away. Or leap over the chasm. I'm not sure how the metaphor is set up."

"Chasm. Okay. I don't mind that idea. I can attest to a chasm or two along the way. Now, but what's keeping you from making this decision on your own?"

I scratched my forehead and wished I had made myself a drink.

"Nothing. Myself. Her, maybe?"

I coughed. She sat up and looked at me like I'd just vomited into her lap.

"And with all the people in the world, you thought to hand this decision over to Stuart *Hurst*. Boy, if that was dumb alone you might be okay, but I got a feeling what's wrong here isn't a problem of dumb. I got a feeling you're a pussy."

"I mean."

"My goodness. You almost had me for a second. Mixed up a stiff drink and handled yourself like a man. Nearly had me fooled. That's the worst kind of pussy too. Sneaky little-boy pussies like yourself."

And as if I owed her further proof, I offered no defense. All I could do was sit there while she pounded the rest of her drink and lay back down into her lounger. Swallowing and smiling with disgust. I couldn't imagine what her eyes might have looked like behind the glasses.

"Little pussy boy, look at you. Who's the tall muscle freak? Edward? Edmund? Least that one's got a set of balls on him. By association I figured you had something going on too. Now I look at you and wish I didn't have to."

"I have to be back at work. Should I get you another drink before I go?"

"There it is—little pussy with that little pussy face. Pussy arms. Pussy legs."

I parked the van inside the warehouse, tossed the MTs into one pile and the flattened cooler boxes into another, then filled out the day's paperwork. At home I bathed and ate a salami sandwich. I found the stack of papers I'd printed in the computer room and put them into a manila folder. I carried the folder out to the garden, where my mother was gardening. She didn't immediately notice me. I pretended to walk in exaggerated comical movement for the audience. She made no acknowledgment of my presence. Her face was in a state unlike any I'd seen on her, violently focused on the task at hand, everything chin to hairline somehow appearing both furrowed and taught, a wrinkled stretch.

I decided this wasn't something I should watch. I left my mother in the garden and continued across the driveway, up to the door of the Hoynes'. I rang the bell and waited, clutching the folder at my waist. Inside the folder were SAT exercises I had stolen from a Web site.

Nancy Hoyne welcomed me into her home. She offered juice or tea or there was also soda if I wanted. I thanked her and said I was fine. No snack, thank you, I'm fine. She led me to the basement door and asked how my summer had been. This, too: fine. Her hand on my shoulder, she thanked me for making time. Carla and Deanna and now this, such array of motherhood. I told Nancy Hoyne it was really my pleasure.

She waited until I'd reached the final step before shutting the door. Like most furnished basements I had known, this one was decorated to take advantage of the little natural light that came through the shoebox windows up high on two of the basement's walls. The walls were off-white, the carpet cream, and the couch in the corner a kind of wheat, or oat color. In the deepest part of the room, in the very elbow of the couch sat Zoe, her legs crossed beneath her, back straight and hair parted in the middle, falling to either side of her face. It was too cool for a tank top, but hers was light green. I tried and failed to not notice her nipples. Lying on the coffee table were a two spiral notebooks and pencils, a Starbucks cup and her cell phone.

Angel on the couch, young man waiting at the bottom of the steps. Mother upstairs mixing one part lemonade with two parts iced tea.

I projected officialdom as best I could, confirming that my role was concrete and without room for movement or discussion. Zoe seemed impressed by this. I had brought with me guidelines for the best way to approach an analogy, and also how to complete a sentence without knowing any of the words. I would save when to guess versus when to not guess for a future lesson. Once she began the practice test, my eyes strayed to the pencil, the hand that held it, the arm, shoulder, the neck. When she looked up from the workbook and caught me watching, I glanced quickly clockward.

"Nine minutes."

After the test we finished with fifteen minutes of vocabulary drills. And here the angel shifted to a position of repose on the couch, which I tried to offset by crossing my legs professorially at the knee.

"*Elegiac.*"

"Spressing sorrow," she said, one arm behind her head.

I nodded and flipped to the next card.

"*Mendacious.*"

"Habbing a false character. Liar, liar, your pants on fire."

"*Non compos mentis.*"

"Not his fault. Him too dumb or him too crazy."

"*Demooterate.*"

"Demooterate?"

Given the alternatives, such childish play was harmless, distraction from the repressed grumblings of desire.

"Wait a second. You make that up, teacher man? You makum upum brand-new word?"

"The English language is an undulating beast, a universe of

flux where meaning and use shifts with context and terms are created according to necessity."

"Demooterate," she said. "Importantizing that which isn't
naturally important."

"Absolutely."

I was performing a service for a client. An educated man sharing his education with a coincidentally beautiful little but not so
little girl. Sanctioned and funded by the family unit upstairs.

four

i drove, I read the billboards out loud, I tried to picture Audrey with a bald head. Certain heads flourish and achieve a new cranial power when stripped of adornment. I carried bottles of Premium water. Other bald heads are bumpy and ridged and misshapen, an embarrassment. From time to time, mistaken tallies from the morning warehouse hour would come to haunt me in the afternoon when I ended up with the wrong bottles for the day's final deliveries. On these occasions I would swap out extra caps from the box I kept between the front seats, dark blue for red, Purified magically turned into Premium. Customer none the wiser. Eddie and Marshall laughed knowingly when I asked whether there was any difference in the waters. I wondered what rule book said I couldn't do this for the rest of my life.

I was in the van when my phone rang. The call was from *SLH!*, and I was dripping sweat, and there are times when a son's instinct is to avoid even the prospect of his father's voice. When the same number called again a minute later, I began to worry. For the most part, I'd gone through life under the presumption that Freddy's drowning had purchased my family a future free from further pain; an unsaid cosmic reparation for the bereaved. But my father never called, and now twice. The closest analogue I knew to worry involved Audrey, and to be honest that was worry perverted by obscene jealousy and idiot anxiety. I grabbed at the phone in the passenger seat.

"Dad? What's wrong?"

"Hi, Potter. It's Sherry."

"Sherry?"

"Hang on a minute and I'll get your dad."

Sweat like a ruptured pipeline.

"Son."

"Dad? What's wrong?"

"Your mother's got one of her things. Something at the zoo. So we're on our own for dinner, you and me. Good game tonight. The Braves. Just swept a series in Cincinnati. Got that young pitcher, the guy, that Ortiz from Colombia. One of these South American guys with an unhittable slider."

Of course everyone was still alive. I couldn't imagine my mother dead. Not the woman who could find life in the tiniest errand or activity. And my father was too weathered; men with catalogs of history and permanently broken noses don't die. He was an institution all his own, imperishable.

"Do you always talk like this at work?"

"How's that."

"Short, clipped proclamations," I said. "Zero inflection."

"You and your old dad. Dinner and a ball game. One of her activities, gluing centerpieces together for a fund-raiser. Hundred fifty bucks a plate, black tie. We'll go somewhere I can wear jeans. When was the last time I wore jeans to dinner? There's your inflection. Need at least two of these three from the Braves. Keep pressure on Chicago."

The rest of the day I took scenic routes and moved slowly. The pool house, end point of end points, had lost my trust. Stuart had, as they say of overgrown lawns, *let the place go*. And in this matter I was helpless. For what recourse was there, really, for the young man who'd lost a friend to unreliability? Was I to plead for more attention? Say *hey, hey, Stuart, pal, look at me?*

At home, I waited on the couch, clean and hungry. Carla was wearing one of her nicer sweaters and black pants that couldn't be confused with pajamas. Clearly she was going somewhere.

"Is there a reason Dad is so gung-ho about eating with me tonight?"

"Reason? No reason," she answered from the kitchen. "He wants to spend time with his son." Now she was in the doorway, drying her hands on a dish towel. "No reason. Wants to talk with his son. I suppose that's a reason."

I asked her to please repeat her plans.

"The Zoo-Ado is a week from Friday. We settled on a theme months ago, now we're beginning the preliminary decorations. The centerpieces and candle fixtures. Don't ask me the theme, because I'm not at liberty to say. Our goal this year is to wow. We want people to walk through those doors and think, *wow*."

"So there's no reason for the dinner," I said.

"He deserves a little of your time, I think. Sit down with your father. No reason."

Out of habit I went to check my e-mail and, after however many hundred previous times proved fruitless, found a message sitting there from Audrey. For a few minutes I stared at the subject line: *the search spreads southward*. I closed the browser window and sat back in the chair. A box at least was something to hold, tangible. I opened another browser window and read the message.

P...
so far no faeries. our search has moved to
swizzerlund. we got bigger nets and sharper focus.
carmel says you'd be a better kisser if you put a little
less heart into it. not sure yet if i agree.

loves.
—a

I deleted the message quickly, but this didn't have nearly the effect I'd hoped. Las Vegas, fall break of senior year. A haggard, early-morning, still-up kiss as just-up joggers and elderly tourists provided context. Following a river's flood of white Russians and much financial ruin. Audrey was asleep in the room six of us were sharing. Carmel and I stumbling from Caesars and sloshing our way to Mandalay Bay, the far end of the Strip. The kiss itself was mostly to signal that we should turn around. An awful kiss. We stopped cold and stepped apart and I felt as if I was staring into some warped mirror, a grotesque and unfeeling reflection of myself—Audrey's other, and potentially realer, love—the gorgeous robot who kissed like she spoke. A wholly soulless and trite moment of imagined desire. Its only sliver of pleasure was that of fulfilled convention: to kiss Carmel was to acquiesce to history and expectation. Complete the unsaid contract of boyfriend and girlfriend's desirable friend. And so a tiny sort of relief for the deflation of that balloon, the release. And then: repulsion and regret and certainty that Audrey would surely find out. Balloon of fear and shame that had floated since that kiss and had now, here at the computer, exploded into a sharp gust of wind, the stink of transgression aged eight months. Stench of my own putrid notions of What's Okay to Do to a Young Woman Who Loves You with All of Her Pure and Wondrous Heart.

Carla left the house humming and, as if choreographed, Richard arrived seconds later. A flash of charred gray suit through the side door, vanishing into the bedroom, then reappearing in jeans and a polo, spinning the car keys around his finger. His shirt was tucked neatly into jeans held up by a needlepoint belt: a series of red birds and yellow bats against a navy blue background, a single black stitch border around each color, giving the whole thing a vaguely digitized look. Needlepointed by Carla sometime in the eighties.

"You get behind the count to Ortiz and you're in trouble. Throws that slider that breaks in the last eight feet."

On these rare nights of nonwork activity, my father would

drive his second car, a silver 1979 Datsun 280Z. The body showed minor signs of wear, enough flaws to save it from the boring sterility of a too-prized thing. These included a rather noticeable dent in the roof that both was and completely was not my fault. The black leather bundled around the base of the stick shift was cracked but clean, Armor All-ed to a semireflective sheen. I always wondered if it was morbid to think, even abstractly, about the day I would inherit the Z.

He drove us to Sportsman's Park, a small restaurant in Ladue named after the former stadium of the St. Louis Cardinals. It was a single-story cottagelike building, split through the middle into a bar on one side, dining area on the other. All walls but one were layered with St. Louis sports memorabilia: baseballs and jerseys and pennants and black-and-white photos of local heroes posing with the restaurant's owners. The sixth wall was dominated by a big-screen projection TV, circa not recently. Sportsman's succeeded at being both cozy and pretentious, with a typical bar menu highlighted by the Heavy Hitter, a pound of wings served with a chilled bottle of Dom. Printed along the bottom of each menu page was the tagline *Where the Elite Meet to Eat*. This was not ironic. This was Ladue, home to the Hursts, meaning wealth, and, tonight, us.

In public, my father was frequently recognized and expected to say hello. People I had never seen. I ducked into the dining side and found an empty table. In a minute he joined me, turning his chair to face the blurry television, and sat. The network wunderkind and former-player color man called the action.

"Have you read what they're saying about this catching prospect? This Brosky. Bresky. Beesk."

"Brandt," I said. "Derril Brandt."

We watched the screen. A waitress appeared who I could have sworn I knew in some old and unspectacular way, and my father ordered two beers.

"People are calling him the next Johnny Bench."

"Except I guess he can't block a pitch in Triple-A to save his life," I said.

The game would triangulate our discussion, a satellite to bounce statements off, replacing eye contact. Mainly I expected we would sit silently, chewing and watching the birds.

The color guy said, *In a situation like this, you're thinking, move the runner over and set the table for the big guns.* The network wunderkind said, *A one–one changeup comes in high.*

The waitress had gone to my high school. Or not. Everybody in this city was beginning to look the same. Half a mile from here was the field where I had been a three-year varsity starter at second base. Batted leadoff, was given a full-time green light on the base paths. District cochamps my junior year, third in state my senior. Named all-district junior and senior years, POTTER MAYS listed in the *Post-Dispatch* with other regional standouts. The clippings went from paper to fridge to framed and hanging on a wall of my father's office downtown. Days when I wore the distinct tan of a ballplayer, arms and neck charred a crispy walnut, one hand pallid. Dad was there almost every game, home or away. In college, I quit during preseason workouts when the prospect of nightly practices and Saturday doubleheaders threatened my drinking and devotion to Audrey. My father had reacted to this decision with a mixture of concurrence and extreme disappointment, a thickness in his voice that had slowly, over the past four years, thinned.

"You've got to jump on this Ortiz early," he said. "Take a strike and he's got you. That slider is vicious."

There was comfort to be found in the alternative time of a ball game. However many seconds and minutes our silences, it all remained relative. A pitch, a foul ball, a brief mound conference before the umpire breaks it up. The formal absence of schedule, something I missed horribly. Even a seven-inning game could drag into darkness, somewhere from two to four hours. Sun setting beyond left field, we held up bullhorn fingers, two down. Play's to first.

I watched my father out of the corner of my eye. He rested one foot on the extra chair, both hands on his elevated knee. His beer was already empty. The color guy said, *Sometimes as a pitcher you'll do that, step off the rubber and give that base runner something to think about.* Richard ordered us two more, even though I hadn't yet finished my first.

"You've got to guess first-pitch heater. Don't let him settle into a groove."

The waitress pretended not to know who I was. My father was drinking at three times his normal rate. My mother had denied it, but I knew some sort of conversation was supposed to happen. Here we were, an occasion, and there was no reason this had to be so difficult. Again I glanced sideways at the primary genetic source of whoever I was, not three feet away. Piece of cake. Here's how it would go. *Dad?* Son. *I could use some answers, Dad.* Of course you could, son.

"You ever have a beard, Pop?"

"Beard? No. Never."

"Were you in Vietnam?"

"I can't tell if this is one of your jokes. Your mother and I are always saying how funny you are."

"Sadly, no. Sort of wish it was."

"My son doesn't know if I was in Vietnam. I can't decide whether to blame you or myself. Probably more my fault than yours."

"We could always blame Mom."

"Your mother." He sipped from his beer, so I quickly sipped from my own. After a few pitches of silence, he continued. "Conscientious objector. As a Mennonite, I never registered. The government never came after me."

"Wait. We're Mennonite?"

"Currently we can't claim to be much of anything. Your grandparents were. So were their parents."

I waited for three pitches to be thrown on-screen. "But you were born in 1948. Please tell me I have that much right."

"I turn fifty-three this year. Fifty-three. Your mother is fifty-one. We've been married thirty-three years. We were twenty and eighteen. You're twenty-two."

Richard leaned back and finished his second beer. Atlanta's second baseman missed a drag-bunt attempt.

"That's actually not true, sport."

"Mennonite."

"About the beard. It's important to understand that a lot of things changed after your brother passed away. Your mother and I struggled. Neither of us slept. We argued. I stopped shaving, I suppose in a sort of protest of the world. Your mother hated it. I ended up making two major concessions that year. One was moving from the city to the county, the other was shaving off my beard. I don't think there are any pictures of me with it. Any pictures we took during that period were of you alone. We would sit you on the couch or in the grass and move away. It was one of the few things we agreed on, back then. She and I had no business in front of a camera."

My dad held up an empty bottle to the waitress. She raised two fingers and he nodded. It was amazing to see this, such cool disaffection, so minimal and right.

"There's no reason to lie about the beard. I don't know why I did that. I'm sorry. There are things I'm supposed to say tonight, Potter. I'm having a hard time."

That morning on the Las Vegas strip, after Carmel had pulled away from our kiss and walked in one direction and I reflexively began in the opposite, I ended up in the MGM Grand at a craps table I could not in any way afford, dropping come bets and hard eights with abandon, bleeding my parents' cash and drowning in a river's flood of white Russians. When my ATM cut me off, I had no choice but to return to our shared room. There I found friends slouched in chairs and curled onto blankets in the bathroom, piled like some denim ad in one of the double beds while Audrey slept alone in the other, curled around one pillow in her stomach while the other was behind her, fresh and new, waiting for me. I lay down onto my back. She rolled over and nestled her head into my shoulder. Whispered, *babes*.

The waitress brought our beers. Richard picked one up and repeated himself. "I'm sorry."

Two words echoing over the restaurant's other voices, overpowering the voices of the broadcast announcers. I couldn't recall my father ever having cause to apologize to me. Surely he must have, at least once, but for what? And now—for what now? I dropped my eyes from the screen to the table in front of me. The game appeared in tiny warped reflection of an empty water glass. Dirty restaurant table right immediately here.

"Your grandfather would be good at this. I wish you could have met him. Of course that's ridiculous. People of his generation always had advice to spare, even when you didn't ask. I remember him sitting me down and talking about love. Only about a month before he died. I was thirteen, and there was this young girl, Angela McIntyre, driving me crazy. He asked whether I was in love with her and I said yes, because I believed I was. The old man nodded and looked me in the eye. He said, *Always make sure you love her more than she loves you, and she will love you even more.*"

The table began to rotate slowly. I watched plates and napkins and empty bottles of beer. Things pulled back, the view grew larger, out now to the table's edges.

"I have always tried to love your mother more."

The hand around the bottle was my hand, it was my Budweiser. I moved my fingers and watched them move.

"We are going through some tough times, son. All marriages do, of course. This is what it means to be married. But recently things have taken a turn for the worse. There are no new problems, nothing beyond two people with conflicting ideas of what constitutes happiness. Anyway, right now, for the past few years, we've been in the middle of something difficult. I'm trying to say this clearly. There has been difficulty, and it's not going away. So there will continue to be difficulty. For everyone. I'm being honest with you. I knew this would be hard. I've been dreading it. But here we are. You and me."

There was my head, and my dad's head, that full head of silver hair. My father's shoulders and arms and hands resting on the edge of the table.

"You're an adult, so I'm not sure how much I have to make clear. Whatever changes, nothing is going to change. This sounds ridiculous, but you know what I mean. I don't have to say that none of this is your fault. Of course you know that much. This is a child's concern, the guilt that drives young people into lives of therapy. You know all of this. What happens is you get to a point when you have to let the past go. To let go. This is one of the things we all know but few of us ever manage to actually do."

Rapt. I saw Richard leaning forward on his elbows, empty bottle beneath interlocked fingers. His knit collared shirt bunched at the shoulders.

"I'm sure you've picked up on feelings around the house. You've seen your mother and me, how we have become. Of course you have. It's difficult to know when to share, and how much. You can't share all of it. But there's a line somewhere. We haven't ever hidden anything from you, but we could have been more up front. You deserve that much."

The scene had been branded, indelibly, into my consciousness. Sportsman's Park, the tasteless burger, more empty bottles than I would have predicted. The news had been shared. Marriage. Trouble. I listened. What other details of note? Table? Hands around beer? I imagined my mother hunched over a fund-raising centerpiece or candle fixture. I doubted there had been much controversy over who was to give me the news. Of course my father. When I looked back at the screen, the ball game had returned. The Braves were switching pitchers. Some time passed. My father was apparently finished speaking.

"Should we get the check?"

"I love your mother very much."

"Me too."

"And I have never, ever in the course of thirty-three years committed any real indiscretion. Not one single indiscreet moment in all those years. Moments. And things are going to be okay. You have to remember that. I have to remember that. We are all going to come out of this thing okay." He spun the dregs of his beer around in the bottle. "I have to use the john."

He stood from the table and I felt two overwhelming desires. The first was to pay for this meal with money I had earned delivering water. The second was to get myself immediately and carelessly laid.

"This is going to sound horrible," I said when the waitress brought the bill. "I don't say this sort of thing ever."

"Right." She stuck both hands into her apron.

"Do I know you? You went to my high school."

"Don't think so. You go to Kirkwood?" She chewed gum, snapped it.

"You have a sister, then. She's my age and went to Ladue."

"I have a brother named Andrew."

"Andrew," I said.

"Unless you're calling Andrew a girl, which is enough to get you messed up pretty good."

I sat at the table and looked upward into the eyes of this young woman in the waiter's apron. I did not know her, nor would I ever.

"My parents are getting a divorce," I said.

"Oh. Sorry. Do you need change?"

I left her twenty-five percent and met my father by the front door. Outside, stars dim and cicadas deafening, we walked silently to the car. I caught myself patting jeans for cigarettes. When he didn't go immediately for keys, we stood on opposite sides of the Datsun.

"You sure you don't want me to drive?"

"I'm fine to drive."

We were both looking at the dent.

"I haven't driven the Z in years," I said. "I'd be happy to."

"We had the same number of beers, you and I. Me."

He ducked into the car and reached over to unlock my door. The Datsun growled as it accelerated back toward home. I turned on the radio and scanned the AM band. The old, beloved radio broadcaster mumbled, *There was one out, now there are two.*

five

h ow even to respond when so natural a fact, a truth thus far assumed and treated as obvious, is exposed as a fake. When the fact becomes fragile, suddenly from out of the sky contingent? I changed subjects and made myself creatively scarce. Days were covered; I developed new appreciation for the morning's stack of papers, rich with instruction. Go *here*, do *this*. No matter that the stack came from Dennis, that bitch of a man with his pockmarks and bitter distaste for any and all people of color. I went down the list, completing the tasks at hand.

When I got there, Ian Worpley was watering the yard with a garden hose. Thumb over the spout to make a spray, he was shirtless and barefoot, standing on the path and turning a slow circle, waving the hose as he spun. When he completed the rotation he set the hose down and approached the van. I met him on the sidewalk.

"Finished early today," I said. "Thought maybe you'd want to go on an adventure."

"Adventure?"

"In the van."

"Where?"

I hadn't thought this through. It was too hot for the batting cage, too hot to stand and water dead grass. Too hot for stasis. Ian began to circle the van and I followed him.

"The airport," I said. "We'll go watch airplanes take off and land."

Because airplanes are massive and they fly and basically blow childish minds. I was confident about this.

"I'm not convinced this van is safe," he said. "My dad always says that by the time you see rust, there's so much going on underneath you don't even want to know."

"Rust is the common name for an extremely common chemical compound. Iron oxide. Ef-ee-two-oh-three."

He nodded and continued around the van. He ran his hand along a dent in the van's sliding door. "Yeah, you got rust like this, something's wrong."

Eventually Ian wandered back into the yard and picked up the hose, then went to the faucet and stopped the hose, then rolled it back up and left it by the foot of the porch before scuffling into the house. When he came out he was wearing a shirt and shoes.

"Come on. Look at this thing," I said. "Safe as a tank."

"It's like a van in the videos they show us at school. About kidnapping."

"I'm not a kidnapper. Kidnappers are pale men with thick mustaches."

He opened the door. "Yeah well, no one admits they're a kidnapper, do they?"

Today the kids in the yard were playing some variation of tag with tennis balls. I saw a blond girl level a brown-haired boy with a throw to the back of his head. Ian fastened his seat belt before I had a chance to tell him to.

I got us onto Highway 44 and took it westward. Ian reached forward for the radio, and there was the old, beloved play-by-play man saying, *headed into the bottom of the fifth, score knotted at three.* Ian opened the glove compartment and pulled out an empty pack of cigarettes, some napkins. He found the cheap plastic tire-pressure gauge and sat back in his seat.

"Dad says we fall six back of the Cubs and we're in trouble." He flipped the tire gauge in his hands.

"Still plenty of time. Plus they're the Cubs, remember."

"Says we have to stop swinging the bats like a bunch of pussies."

Sometimes in etcetera, motion alone is a value in and of itself. It was early enough that we beat the traffic exile from the city. We passed small mountains of earth and rock, the yellow machinery that signaled change. Stacks and stacks of light-blue piping. The landscape out here evolved, always. The buildings themselves, huge, reminded me of models, a set of tabs and slots.

"Your thing is beeping," he said.

"I usually ignore that."

"And! You're going the wrong way. This isn't how you get to the airport."

I reevaluated the plan, thinking for a minute to confirm that I did in fact know what was what.

"Not Lambert. The airport we're going to is smaller," I said.

"Yeah, I *know*. Spirit of St. Louis, the small one."

"Named for the silver prop that carried Lindbergh to Paris."

"Yeah," he said. "It's off Highway 40. We're on 44."

"That's right. That's right. North of here. Minor adjustment. Hold on."

Our path righted, soon we passed the network of fields where I'd played summer ball, and I thought of my mother sitting cross-legged in the stands, chatting with other parents while my father paced behind the dugout. How far back did it go? Could memory, if I looked hard enough, provide evidence of unhappiness even then? It was out here that I put the dent in the Z's roof. The foul ball I hit late one summer afternoon, how the moment it left my bat I knew it would land on his car. The *tink* of a barely tipped foul ball, the ball rising with menace, irrationally seeming to grow larger as it went, then the hollow moment of collision, the roof of a Datsun. Crowd response, *ooh*. I stepped out of the box, ostensibly for practice cuts, and my father and I shared a quick look rich with blurred meaning. And once the game was over and I had squeezed into the backseat, my parents lingered outside and

I heard my mother's muffled voice travel overhead. And if I found the right dial, maybe I could adjust the memory's volume and discover what she said.

I exited 40 and followed a mile of frontage road along the side of the highway. Ian unfastened his seat belt so he could lean out the window. I imagined how it would look through his eyes, this world. The control tower, the paved lot with fading parking spots, the swath of green separating the lot from the penitential fence that circled the place. The spirals of barbed wire proved that this was a place of serious consequence. I turned up the radio and we got out of the van to sit in front of the fence. Eight or nine planes were in a staggered line to the side of the tarmac, with blocks wedged under their wheels.

He said, "I don't understand. How does anyone make money selling tickets for these dumb little planes?"

"They don't. These are privately owned. There aren't tickets; it's just a pilot and a few passengers. No peanuts or pretzels."

He looked at me. "What kind of person owns an entire plane?"

Mr. John Hurst, father of three. Divorcé. Payer of settlement. Marrier of his secretary. Driver of: Jaguar XK8, Mercedes CLK, Land Rover Discovery. Maker of very much income. Secretary adulterer. Owner of private jet, Cessna.

"They must be Jewish."

"What? No. That's not important."

A jet appeared from out of a hangar and taxied around the others before turning onto the runway, facing more or less exactly where we sat, waiting for clearance. I watched Ian watching the plane and firmly believed the process of takeoff was going to be of great satisfaction for the kid. We waited. After several minutes the plane turned and left the runway completely, back to the row with the others.

He stood and went to the fence briefly before moving off to my left. I was beginning to fear that we'd come on an off day and that we might end up sitting here staring like cows at this tableau of overgrown blacktop and fence and small unimpressive machine. I got up and followed him at a distance, stopping when he stopped and watching him bend to pick something from the grass. I took a step closer as he held it up to his face with both hands, worried that he was going to eat something little boys should not eat. He dropped it and bent for something else and I realized what was happening. You stretched the grass between your two thumbs and brought your hands up to your face, and if you blew just right it made a sound like a tiny woodwind instrument.

My father buzzing grass and walking through grass, playing catch in and among grass. Good old Dad, my father who only ever wanted what was best for those of us he still had left. Ian turned to face me and blew into his hands. No sound came out. He dropped the grass and leaned to pick a fresh blade.

"My mom showed me this. If you do it right it'll buzz."

"I like the one where you take that long grass with the fuzzy bulb on the top, and you wrap the stalk around itself and use it to shoot off the top."

"Buck*weed*," Ian said. "It's not grass. Yeah, Mom likes that one too. Mom knows all sorts of things to do with grass."

There was still no activity on the runways. There was a man in an orange vest holding a set of those noise-canceling earmuffs, but he was just standing there, speaking into a walkie-talkie. I remained incapable of coming up with anything to say to Ian about his mother.

"What about that girl you used to sit with by the creek?"

"Yeah. Two days ago she showed up at my house wearing a backpack and said she was running away because her parents wouldn't buy her a pony. She asked if I wanted to go with her."

I was surprised to hear little girls still wanted ponies.

"What did you say?"

"I told her running away from your problems doesn't solve anything. Really it just hurts the people who count on you. Then she came inside and we watched DinoChamps until my dad came home and made her leave."

We turned and moved back to the van. One of the planes began moving onto the runway. After a few minutes, it accelerated toward where we were sitting, front wheels lifting without ceremony and the rear soon after. Takeoff. But the whole thing was too quiet; I wanted explosions of sound I could claim as my own. To say, *Listen, Ian, to the massive noise. Cover your ears. This is bigger than all of us.*

"Does she ever talk about faeries, this girl?"

"Fairies? She's eleven. Not six."

"My girlfriend cut off all her hair, and now she and this robot girl named Carmel are scouring the European countryside in search of faeries. They have moved from Germany southward with faerie nets strapped to their backpacks."

"That's the stupidest thing I ever heard."

"That's right! Jesus, it's good to hear you say that."

"Fairies won't have anything to do with robots. And you shouldn't say *Jesus* like that! You only get two a year and you just wasted one for no reason."

How laid-back this God of his to forgive blasphemy up to twice a year. I wondered if the same rule applied to the other commandments and whether the parents had created this version of religion together.

"This is kind of boring," he said.

"But you love planes. Planes are awesome."

"Sort of. I mean, I'm not six."

"The first flight on record only went one hundred and twenty feet," I said. "In Kitty Hawk, North Carolina."

"Yeah, and when he was young, Orville had typhoid. Wilbur had to take care of him."

"Alright. But I bet you a Coke you can't tell me what they worked on before planes."

"Bikes," Ian said. "We did all of this in fourth grade."

"Alright. One Coke."

We continued along the frontage road back toward the city and Ian flipped the tire gauge in his little fingers while I looked for somewhere more interesting than a gas station to buy his Coke. When I saw a diner ahead, I signaled and pulled into a large old vacant lot.

"Wait, stop. Stop, stop, stopstop*stop*!"

I stopped the van a good thirty yards from the restaurant. Ian looked carsick and confused, face white and eyes glazed. He bounced shoes on the rubber floor mat and passed the tire gauge from hand to hand.

"I'll wait here," he said.

"Okay," I said.

"I don't want to go in there. My mom and I used to come here sometimes."

I scanned the lot and wondered if I was allowed to leave him here alone. I had seen enough local news to know of the city threats, the poor and desperate victims of the world. But this was practically the country.

"I'm okay by myself," he said, and held up the tire gauge. "I got this thing."

So I left him there and went into the diner. When I got back, Ian had the hood of the van open and was looking inside. I handed him a forty-two-ounce Coke and he stepped back and to-gether we stared at the filthy old engine.

"It's a V8," he said.

And in the next few minutes while we drank our Cokes, I did not mention his mother or his father, or my own father or mother, or discuss with him what we were supposed to make of marriage, ask how either of us could ever believe in the porcelain institution we'd both seen crumble. And I most certainly did *not* reveal that I'd aged twenty-two years without knowing what the V stood for in V8.

Through the ride home, Ian stared out the window and

clenched the tire gauge. It was a willed quietness, one he believed in. And if silence was what he wanted, I would let him have it. Soon I was steering us back onto Waldwick Drive. I was surprised when he finally broke the silence.

"I got a postcard in the mail the other day. I'll show you if you want. It's not like she left forever or is gonna leave me alone forever with Dad. I just don't want you thinking she like forgot me or something. Because she didn't."

Ian slipped out and closed the door without turning. I watched him walk back to the house. If I kept going at this pace, by September I'd be in love with the whole Midwest.

six

there are stages of swelter, and as summer progresses, each stage trumps the last. Around mid-July the heat reaches the sort where mere digits lose meaning and even the heat index, that fetish of meteorology, fails, leaving the city's elderly as our de facto authorities, both for their spookily accurate ability to rank current conditions against history and their tendency to expire in these conditions. A city of seniors, already withered, further withering in their un-air-conditioned rooms, stoically riding out a heat wave that can't hold a flame to the Great Heat of 1968, fanning themselves with an old framed photograph or church program until they quietly give in to exhaustion or stroke. One more dead. But then, these are people so old that their passing requires little explanation. They're OLD, is the thing, and the journey from old to dead is one so brief it's hardly worth packing.

Five of these elderly died of heat-related causes during the second week of July, only two short of the record. I myself stuffed cargo pockets full of twelve-ounce bottles each morning before leaving the warehouse, though a part of me secretly adored the possible irony of falling down in pathetic drama, succumbing to dehydration while working for a water company.

My other employment brought a sweat that simmered only within. Cool basement sealed away from outside world, cool color of walls and furniture, cool air pumping through vents. What was it about the Midwest and our furnished basements? The heat of the angel surrounded on all sides by the cool of subterranean academic pursuance.

"Begin," the official timekeeper said.

I would not have claimed to be a good tutor. My illusion of authority was thin and translucent, and it was therefore semimiraculous to watch Zoe listen attentively and take occasional notes. I marveled at the innocence of it all, the purity of intention. The mother happily opening the basement door. Zoe with hair and eyes and bare arms, shoulders. Neck.

I stood up and began walking circles through the basement. I swung my arms and hopped. Outside, movement was limited to the slow and gentle. You operated within the rules of the atmosphere and did whatever you could to minimize your confrontation with the air around you. To move with any quickness was to risk angering the tyrant.

"Twelve minutes."

Down here I was free to dart and cut. In the free space by the stairs I went through a series of basic calisthenics, ending with thirty jumping jacks. Zoe, consummate student, was not distracted. I dropped and did push-ups, then hustled back to my chair.

"All done," she said, lifting herself from the floor to the couch.

"If you finish early you're supposed to go back and review your answers."

"Reviewed. Think I aced this one."

All of the sun tea in the world, all of the lemonade.

Rarely were all three of us in the same room. There was a new presence in the house, floating shapelessly, this looming conversation that was sure to come soon: the technicalities of our family's situation. More than once Carla had approached me, but I had sensed an explanation coming, perhaps seen something in her posture that warned me of her intention, and I had changed rooms, stepped outside, or driven away completely. They continued to share their bed in the first floor's master bedroom, which seemed impossible until I realized that, between them, there was nothing new here. This secret of theirs, fresh to me, may in fact have been old, stale, a gradual and slow decay of which they'd known and adapted to.

Late one night I drafted a message to Audrey, taking my parents and their split as a perfect excuse. But reading over it I realized it was all wrong, too much us, so I clicked delete and confirmed, yes I really mean it, computer.

And when my mother brought home a new water-filter pitcher, her timing struck me as drastically wrong. What could she have meant by introducing a new kitchen appliance at a time like this? She walked through the door carrying a single plastic grocery bag. Inside were two boxes, the pitcher and a six-pack of replacement filters. I sat at the counter and watched her open the box and read through the instruction packet. She submerged the filter in cold water and left it to soak as she went about her household business, while the replacement filters sat on the counter like some cruel reminder of time's passing. Three months each, a full year and a half embodied by that box. Who could say where Carla would be by then? Or Richard? Not to mention, not to mention.

I was eating breakfast when my father first encountered the pitcher. Carla was in the garden. He removed the full pitcher and held it like some mysterious alien technology, then set it on the island. He stepped back slightly and considered the pitcher before looking at me. I shrugged and quietly mopped up yolk with toast. The silent offense here had to do with our stellar record of public water filtration. To my father, the city's consistent performance in national tap-water rankings was a source of great pride, our small modern version of the ancient Roman feats of aqueduct design and upkeep. And now it occurred to me how redundant he must have thought my chosen profession. Insults, insults; both of us turning on him, only son and only wife.

Good old Dad.

The argument, once they got around to it, was a quiet affair, endearing almost, not unlike two new lovers' first experiments with contact. It was Sunday afternoon and they seemed unsure exactly what behavior they were allowed to exhibit in front of me. They stood in the kitchen while I sat on the couch. The sentences I caught were fragmentary and full of gaps.

"I have to wonder when we became too good for tap water."

"Tastes better, for one. And safer, Richard. All the impurities."

From the couch it was difficult to know how much of their fight was taking place at the subsonic level. What body language and nuance of posture? She would busy herself with drying a dish or wiping the counter. He would stand still and maneuver his hands through the air over the island.

"Impurities, chemicals, things I don't want in my body. This is my body. My only."

"Simply no reason. It's *unfounded,* Carla, based on fear alone."

"Then don't *use* it, Richard. It will be *mine.*"

"These are good, hardworking people, Carla. The record is there. I can show you the numbers."

They went on like this, an argument that couldn't possibly matter as much as it did. It was like a contest to see who could say the other's name more. Such emphasis on those syllables. *Richard.* Perhaps this was the point of bringing the pitcher home: stage a fight for the boy, illustrate the rift. *Car-la.*

They stopped talking when I stood from the couch. My mother moved to the sink and my father opened the refrigerator. I sat at the counter.

"Let's try to all three of us say the word *divorce* at the same time. See if anything happens."

My mother looked through the window above the sink into

the backyard. She waved her hand in front of her face as if at a fly. My father began to make himself a sandwich on the island, folding slices of meat onto bread. Without once looking at him, my mother opened a cabinet and handed my father a plate. Damn impressive, that, and it seemed to me that this would be their greatest loss of all, the routine comfort of spousal awareness. To know a person so deeply so long, but to what end? Once that person was gone away to someplace else?

"We're giving ourselves some time to think. This is hard for all three of us. Neither your father nor I has said anything about divorce. Have we, Richard."

"There's someone at the front door," he said.

A few seconds later the doorbell rang. Stuart, with Marianne at his side. She raised a hand in a short little wave.

"Where have you been?" Stuart asked.

"Me?" I said, letting them inside. "Where have I been?"

Their arrival immediately transformed the scene into one of reunion and introduction. It was difficult to gather five people into a kitchen without feeling some kind of joy. My parents were happy to see my old friend after all these months, happy to meet his girlfriend, who was happy back, nodding hello with her hands pouched into overalls. Stuart explained they'd come on their way to the riverfront for the final day of Fair St. Louis, the annual riverside whoop-de-do of independence. Tonight there would be fireworks launched from barges on the river, screaming skyward and booming, colorful bursts glittering against pitch black, silver light reflected off the Arch. Originally a Fourth of July event, the fair had fallen later and later each year as city organizers and *SLH!* compiled resident/consumer research.

"You should come, Potsky. Obviously."

"Have you all gone down yet?" Marianne asked my mother.

"Not this year. No."

Stuart and my father began a conversation about work, and I listened as Stuart shared his most recent idea, a diet technique no

crazier, he insisted, than jaw wiring or stomach stapling. My father chewed his sandwich.

"We introduce a tapeworm into the client that will feed on
whatever the client feeds on, like any good parasite will. Then,
after a predetermined time—based on how much weight this
client wants to lose—the tapeworm, which has been geneti-
cally engineered to live for precisely as long as the client wants,
dies. Expires. We introduce it to the market as a quick-fix kind of
treatment, optimal if you've got, say, the Oscars coming up.
What got me here was realizing you can't get fat if there's something inside you intercepting the food before it reaches your in-
testine."

I watched my father's face for a clue as to whether this was a
ridiculous idea or a sort of good idea. His eyebrows appeared to
climb slightly. Meanwhile, my mother and Marianne left the
kitchen for a tour of the house. Richard took another bite and
Stuart poured himself a glass of water from the pitcher in question. My father set the plate on the counter and slid it toward the
sink. He wiped the mustard from the corner of his mouth, then
wiped his hands in the napkin.

"How do you plan on introducing the parasite into the client's
system?"

"Thinking a soluble gel-cap enclosure. I've got the ear of a guy
at Monsanto."

"What did I hear about your father the other day. Is there a
new account, something big? A national firm, a New York coup
of sorts."

I heard the women moving through the house and caught up
with them in the living room. I wasn't certain why, but I didn't
like the thought of Marianne and Carla alone together. Then the
house's phones came alive, the staggered multipitched ringing,
and my mother excused herself, leaving me standing with
Marianne, the simple country girl. She stood at the fireplace,
looking at a picture on the mantel.

"I told your mom that she did a great job decorating this place. Except I think that made her sad for whatever reason."

I saw her shoulders from behind and felt something warm and lurid rising through my chest. No, no, I didn't care for this Marianne girl one bit. I wanted her out of my living room immediately. She moved to a window and brushed aside the curtain, looking outside.

"They're thinking about moving into something smaller," I said. "Once I get my own place."

She turned from the window and approached slowly. I saw her forehead coming at me and was grateful to have a full head's height on her. She stopped once she was very close.

"Let me ask you something," I said.

"Go right ahead."

"This thing of yours about meeting all of Stuart's friends. He's mentioned it several times."

"And you're concerned that maybe something ungood is going on."

"I have to wonder how you decided everything you needed to decide about me within those first few minutes."

"We're talking about that first day, when you were staring at my tits."

"No, see, I *defended* your tits."

"That right? To who?"

"To me. I convinced myself to excuse your arrogant nakedness."

"How about we make this deal. You tell me about Stuart's finger and I'll describe what I saw."

"Can't. It's a long-held secret source of Stuart's power. I think only three people know the story outside of his immediate family."

"Plus one," she said. "He told me the first night I met him, over our uncooked cake."

She walked past me and down the steps. I heard them saying goodbyes and weighed the options, which right now felt like the only two options in the entire world, ever. I descended the stairs and yelled goodbye to parents who, by now, were surely in different rooms.

To ride in the ad was to participate in a complex and devious system of promotion. I sat in the backseat and watched Marianne's hand outside the passenger window cut a rising and falling curve through the wind. Occasionally we met eyes in the rearview mirror, though I couldn't say who was catching whom.

Stuart lit them two cigarettes.

"I thought you weren't supposed to smoke in the ad," I said.

"My relationship to the ad has evolved. I'm exploring the boundaries between us. Which is why I can't just hand it over to Edsel, no matter how much he wants or thinks he should have it. He said he's meeting us at the fair also."

He inhaled, then leaned forward to blow the smoke directly into the stereo. He dropped the rest of the cigarette onto the floor mat and let it burn briefly before stomping it out.

We passed Forest Park and the community colleges along the highway. I had begun to fear her in small but meaningful ways, this simple country girl who was growing less simple and less country each minute.

When she said something I didn't catch, Stuart responded, "We'll find a funnel cake, I assure you of that."

The downtown streets were like my father's dream, dense with pedestrians. We parked and began walking. The crowd had its own rhythm, bobbing heads and shuffling feet. For a second I saw the vision, the St. Louis Hooray! master plan. Wasn't this what the city was missing? With no urban center there was no crowd, and with no crowd as its opposite, how strong was our sense of the individual? Maybe this explained the region's primary obsession: the crowded ballpark.

The three of us entered the sweeping fairgrounds through enormous inflated Budweiser gates, flanked on either side by enormous inflated Clydesdales. Here among the happening came a fuzzy and numb wave of community. We made our way into the crowd until we came upon two lines stretching in opposite directions, one to purchase tickets, three to the dollar, the other to exchange tickets for sixteen-ounce cups of Budweiser, thirteen tickets to the beer. My head pounded.

"I have pockets full of money," Stuart said. "I'll wait for tickets, then catch up with you two in the beer line. We're going to show this system who's boss."

He poked Marianne's bare shoulder and left us. Deceit, gullibility, monogamy. Two men in front of us wore Blues hockey jerseys and jean shorts and smoked menthols. The line moved us forward and I remained quiet because this was the pattern we'd set within the fairground chatter around us, the children and their tantrums, man talk and woman laughter and the reverse of that. Stuart had spoken of honesty and their unprecedented version of nakedness, sweeping admissions and revelations of long-held beliefs. *Eliminating the metaphor.* The air smelled sweaty and alcoholic. Slightly in front of me, her neck was dark beneath hair gathered into the loosest, most vague version of a ponytail. I wondered what would happen if I just reached for it, wrapped fingers around her hair, and jerked downward, just to see. She'd, what, scream?

Without turning to face me, she said, "He'd better get enough tickets for a funnel cake."

"What percentage of you, approximately, would you say is full of shit?"

"No more than you, pally."

"Nice fucking overalls."

"Coveralls," she said, turning. "Where I'm from we call them coveralls."

"No. Coveralls are jumpsuits with sleeves. Onesies."

"Says you."

And then Stuart was back, emerging from the crowd to lace an arm between Marianne's tanned back and her dishonest denim.

"I handed them dollars and they ripped pieces of cardboard from a giant spool and expected me to say thank you. Deal of the century."

A volunteer checked our IDs while the troop in yellow collared shirts behind her filled millions of beers and set them onto a plastic table. We were given bright-green bracelets to prove we were of age. As we left the table I began playing with the bracelet and accidentally broke it. I went back to the table for a replacement, and when I returned Stuart and Marianne were gone. I continued deeper into the fair, through the rows of booths and attractions. I watched darts thrown at a wall of balloons and peered into a cotton-candy machine, relieved to be alone and anonymous among the throng of strangers.

Turning a corner, I caught sight of Edsel in one of the booths, leaning to speak into the ear of a man behind a vending table. The man nodded slowly. For a moment Edsel and I locked eyes, and I nearly smiled at the thought of a beard on an evening like this one. I stood still as heads and shoulders passed between us, only slightly curious what he was saying into the vendor's ear. Some words of trade and exchange value. Simple numbers game here in our tiny little town on the river.

I left the maze of booths and attractions and moved into the crowded lawn beneath the Arch, stepping lightly around the feet and fingers of those already settled. I found a small plot of grass and dropped to the ground, untied shoes, piled my socks to my right, and lay down flat on my back.

Everything about the fair was growing louder, the mayhem of communal glee. I closed my eyes and imagined the lawn packed with men and women and blankets and coolers and those collapsible canvas chairs everyone was buying. I foresaw the arrival of vendors selling thin glow-in-the-dark tube lights that would make it home wrapped around children's necks and wrists. Money would be exchanged. There would be mosquitoes like all get out, clouds of vile mosquitoes, and nobody here would care a bit.

I saw Stuart and Marianne moving across the lawn, not forty feet from me. I dialed his number quickly and saw them stop. Stuart pulled out his phone, looked at it, and put the phone away. I watched them take several steps across the lawn, then I lay back down.

seven

d ennis rested thick and bitter on his stool and told me to load as many bottles as I could into the van. I stood waiting for an invoice.

"Hell are you doing?"

"Rule one of delivery, you said. No paper, no water. You were adamant. You gestured and deployed intonation to punctuate your point."

"This ain't business today. This is a gift, kid, compliments of Debbie Dinkles. Here's your paper. Directions so you don't get lost, have to call big Dennis come save your hide."

I loaded as many bottles as would fit inside, then reversed down the ramp. I was to go west—deep into rural backwater Missouri until I reached something called Irenia Winery. My only delivery of the day, off the books, no official delivery at all. I followed directions onto Highway 40 and traveled beyond the Spirit of St. Louis airport and baseball fields, beyond the stores and dealerships and everything else until I reached Route 94, where I was to turn left and follow as it snaked south. I passed a police station and shooting range, then came upon a tight set of curves flanked by bosky walls of the most brilliant natural green. And here the road stayed for a bit beneath a canopy of overarching leaves that allowed sunlight through in disco-ball rays, splattering the blacktop roadway.

Signs said I was approaching the town of Defiance. Four or five short white houses with porches on either side of the road, a yard packed with rusted tractor parts, two roadside bars along one mellow left-hand curve, two empty parking lots, and then no more Defiance.

Back into the trees for a while, around blind curves, strict no-passing zones. I slowed to a near crawl, taking it in. By now I'd given myself over to the delivery, whatever its length. Today I would be subsumed by this one task. Tomorrow would be different. I followed a long, gradual descent around an arching right-hand turn, and here the foliage parted, opening into a scene of great countryside, fields stretching to a river and beyond, where they stopped at a sheer gray wall of bluffs. And it felt that up until this point, the whole summer so far, I could have been anywhere, any of a hundred middling American cities pocketed by wealth and poverty and sex and violence, faith and despair, contrived success and palpable failure. But with these fields and this river, those legendary bluffs of song and portrait, I knew where I was. *Missouri,* her naked body hidden away for anyone who knew enough to want her.

Southwest, fields and bluffs on left, hills and wineries on right. How long had these places been out here? I passed the Sugar Hill Winery, Stone Creek Winery, Augusta Winery. Several others marked by signs with arrows and promises of live music or scenic gazebos. I held Dennis's directions up against the steering wheel. *Stay on 94. Keep going.*

I saw the sign appear as I came onto a particularly straight section of whatever name this road went by out here, an inconspicuous sign of natural wood.

"Eye-ree-nee-ahhh."

The van, gravid with as much weight as it had likely ever known, could only inch up the steep dirt driveway. And this seemed a much more appropriate rate of travel for a delivery of this size. How reckless I'd been on Highway 40, how inconsiderate of my cargo.

Standing at the lot's edge was a bald man wearing a pale-blue collared polo shirt tucked into khakis. He approached my van with a raised hand and something approximating a smile.

"You must be from Deborah. Welcome."

I extended my hand through the window and we shook.

"Potter Mays," I said.

"Mays. Glad you made it. We were starting to run low. Follow this path around to the back and the others will be out in a minute to give you a hand."

I drove along the side of the winery's central building, a squat home that looked like an old plantation mansion squished down to just one floor. The gravel path ended in a small circular lot behind the building. Here, four white Econoline vans much like my own were parked facing outward, as if ready to flee if the need arose. I got out of the van and walked a few steps for a better view of the land. The grounds were beautiful, gentle hills and walls of forest, the better part of a valley cultivated with sparse rows of grape plants. I turned back to the building in time to see a door open from inside where I didn't think there was a door. Two men emerged, both dressed like the man out front, in khaki pants and light-blue collared shirt. I met them at the side of the van and we shook hands. They were both somewhere in their forties and had hair shaved to the skull, fingers blunted by years of work, and the quietly stunning musculature that can only come from true, purposeful labor. One was slightly taller, and the shorter was a bit bulkier in the shoulders.

"It's good you made it," the shorter man said. "Any trouble finding us?"

"Not at all. I had directions."

The taller man had his arms crossed and his gaze fixed on a spot somewhere above my head.

"Any problem getting up the hill? Guess it depends which engine you've got in there."

"This is the V8," I said.

Tall one cracked a smile.

"After '92, about all you find are the V8," the other said. "Wondering if it was the 4.6 or 5.4, is all. Either way. Important thing is you made it. That's good. We're here to give you a hand with those bottles."

"Mighty kind of you."

"Pleasure's ours. Job to be done, so let's do what we can to get that job done."

"Potter Mays." I shook the shorter man's hand firmly and then reached to meet that of the taller man, which consumed my tiny rabbit paw inside a great limestone cave of a palm while his eyes locked onto mine as if that's where I kept my records of lies and cheating and mismanaged worth. My hand compressed inside his and I squinted, fighting the traditional battle of masculine will. When we released I slid open the door, revealing the wall of bottles stacked within.

They took two bottles each and waited as I unloaded two of my own. I had always carried the bottles one at a time, but to do so here seemed an insult to everyone involved. I followed through the unmarked door into an undecorated stairwell; we descended immediately and moved through a long, plain hallway. The two men in blue moved with diligence that seemed a necessary part of who they were. I shuffled to keep pace, my hands burning. At the end of this hallway we descended another stairway into a slightly darker hallway lit by single lightbulbs at irregular intervals. The walls were unpainted cinder block, the floor smooth cement marked only by the occasional circular drain. I longed to stop and rest my hands. Sound of six shoes echoed in this hallway. Until finally we arrived at a double door that opened into a cavernous storage room, where I followed the men to a dark corner and dropped my load next to theirs.

"Jesus," I said. "Long way down."

The men backtracked silently to the van.

The job went on like this for half an hour. Through it all, not a single word was uttered among us. After my initial mistake I understood: language in this place, at this time, was frivolous. What could we have said? What could talk, large or small, do for our task? We were lifting and we were carrying. We descended and stepped quickly through hallways, determined. This was toil to transcend words, to simplify and reduce and deliver us to that ancient realm of human existence. There was a job at hand that would have taken me all day to complete alone. We were wearing our collared shirts, uniform of American labor, and we were *working*.

Once the last bottles were set into the storage room's back corner, I followed the two men silently back to the surface, where we stood beside my van. During the job I'd caught flashes of the occasional worker moving into or out of a door. At least one was a woman, which initially surprised me and then seemed perfectly appropriate, even necessary. I was aware of an unnameable something transpiring at the winery, but it was so secondary to the greater thing at play, which was assistance. Which was reaching out with heartfelt aid.

The tall one brushed his hands. "Ford's talking about canceling the E-series altogether."

"The van," I said. "The Econoline."

"I got a brother over at the Avon Lake plant," said the other. "Tells me the whole state of Ohio is on edge. Whole lot of good people working those plants."

"But that doesn't make sense," I said. "Those vans are everywhere."

"Yeah well, Ford's doing a lot that don't make much sense, aren't they?"

"I had no idea," I said.

We stood quietly for several minutes. Clouds had moved in to cover the sun and plaster the sky in gray that stretched across the land. When my pager beeped inside the van, the men shook my hand again and I shut the sliding van door.

"Thank you for the water."

"Thank you," the tall one said.

"Thank you for the help," I said.

"Not at all. Anytime."

"Anytime."

The third bald man, who stood guard out front, waved as I left the winery. Again I examined my hands and these calluses that could always, always grow thicker. It occurred to me I hadn't caught any of the bald men's names. I descended the steep driveway in a van comparatively weightless since shedding its burden, my Ford Econoline V8. Probably the 4.6, if I had to guess.

eight

It was within the private rapture of sustained focus that she was most angelic. She sat with legs straight beneath the coffee table, elbows wide, chewing her bottom lip or pencil. The teacher and student and the barriers between. I imagined Stuart telling the story of his finger to Marianne. Were they naked? They might have been naked. They were naked and he was speaking in the first person about that defining experience of his childhood, baring his inner self, and she was nodding. But were the nods sufficiently appreciative? Were they even somewhat bored or rote or feigned? This was a gift of terrific magnitude, the private childhood secret, one to alter the very DNA of a relationship. I looked at the clock hanging on the wall, then watched the angel finish her test. When she looked up, I asked if she would like to hear the true story of my best friend Stuart Hurst's missing finger.

"Hell yes," she said, climbing onto the couch. "Totally."

"Stuart's family used to live in Tokyo. His father does some variation of financial advising that's almost covert, something there's really no point even trying to understand. So in Tokyo there was something tainted about a transaction between his dad's then up-and-coming small firm and a huge Japanese conglomerate. Allegedly. One afternoon, Stuart and his mom were walking through Tokyo and she turned to tell him to hurry up and he wasn't there. The kidnappers mailed his right index finger to his father so he understood the gravity of the situation. His parents went to the authorities, but apparently the group that took Stuart was such a force in the Japanese underground that when the police read the ransom note with the little freckles and streaks of Stuart's finger blood, they were visibly shaken. What's the name I want for the gangsters?"

"Yakuza," she said.

"Which is why nobody would help. Stuart was seven. They kept him in a windowless room with only a small table and three chairs. They addressed him in English as if he were a full-grown man, speaking formally even as they made a fist of all but that one finger, then laid it across the table. He describes the pain as something he felt everywhere but his finger. Then they left him to wait in that room while his dad gathered the cash, arranged the exchange, and so on. They provided soup and bandages, very organized and businesslike. All told, he was gone for just under forty-eight hours."

"Jesus, is that sexy," she said, and I quickly gathered my papers and said goodbye.

The door from the basement opened into the Hoyne kitchen, a softer-hued and more sheep-covered reflection of my own mother's kitchen. There were sheep on oven mitts and towels and the small chalkboard by the phone. I stood lingering at the kitchen island across from Zoe's mother, my mother's dear friend. I assumed she had known long before me of Carla's displeasure, and I wanted to ask her about the progression as she saw it. When had she first noticed a change in my mother's behavior? Did Carla point, when pressed, to a small but ultimately devastating moment when she knew the marriage was finished? But all I could muster was a halfhearted question about the origin of her kitchen sheep.

"About six years ago we found that stool at an antique store in

Herman. Then Derrick brought this home one day." She reached both hands across the sink for a painted clay jar sitting in the windowsill. "From there it just kind of snowballed for us both. There are cookies in here if you'd like one."

"Would you say the sheep have had a positive effect on your marriage? Life in general?"

She looked at me the way you might look at a three-legged dog. "Have a cookie, Potter. Go ahead."

When I made it to our sheepless kitchen, Carla was in the middle of pouring herself a glass of wine. I sat at the counter and she was at the sink, no more than three feet away.

"Are you enjoying the tutoring?"

"To be honest I feel redundant down there. I'm basically a glorified egg timer."

"I'm sure that's not the case."

"There's just so much trust coming from every angle. To instruct another person, in basically anything, is to approach volatility. So many things hang in so many states of balance."

"I loved teaching. I really did. I could have taught forever."

Her shoulders were pulled forward to accommodate her crossed arm and drinking posture, the glass held a few inches in front of her chest. Her upper arms were strong where they showed at blouse-sleeve ends. Her hair parted in the middle and spread outward like mist—thin, increasingly gray hair mist. Here was a woman I'd looked at so many times that I had no option but to take her for granted. A face too much like my own to register as anything else. Halfway-to-death woman, twice mother, future divorcée, looking down on me. I looked to the wine bottle on the counter briefly, then back into her face. Older female mirror of ancestral me.

"What's news from the garden?"

"It's not easy, son, figuring out how to be a mother once the normal duties are complete. Of course they keep going, I'll always be your mother. But once you were gone and schooled and now ready to begin your life."

"Mom."

"I'm sure you understand that none of this is easy. And that right now your father and I are in the middle of a very difficult time."

"I have to be going in a minute."

But going meant deciding where. I remained at the counter, sitting quietly and staring into the face of my mother. As she sipped her wine, I found myself blaming her for almost everything.

"I can see that you're upset. Of course. Your father's upset and I'm upset."

"We're like a club."

"Honey."

I reached for the glass, took enough of a sip to finish it. She poured another.

"You and your father didn't make it to a game."

"No. And now they're in the middle of a major West Coast road stretch of Giants, Dodgers, then Diamondbacks. Then it's here against Chicago, which will be sold out. Then they're in Houston."

"I know he was really hoping to go," she said.

"Tell me this much. Be honest for one second."

"Don't attack me, Potter. Don't use that tone."

"Tell me this much. How often do you see Freddy?"

"Oh. Son."

"Please don't make me feel crazy. Asshole is plenty for now."

"How are you an asshole?" she said. "You haven't done anything wrong."

"That is false."

"There's no reason to yell."

"I don't mean to!"

My mother set down the empty glass and poured another before recrossing her arms in the manner from before.

"We never lied to you, Potter."

"Fuck."

Still holding the wine, she leaned over the sink and spoke calmly into my face.

"I see Freddy everywhere I look. I see him in the basement by the washing machine and in our closet while I'm getting dressed and in the office. Right now your brother is sitting next to you. He's right there, Potter."

I left her in the kitchen and went to my car. I was halfway to Ian's before I realized his father would be home, and I turned around.

At Stuart's, a man was standing among the automobiles. I waited at the end of the driveway and watched him peer into one car, bending at the waist before stepping back and glancing over each shoulder, at which point he spotted my car and came toward me. It took me a minute to realize who it was. He was dressed in a clean white button-down shirt, a slim blue tie, shiny black loafers, and dark-gray dress pants. Dark-gray slacks. As he approached the passenger side of my car, I saw he was freshly shaven, leaving stark tan lines where the beard had been.

"If it isn't Potter Mays."

He got inside and held down the button to move the seat backward. The last person to sit there was Ian.

"Edsel."

"I have to get to Shannon's Bar and Grill downtown."

"You were going to steal one of these cars. Tell me I'm wrong."

"Seven cars sitting here and the cockblower won't let me drive the ugly one he got for free."

"Is that gabardine?"

"Big event tonight. Start of a new moment, crucial step in what I plan to become. You'll be underdressed, but so what. Lessgo."

I had no reason to resist a trip downtown. Yes, why not, Richard's downtown, surely something to learn from the deserted shells of once-prosperous buildings and the ignored,

the slide 185

downtrodden people who lived among them. As I drove, Edsel read to me from the pamphlet he was holding.

"Successful St. Louisan's monthly Meet 'n' Greet Happy Hour is the region's premier opportunity for fiscally motivated, success-driven men and women to expand their network of connections and further their goals of career triumph."

Behind us, the sun dipped into a sky the color of scotch and water.

"There's a two-dollar lot just around the corner."

I paid the attendant and found a spot. Here was the ogre, beardless and wearing some sort of costume. I sensed we might be sitting in the car for a bit and left the windows down. He pulled a crumble of aluminum foil from a pocket along with a palm-sized vanity mirror. Inside the foil were two milky-green trapezoidal pills. He placed the pills and mirror in the console's cup holder, then leaned back in his seat.

"What are you doing here, Edsel?"

"You're here," he said.

I considered this.

"Making my move," he said. "Everything I've done in the past six years has been preparation for this moment. I've hustled Talkative and Relaxation. I went to bed with roughly a hundred different women. Give or take. I have traveled and treated my body like it's my favorite hammer. I got no other option but some bovine cattle commitment to following this thing through to its end."

"You shaved. I assumed the beard was linked to the size issue. Your force."

"One way these people level the playing field is by frowning officially on facial hair at the lower levels. This world of theirs believes in the concept of reward. Facial hair is part of this. If I ever get high enough here, I promise you I'll grow another beard. I'll look forward to it. By the way, Stuart paid me five hundred dollars to take you off his hands. Did you know that?"

I didn't, but it sounded about right. A sedan parked next to us on my side and two men in business attire got out, each holding a suit jacket in one hand. These men had careers. The driver of the car had bought the car. It was his.

"Bigger point is, I agreed to a job and plan on following through on that job. Stuart is gone. Found himself a woman and he's made his way into commitment. And part of me understands, because a woman like that will make anyone think twice. Even me. Even me. As for you, personally I give half a nut what you think. But the bigger thing here is customer satisfaction. I agreed to do a service. I intend on following through on that."

"It's not just your appearance. Your voice has less country in it."

"If you're not refining, then all you're doing is waiting around and sitting still. You should learn that soon as you can. I got the uniform and the necessary personal skills. I have learned the languages. Now I go in there and perform. Wish I could have rustled up a jacket, though."

There was a warble. His voice shook a bit. I heard it in *gu-o* and in *perforum*. And if it didn't seem impossible it would have been obvious: Edsel was nervous. He placed the mirror and pills on his left thigh, then held out his hand. I pulled the Visa from my wallet and gave it to him. Edsel carefully crushed the pills and herded their powder toward the center of the small mirror.

"Here. Smell this."

"You going to tell me what it is?"

"Placebo."

When we got inside, Shannon's Bar and Grill was in that early stage of attendance when any slight move would reverberate through the rest of the night. The few who were there watched us enter. Vacant pool tables and bar stools, an unused pinball machine. A small group of men and one woman huddled around a video golf game in a corner. We secured a table smack in the middle of the room. My nasal passage wanted to bust free and whip about like some balloon slipped from a clown's fingers. A slow trickle of nicely dressed young adults filed through the door, and Edsel went for beer.

I watched him at the bar and felt the confessional momentum gathering steam. I had no therapist, no priest behind a screen, just this depraved, remorseless soul. I imagined a wet cloth wiped across a countertop, requisite purgation and atonement. Edsel sat back down and handed me a beer.

"Took that out of Stuart's five hundred."

"I fear you, Edsel. You scare me in a way I want to go find somewhere else to live. I fear the implications of you. I fear the reality of a world run by people like you."

"Good," he said. "Keep talking. I'm going to try to appear interested and nod my head. Don't be scared to move your hands. Try and give the impression you're discussing something financial."

"I've been tutoring the daughter who lives next door for the SATs. She's sixteen. I think based on her test scores and the way she laughs at me that she's very smart."

Edsel nodded and looked around the room. "And you wanna wrestle with this girl."

"If I call her blond, it's a clear case of a word not doing justice. Last night I counted eight different shades on her head."

His pretend listening skills were stellar. His eyebrows rose. He shifted his weight and opened a palm to ask follow-up questions.

"This girl, she's around all the time?"

"If I'm home later, she'll be there. It's as if she knows exactly when I'll look outside my house, either just coming out or just going in. So I'm forced to either think long and hard about going and talking to her, or think how I wish I had seen her earlier. Yes. Tonight we'll talk and she'll be there and I'll try not to want her."

"Now shake my hand and I'll walk away."

As soon as he left, another hand smacked my shoulder. I turned and was looking up at Matt from Saturdays at the pool house. He wore a blue shirt with a white collar and a solid red tie.

He set a bottle of Budweiser on the table and draped his suit jacket over the back of a chair. Eric was a step behind him, also holding a Budweiser.

We all touched bottles and drank and then sat quietly for a few minutes. Shannon's was filling up quickly. Groups were forming around the bar, then being pushed into the middle of the room as newer groups formed closer in. The smoke was growing thicker, and the layers of chatter soon became loud enough to drown out the music. I saw Edsel on the outskirts of a group, working his way to its inner circle. He nodded and shrugged and shook hands. It was a terrific sight to behold, his first nibbles at legitimacy. Reminded me of that movie where the reformed hooker runs for Congress. Soon he was inside, centrally located, towering over the heads around him, having punctured their circle and this new world. He was just so *big*. Someone behind the bar turned up the music.

I must have blinked, because suddenly something had changed—the group had moved several feet away, leaving the ogre standing alone. I couldn't believe how quickly it went down. He seemed dazed, then began looking for another group.

Matt leaned in and said, "He overshot."

"By a good yard, at least," Eric said.

"Who can be comfortable around a person that size? Look at him. He was already tall. Still is. Then he added all that muscle and he became a cartoon."

"It would be another thing for a guy who wasn't coming in cold."

"You're right. Nobody here has any idea who he is."

"The contrast between his cheeks upward compared to the mouth and chin area isn't helping. It looks like some spa treatment Melissa gets."

"Did he shave with bleach? Is this some attempt at a joke?"

"Good look, otherwise. Good slacks."

"But where's the jacket? Does he even have a jacket?"

They were right. Though he'd made his way into the circle, nobody around Edsel seemed to be interested in his presence. He stood peering over shoulders, his massive head jutting upward like an unwanted thumb. They had regarded him, humored him, and now he'd become the eight-hundred-pound ogre no one would discuss. It was almost heartbreaking. Matt and Eric were extremely satisfied with their cool piece of judgment. They sat on their diagnosis like telephone books. Edsel leaned in and said something to the group's lone woman and she ignored him. They all ignored him.

"He's done for. What a clown."

"Jesus. He totally blew this, huh?"

"It's a joke. He's a clown."

Matt tapped a finger to the music. Eric sipped beer, then inhaled through his teeth. Here was the risk of the attempt: failure, public, spotlighted for these hundred eyes, the opinions and pity and casual judgment. Edsel's attempt at climbing out of his personal muck, and these young men with their voices, words, eyes and faces, ties and glittery watches. I thought of the right word and leaned across the table for their attention.

"Smug," I said. "Both of you. I never liked you guys but until now I couldn't say exactly why. It's smugness. You assholes ooze it with the grins, shit-eating grins and smugness to spare, wearing your slacks, talking your smug shit. Festering smugness, all cozy and smug, got your wives, income, why bother to even try anything. Try something."

I stood up and waded through the thin crowd of people, most of whom appeared to be in their twenties. At the bar, I turned and stepped onto the foot railing to boost myself over the canopy of heads. *Improvement.* The legendary notion of personal advancement, of bootstraps and pulling upward, here condensed to its purest form.

Edsel was sitting alone at the table when I returned. I sat with him. The beard had served as both weapon and shield. Now he was naked and revealing more than he should have. Didn't he know this was no place to exhibit gloom? I slid one of the two beers across to the maudlin ogre.

"Something's gone wrong. I miscalculated, Mays. I shit the bed."

"It was your rookie attempt," I said. "They say disappointment keeps you irritated and therefore motivated."

He spent the next minute staring into my face while I took sips from my beer and tried to act naturally. Occasionally I watched back. Soon enough, I witnessed a change. His features went from those of the rebuked failure to something else, a hopefulness. He shrugged and settled into confidence. Just like that.

"Yeah well, no shit. So I need more training. So what. The beauty of hopping rails is that the old rail doesn't go away. There are still women. The old rail is the same as always. Skills like mine don't disappear. Nor's this mean the night has to be ruined. Look at the night. It is young. Younger than that neighbor you should avoid at all costs. What we'll do, Potter Mays, is find us some women."

The bar was thick with smoke and the noise of language. So many words with so many intentions, words born from desirous agenda, well aimed, everyone in this room aiming, aiming. The ogre had not excelled at this exchange. But now, having failed at professionalism, he would retreat to the effortless realm of seduction. And he would take me with him.

"This girl, Edsel, I'm telling you. She comforts."

"Forget the child for tonight," he said. "I forbid you to touch that little girl. Trust me. You remember what sex was like at sixteen? The awkwardness? The are-you-sure-this-is-what-you-wants? Is this how a condom goes on? Why won't it roll on? See you next time my parents are out of town. Be a grown-up for once, Potter. Grown-up sex is a violent struggle. You don't want comfort. You want powpow and the bang train. Comfort is for the meek. Look over there. Not like that, easy with the stare. Just look. See them? Two friendly girls, all smiles. I'm about ninety-nine percent sure one of them is willing to lie down with you. And now before you say something, yes, she's got something in her face. Alright fine. Maybe she's a little bit downy. But cute still. What am I saying?

Look who I'm talking to. Monsieur liberal art. You with the open mind. Plus I bet you've heard about the sex drives of the retarded, right? You put two retards in a room, they'll fuck for hours."

Escape. There was always escape.

I drove home with every window open, radio off, sound of wind like whiteout. The house was dark and still. I slid into my dad's office and sat down to my empty e-mail in-box. I began to put together an album of songs. Her silver Jetta was full of shit music programmed into boy-scrawled CDs. She was out there now—I could see her through the crack where the curtain met wall—wandering circles in her parents' driveway. I removed one disc and replaced it with another, and watched her. *Time takes a cigarette, puts it in your mouth . . .*

I left the computer and stepped back into the evening. Now she was talking on the phone, one hand against the side of the garage, lifting and lowering herself through a series of careless pliés. I approached and she handed me a cigarette with the lighter. I smoked and made small circles of my own in our driveway. She looked up and mouthed *sorry* with tiny delicate angel lips. I picked up the basketball from her driveway and shot some jumpers. I walked circles and smoked my cigarette. I pulled a quarter from my pocket and flipped it, thinking heads I would go back inside, tails I would stay. Simplest of equations. T means stay. H means go. It was heads. I flipped it again. Heads. H, then H.

She closed her phone and approached me. I stepped backward from the driveway into the grass of her family's backyard, moving beyond the limits of the garage light. She was part of it, I wasn't alone in the process. Hello, body. Within her grasp I felt quiet and I felt warmth. We stood and collected each other. When I pulled, so did she. And grabbed. She went down to the grass, and I did too, and it was wet from the day's storm, and soft. Then lips and darkness and hair in my fingers and wet soft grass. My knees were between her knees. And for some time we stayed this way. We kissed playfully and then seriously, and then when the kissing moved from serious to necessary, our knees touched, and hers moved outward, and mine followed. I lifted her shirt from her waist and descended down to her bare stomach, brushed lips against untouchably soft skin, the smell of peaches or apple, a flash of light. I moved back upward and her hands went to my waist, fumbling at belt and zipper but not underwear. Pressure. More flashes of light somewhere off to our side, car passing, maybe, or a dog walker's safety measure. So forgotten an experience I didn't realize until it was happening. Tightness, pressure. Two layers of cotton, but I was inside her. Barely. Tiny sounds rising, and I stayed with her until I felt the first hints of something approaching slowly from somewhere down this dry road. Then I pulled back and moved my head down to her stomach and laid it there on its side, half deaf to the world.

"*Diadem.*"

"Whatsits . . . jeweled headband used as a royal crown."

"*Finial.*"

"The thingy on top of the other thingy," she whispered. "An ornament."

"You are going to be accepted at a top-tier school and have the time of your life."

When I stood, I found myself sore, tired. I pulled her up and kissed each of her temples, then briefly her lips, resisting the urge to replay the whole sequence again, return to the ground with her in my possession. A girl within arms. But then we were apart, and she moved through light into the darkness of garage, and I slid quietly through the side door into my parents' unstable home. I walked calmly through the living room, up the stairs to bed, leaving the computer glowing into an otherwise dark office.

august

one

there was sun all over the place, and glare, in this season of squint. I parked in whatever shade I could find and ate the bagged lunch my mother kept preparing for me, sitting at the foot of trees. We had reached the month of legend and woe. August, dank and brutal, sucking from the city a steady sour tang of human sweat.

Then there was the other thing, the narrowly averted debasement of my angelic neighbor. I worked very hard to keep her out of the daydreams that came at me with increasingly sexual overtones. Sometimes I fell into a whirlwind of sexual memory, Audrey and others and Audrey again, and I found myself longing for her distant frame—an hour, ten minutes with her familiar body. Thirty seconds, her neck only. Single glancing touch.

Was Zoe a virgin? I told myself: *do not even wonder.* Far more important was that, when asked, I could tell Audrey that, NO, I had not slept with anyone this summer. Because actually this was technically true—if I had pressed myself into anything, it was *cotton,* the underwear had remained throughout, which meant at most what we had done was a kind of play, technical recreation and nothing more—and it was important to milk these rare moral victories when they came.

And look what else I could do! With one minor sleight of

hand, one negligible benevolent fraud, I could instantly upgrade the generosity of my existence. Every bottle could be made into Premium with a quick swap of the caps, these "Premium" bottles substituted into orders for Purified or Natural Spring. Compliments of me, no no, you're welcome. Please, really, it's my pleasure. If this qualified me as a liar, it was a title well worth the bright looks of gratitude on my customers' faces. The spread of eye, curl of lip, tilt of head that captured their disbelief. How clear the happiness. *Premium.* Postures changed at the sound of this word. Meaning: the highest grade of drinking water available. And if they pressed why, exactly, I was willing to do this? I said *we'll just keep it between us,* with a wink and sly nod, and here they grew even further grateful, charmed into one of these minor conspiracies we all so dearly crave.

I returned home one afternoon and opened the front door to the sound of my mother yelling. I stood for a minute, stunned. In the computer room, she yelled a short word and then *stupid.* The computer wasn't working. I heard a series of clicks, that blandly infuriating *chirnk,* meaning, in computer, *no, that won't work.* The living room between us was not dark and not light, striped with shadow. Her short bursts of voice came out shrill. She was enraged and breathing loud enough for me to hear from where I stood. And I knew: she hated that room. The computer room, she called it. Angry at the computer and the room that housed it, the house that housed it. I told myself only a jerk would stand there and listen without announcing his presence. She yelled again and I went upstairs to take what turned into the longest and coldest shower of my life. By the time I came back downstairs, the house was empty.

When the second week of August came around, so did the Cardinals. They began hitting the ball with a ferocity that caught the rest of the league off guard: opposing pitchers shook their heads and spoke of mistakes, how they were made to pay. Dinkers fell for singles, gappers stretched to doubles, and hit-and-runs found holes where fielders would have been. We passed Houston and were catching the Cubs.

The city, in turn, was gathering the only real energy it knew. We all began to BELIEVE. Small flags fluttered from hoods and trunks of cars, posters appeared in the windows of businesses. *Go Cards!!* Local supermarkets ran specials on hot dogs and pork steaks. By this point the salt lines on my hat were whiter than the team's logo.

Stuart called with an invitation to a night game against the Mets. I made what I considered a pretty solid joke about maybe he had dialed the wrong number, and he said, "Five minutes." The rolling ad pulled into our driveway, a filthy shadow of its former promotional radiance. There was mud caked into places I didn't fully understand how mud could get. I opened the door to an interior scarred with cigarette pocks and a deep, deliberate-looking slash across the lumbar. Marianne was not in the car.

"It's really good to see you, Stubes."

"Stop right there. No talking in the ad. The ad has become an experimental silent zone."

"You're serious."

He raised his hand from the wheel to quiet me. I nodded and fastened my seat belt.

We arrived at a stadium that was all crowd and cheer. We shuffled among the throng of strangers and their infectious feeling of community, men and women sharing random high fives while beer spilled over the rims of big plastic cups. The panoply of red was about your sense of pride and your sense of place, and pretty much *compulsory.*

I had to wonder how long Stuart and I would go without speaking. It was a loaded silence that gave me the impression there was a reason he'd brought me here tonight. When we found his father's seats six rows back from the visitors' dugout, I

held my big fresh Budweiser and turned a slow rotation to take in
the growing crowd. These people were St. Louis, all of them, regardless of how long they drove to get here. These guys over
there, sure. Those guys. And the women two sections above us,
in the hats. Them. The center-field jumbotron blinked the message *The New West County: If you're not there, why be anywhere?*

I asked my friend who it was that had written about being *in*
but not *of*.

"Heidegger," he said. "Among others. Sit down. You're making
people nervous."

Two innings passed without further conversation. Stuart
flagged down an ancient black man lugging his tub of beers and
hollering *Cold beer here!* so it had five syllables. The man poured
like a true professional of his craft, one old scarred hand over-
turning two cans at once, a system of angles and air pressure and
perfect foam. Stuart paid and the old man continued up the stairs,
hollering into the clamor.

We went two more innings before Stuart broke our silence.

"Edsel came by the other day."

"Oh man, you should have seen it. I've never imagined that
guy failing at anything. But these businesspeople at the bar the
other night didn't even blink in his direction. And once I saw it
happen it was suddenly so clear. He's as human as the rest of us.
Your buddies Dickbrain and Shitmouth were there also."

"Matt and Eric mentioned that you were extremely rude. That
on top of the way you treated Marianne at the fair was enough
for me to start to wonder what was happening to you. Then came
Edsel, with his photographs."

He took a long sip of his beer before setting it down. He
reached into his pocket and removed a small envelope and folded
back the flap. He handed me four pictures, each split between
green of lawn on the bottom and a solid half of black toward the
top. I flipped through them quickly, then took my time looking at
each one.

"There's an official term for what you're doing there," he said.

I left the photos in my lap and stared intently at the field. Ball goes here, you move here, back up this man.

"Potter."

"Dry humping," I said.

"I was thinking *statutory rape.*"

There is no mystery to the past. At any time you could stop and glance behind you and see the steps, how this then this, this, and now here you were. I was at the Meet 'n' Greet Happy Hour sympathizing for the failed ogre, poor failed Edsel, and admitting things to him that I should not have admitted. He was failing so badly at legitimate business that he relapsed into his natural state of assholery, to dangle filthy notions of the developmentally disabled in front of me like some reverse bait, some catalyzing atrocity on a string. I was fleeing and stumbling headfirst to the safety of home and the angel next door, Edsel's first success of the night.

"How did he get there?" I said. "A cab? He hailed a cab, said Arbor Drive and step on it. And he carries a camera around with him?"

"Not the most important thing, here."

"That devious piece of. My God, I reached out to him, Stubes! I saw him fail. I watched it happen. And he turns that around? Uses failure to catch me off guard? What kind of person? And you're friends with this ogre shit? Fine. That's fine. But you have to listen to me on one thing. This was not sex. I will stand by this all night long."

"Those pictures would seem to basically obliterate doubt."

"Explain that neither of us removed underpants."

"You are on top of her like some ravenous beast. Look at the poor girl. She looks like a victim."

I flipped through the pictures. We were standing. Next we were horizontal in the grass, legs flat. Zoe looked small and helpless beneath me, and there was no pleasure in what could be seen of the girl's face. Next her little shoeless feet were flat on the ground, knees up and bent. I looked like some invading army between her legs. Next I was holding one of them, lifting it to my waist.

"I am not a bad person. I have done bad things but I am mostly good. I am overall good. I'm not a rapist."

"I know that," he said. "Except, also, yes you are."

"What am I supposed to do here? How many copies of these pictures exist? They should be mine, shouldn't they? They're of me. This is me, my body, a private moment. Edsel. Goddammit all. I have to find him, don't I? I'll face him and demand he hand over the pictures. This is not his concern, this private moment. But Jesus, Stubes, he's so big. What if he says no? I can't possibly overpower him."

"Fighting with him will get you nothing but hurt," he said.

"I've never felt so helpless in my life. Come on, Stubes. You two are friends. Aren't you? My stomach, Jesus. Talk to him for me. These pictures should mean nothing to him. Okay, it's funny, isn't it? We'll have a laugh over it. Jesus. Stuart. I said he was trouble. Didn't I? I said, what's that asshole doing at the pool house."

"If I'm you, Potter, I might accept that he has the pictures. You can't change that. You can't un–statutory rape this girl. Edsel is treating the pictures as a commodity with a value yet to be determined. He knows he has something and he wants something else. The only power you have here is doing what you can to give Edsel what he wants. He has proposed a sit-down with the four of us together, a frank, levelheaded examination of the situation as it stands."

A new beer vendor had a mustache with tips pinned by sweat to his cheeks. Above center field, the jumbotron flashed words and chants. I had a terrible image of my father and Derrick Hoyne dining together at Sportsman's Park, an amicable neighborly meal until the photographs appeared on the restaurant's TV. I saw my mother and Nancy Hoyne in their book club, each woman holding an album full of these pictures. I tasted puke, anxious in the back of my mouth.

"Four of us?" I said.

"Including Marianne. As an independent observer and moderator. She's already agreed."

Soon a group of fans above left field threw their hands to the sky and stood from their seats, the first lame tries for a wave. This attempt spread clockwise twenty or thirty degrees and the faithful wavers tried again, again, until they scrapped through a very thin but full first revolution. With this success came more faith and energy, and I watched the cheer gather momentum as it swept rotations across the ocean of Cardinals loyal, dual-action source and signifier of their joy.

While those around me rose and cheered, I remained seated, clenching the photographs. For the sons among us, it was simple: admire the fathers, watch and ape the ways they sat and moved their hands. We sons of these men, these factories of pride and shame, these creators, bar-setters, and judges. These fathers. And they likewise were to watch us back, see reflections in our shapes and behaviors, echoes of how they defined themselves. We boys of theirs, emulating traits they once emulated in their own fathers. These ties.

People around me stood and waved.

But what of the aberrations? We half-mirror sons, smudged, foreign. These deviations from values. We who survived only to tarnish the men we admire. We failures, broken models. We gauche wardens of history, entrusted with treasure, carrying hopes inside clumsy shaking hands while our fathers kept watch, appraising, eyes falling shut under the weight of shame. We who managed to crumble beneath pressure's absence. Crying aloud, *here!,* Father, here is what I do with our name. Here, here, now call me son and love me until you die.

Once the wave died down, Stuart said he was going for a bratwurst and did I want one.

"Take some money. Let me pay."

He didn't take the money. Later, we saw the Mets score seven runs on a series of roped base hits and embarrassing fielding miscues and one astoundingly bad curveball that hung like a butchered cow before it was launched into the center-field bleachers. As hope dwindled, I stood to let Midwesterners squeeze past. At some point I had slipped the pictures into my pocket. We sat among increasingly vacant red seats until we were more or less alone in the stadium, today's loss now finalized into the records. It seemed Stuart was waiting for me to make the first move into this new era of looming photographic evidence. I thought, *Stand up and move, navigate the situation you've made here, with your mixture of pathetic neediness and nostalgic sexuality, you small dumb little excuse for a grown man.* Eventually an usher came by and told us she was going to have to call security.

I could not believe how many silver Volkswagen Jettas there were in this city. As if I required reminding. Each one I saw belonged to Zoe until proven otherwise, which gave the day's work a sense of pursuit, though I couldn't decide if I was chasing or running away. Most turned out to be driven by people who looked not unlike myself, sensible white males in their twenties who were probably not rapists.

When I ended up behind her silver Jetta moving eastbound on Highway 40, I found her number in my phone's list of recent incoming calls.

"Raise your hand and wave," I said.

"Weirdo," she said.

"Yeah. In the van behind you."

"That's odd, because I'm at my friend's house." People or a TV in the background laughed. "But I was going to call you. Meet for coffee in an hour?"

I arrived at our closest branch of the giant coffee chain early so

I could case the joint and see what advantage might be gained by
positioning. These plush chairs and pleasant lighting and pockets
of conversation. What lighthearted words were the law-abiding
men and women sharing over afternoon beverages?

I secured a chair with my hat and went to the counter for an
iced coffee, which I took into the bathroom, only to remember
that you weren't supposed to take drinks into the bathroom, so I
quickly put my lips around the straw to protect it from the floating bits of pee and shit.

Zoe was in the purple chair when I returned, flipping through
a clothing catalog.

"If I'm to believe these people from Delia's, stripes and oversize necklines are going to be everywhere this winter. Pointelle
yokes with ruffles. I can't wait."

I quickly assumed my preferred state of rest, sitting in a composed manner with legs crossed. After a few seconds I switched
the crossing of my legs and shifted in the chair. The music went
to Ella or was it Billie or maybe Etta.

"I might as well just come out and say this."

"Good," I said. "You start."

"I have a boyfriend."

"That's. No you don't."

"It's true. At this party two nights ago there was this guy Luke
who I've known forever. And he asked if I would go out with him.
Nobody's ever asked me to go out with him before. I didn't know
what to say. I asked if he meant like to a movie or something and
he said, no, he meant, like, to be his girl. I couldn't believe that's
what he meant."

"He asked you to be his girl? Just like that."

She nodded.

"Luke the swimmer? You can't go out with Luke the swimmer.
There's something weird about his ears. You told me about
them."

"That's Jeremy," she said. "Luke is nothing. I mean, he's not someone we've talked about. He really has no thing. He's just Luke. You'd like him."

"Why would I like him?"

"Jesus, Potter. I don't know."

I put my fingers to my temples and closed my eyes. The plot churned in the background, wheels greased to spin silently, high-grade Swiss precision bearings. And now the pictures had sucked another person into the affair, this courageous Luke boy with his forthright invitations.

"Listen, I'm sorry," she said. "Honestly I didn't expect you to be so sad."

"Do you want coffee? Let me get you a coffee. Some kind of latte. Shot of vanilla."

I stood and went to the counter and, facing away from her, ordered a complex and stupidly named drink. I could tell her about the photographs or I could not. She was a responsible young woman with a firm grasp of the world's ways, a generational forbearance that must have emerged since I left high school. I could pad the truth. The sheer potential here was impressive, the number of ways this could go. The door was not far away. I could stay here or run away. They weren't all that different. Her drink came, tall, pale, blended, and topped *appropriately* with whipped cream.

"I didn't realize I was ordering something pink."

She said, "Listen, I get it. You're going to say don't tell anyone about what happened because you could get in trouble. Technically. You're going to say our fathers are friends and you know my brother and nobody should know, probably. And I'm going to say don't worry, please, it's not that big of a deal. It will be our own little secret. Like it never happened. This is good, the drink, thanks. But I probably won't finish the whole thing. I'm supposed to meet Luke in a minute."

"You're being so polite. Stop it. We have to talk about this."

"But not really," she said. "As I understand it, things like this happen, then they end, and then you appreciate them as something that happened sometime in the past. And together they make up memory and shape who you are as an adult person."

"Just a couple things to iron out. First on the list is the question of whether or not you were a virgin. I'm sorry to speak so bluntly, but it's something I'd like to know."

"What?"

"Were you? A virgin."

"I was at one point a virgin. Yes. But it has been a while. I continue to not be a virgin."

"And would you agree that I never abused the inherent power dynamic of the student–teacher interface to coerce you in any way? This is a yes-or-no question."

"Sure. Okay. I agree."

"The point here is just to achieve closure."

She was smiling at me and I did not like it. "Closure for what?"

"Okay, fair enough, ha, good point. Good point."

Zoe picked up her drink. I watched her lower her head, lips meeting the bright novelty straw. Her hair today was pulled into pigtails. Then she stood, and I knew that in this place of bitter coffee and watery jazz, the girl standing across from me was gravity, centripetal in every way.

She pulled out her cell phone. "I'm meeting Luke for a coffee date up the street."

I began nodding and kept nodding. Once she'd walked past me, I switched to her vacated seat so I had visual confirmation of her leaving the premises.

That night, I sat with my mother on the couch watching the six o'clock local news. She sipped from a glass of wine. The female anchor was one I recognized from growing up, except she must have had some sort of work done to her face. The man was the former sportscaster who transitioned to general news a couple years back. He took us live to on-the-scene coverage of a foiled abduction in Warrenton, about forty miles to our west. Police weren't yet releasing the name of the thirty-year-old suspect in custody. I thought back to my mother's flash of anger on that afternoon with the computer. Now she was completely still; aside from her eyes, open and glazed, she could have been sleeping. The female anchor introduced part three in their ongoing coverage of the approaching grand opening of the New West County Mall.

I moved from the couch to the breakfast counter and watched my father, who tonight for whatever reason was cooking. I tried not to read into this or see it as practice for bachelorhood. He had a dish towel draped over his left shoulder and an oven mitt on his right hand. It took opening three cabinets before he found the serving dish he wanted. As he cooked, he drank from his old law school beer stein.

I poured myself a glass of whiskey and went back to the couch. The weatherman mentioned a possible break in the heat but said not to hold our breath. From my seat I could see a stack of mail sitting on my father's desk. And what if one of the envelopes contained the pictures? What if they were accompanied by a note, a collage of mismatched letters cut from magazines, glued messily back into demands? Holding the remote with a straight arm, my mother began slowly climbing through the channels.

At dinner, my father and I spoke about baseball while my mother shook salt over her entire plate. The food was passable and I think better than she would have liked to admit. Now that I had my own scandal, every minute inside this house had become charged with implication, as if the rise in our calamitous prospects had given us something to look forward to. Was this instinctual, this secret desire for things to go wrong so we'd at least have guiding principles for what to do next? The three of us drank our alcohol. At any second it was all liable to crumble into a cloud of dust.

Much later, I found myself awake and made my way back downstairs. In the living room, I sat in my father's chair and listened to the wheels spinning in the shadows, the secret machinations whirring away.

It seemed my parents, likely distracted by their marital catastrophe, had forgotten to turn off one of the outdoor lights. I crossed the room for the switch but stopped when I saw my mother out there gardening. The clock read 2:30.

I stood at the window and watched. She was down on two knees as if genuflecting to some pagan feminine earth spirit. She was barefoot and wearing her purple nightgown, wristbands on each arm. Who knew what cruel circus of thought might possibly be going through her mind. She had a trowel in her hand and was stabbing into the soil to get at something that wouldn't budge. I stood until I couldn't watch anymore, then a little longer. I left the light on for her, though I doubted she really even needed it.

two

the heat had become something you wouldn't even discuss. It was three digits—what else was there to say? The city's old population was passing away at an alarming rate. As these tragedies grew more common, the news gradually eliminated their segments on heatstroke victims, interviews with surviving kin. In their place we had all variations of expert advising us on how to stay safe in what one network termed *Radical, Perilous Heat* and another, simply, *The Danger Zone*. How comforting the advice of these authorities, how nice to sit and listen to their simple, organized precautions.

We were two and a half games behind the first-place Cubs in the National League Central.

My mother cultivated her therapy of voluntary service. Without fanfare or even announcement, she joined a civilian group that drove Econoline vans through low-income neighborhoods with small bottles of water and battery-operated fans. This was a massive step forward from wrapping Christmas gifts at the Galleria for children's charities. The more selfless her volunteering, the harder it was to continue seeing her as the villain of this domestic drama.

The meeting was to begin at midnight. Once the sun went down, I covered myself in mosquito repellent and set off walking vaguely in the direction of Stuart's. Since I blamed at least some of my behavior on the place that had raised me, perhaps moving through it at the ground level could provide the logic for my defense. I began along familiar roads, blacktop, beneath overhanging trees, elm, and cars, mostly silver. I left the neighborhood by the less decorative back way, taking the pedestrian bridge halfway across Forest Park Parkway. I gripped the chain-link fence that rose ten or so feet from the waist-high concrete barrier. Occasional white lights sped toward me, red lights sped away. Four lanes total. I had never even considered the consideration of suicide, but this struck me as exactly the sort of spot where it could happen, provided one made it over the fence. A fair, reasonable challenge for a final small triumph at life's end. Down the road, I spotted a police cruiser hidden in the shadows waiting for speeders. I walked quickly away.

The photographs were in my back pocket, and with each step I felt them rub against my thigh. Otherwise, my attention was focused fiercely outward on whatever answers might emerge from this exterior world. Flooded by yellowish gaze of streetlight, the colors appeared suddenly retouched, somehow more essential. The forms of buildings struck me as more relevant than ever, each different manner by which lines met and diverged, framing other shapes within. It was as if some hand had reached out and spun the city's master dials clockwise: resolution, volume, contrast, brightness. The menacing dark, empty enclosures inside common garden ivy, a sidewalk seam tall enough to trip over. Everything was here, the facts of the world, the truth of details.

I crossed a street and entered Shaw Park under the watch of a gazillion cicada eyes and the tidal pattern of their call. *Skee-her.* The park was empty of course, municipal sporting fields and water houses abandoned at dusk. *Skee-her.* I sat against a tree and felt the bark press some fractal design into my back. I wasn't sure what I was expecting to find here. Some dark rendezvous, perhaps, any variety of nefarious nighttime business, something to make my own moral decay seem tame in comparison. But I was in the wrong part of the county.

After an hour, I stood and brushed myself off, then continued across the park and eventually along a series of dark, quiet streets while details continued to scream my name. Soon I came upon what appeared to be teenage boys and girls in a circle of chairs in the yard of a modest brick home. There was one man sitting among them, light-haired and boy-faced, with the enthusiastic demeanor of faith. It was a youth group meeting. He wore a collared shirt and khaki shorts and leather sandals.

"Good evening," he called as I passed. I paused and nodded back. Then one of the young men stood from the chairs and walked crisply to meet me. I saw others in the group smile to one another at his enthusiasm. I reached back to make sure the pictures were secure in my pocket.

"Are you lost?" he asked, and I suspected he wasn't speaking of geographical bearings.

"Not really."

I waited for what he would say next, but instead he stood there, weirdly silent, smiling, and big-eyed. Was this how people found religion? Were they awkwarded in?

"What are you doing out here? It's so hot."

"Our group prefers to meet under His watchful eye. It allows us to look back up at Him too."

"And marvel?" I asked.

"That's right."

Behind him, some of the others raised hands in greeting. I nodded and continued down the sidewalk.

The pool house was dark, as was the pool itself. I could hear voices, though, a series of syllables wrapped in our Missouri cadence of reluctant twang. As I got closer I saw them: beastly ogre, lithe vamp, and fallen sage.

My God, did I smell awful.

I shut the fence gate behind me. The deck was dry. I stepped over the rafts and recliners that had been dragged ashore and took a seat at the table with my three arbiters. Gray faces, shadowed. They had stopped talking when I reached the gate, leaving a silence of the sort I could tell was my responsibility to break. Marianne pulled on her cigarette and we heard the crispy burn of tobacco and paper backed by the slosh of pool drainage system. My eyes went from my old friend, shirtless and weary-eyed, to the girl and her long, knobby-knuckled fingers raised to hold her smoke. I brushed a mosquito away from my face and looked at Edsel. Countenance of cardboard.

"These pictures are nothing. You've got nothing."

"Don't be a fool," he said.

The beard had grown back into something thick and bushy. I maintained steady eye contact and labored to project calm disinterest. He leaned back in his chair, raised his hands to his head, elbows out. He wore a T-shirt with cutoff sleeves, those ridiculous arms flexing convulsively. How selfish and paranoid his arms were tonight, hoarding strength like this, taunting our own meager limbs.

Marianne reached for the ashtray and snuffed her cigarette. "Just to be clear, Potter, anyone over twenty-one who has sexual intercourse with a person less than seventeen is guilty of statutory rape in the second degree."

"Didn't ask. Did not ask you a question."

No shadows could conceal the truth of tonight's caucus. Stuart lit another cigarette and passed it to her. I knew of this girl's drive to alienate wealthy, generous Stuart from his closest male friend. Lithe and prettier than I had previously admitted, she was circling, closing in on her lame, confused kill.

"You should know also that our state of Missouri defines *sexual intercourse* as any penetration, however slight. Whether or not there's emission."

"Don't like you," I said. "Never have. Don't trust you. Don't like looking at you. Don't think I'd mind if you disappeared forever."

"That's plenty," Stuart said.

In the moments that followed, there was momentum gathering. I was certain we all felt it. The force had been revealed the first time I saw the photographs at the game. Plain envelope opened to reveal images of stark confirmation, heavy iron ball set into motion along this steady downhill road. And now details were falling into place, exit ramps were closing, alternatives erased as part of this narcotic certitude.

I felt something tickly on my arm and waved it away. If the lights were indeed turned off to keep away mosquitoes, why wasn't the citronella candle lit? I waved away another one.

"We're looking at a blackmail of the classic model," Edsel said. "Industry standard."

I could sense a smirk beneath the beard. As with Marianne, there was little ambiguity to the ogre this evening. I had told him I feared him and I meant it in every possible way. He was first and foremost an asshole, but he was also a plotter, a man who found happiness in the creation and performance of schemes, which admittedly required commitment and a strong sense of organization.

"I will give you a list of demands you will have to meet. You don't meet them, the pictures will go first to your father, then to Derrick Hoyne, former State Senator John Dunleavy, the Ladue police department, and whoever else I can come up with."

"You conniving son of a bitch."

"All the names you want, bucko. Blow off steam."

Time passed loudly. How foolish I'd been to think the spinning I had heard these past nights, that not-unpleasant whirring from the shadows, was plot. Such was my inexperience with the device. In actuality, that sound was freedom, rotating contingencies, the many things that might but might not come to be. Now options were being dislodged from the spin, launched into darkness, leaving the ambient grinding of something increasingly certain, the grating clatter of truth and consequence and impending doom.

"What do you want?"

"The big ones are your car and ten thousand dollars. Few other trifling items for posterity."

"The car's not in my name, and I don't have anything even close to ten thousand dollars."

"Should start work on a list of people who might."

Stuart and Marianne were momentarily put on display by the quick orange bloom of his lighter. My friend would not look at me. It occurred to me the darkness around us might have been less about mosquitoes and more about shielding me from the memories of this place, to render what was familiar foreign. I wasn't sure whether this was something he did to make this easier on me or something he did so I wouldn't feel compelled to stay very long.

"But it's still the pool house, isn't it?" I said, and reached down to remove my shoes and socks. I walked to the pool's edge and lifted off my shirt before falling into the black water. I let myself sink naturally, then maneuvered myself deeper until I reached the cement floor, where I searched blindly for Audrey's starfish, canvassing the pool's deep end with waving hands. My lungs began to ache. It was not here. Of course not. But how many legs did it have by now? Three still? Were there three when it came in the box? Did she have the other two? Had she kept one and given one to Carmel? I kicked to the surface and gasped for air.

Out of the pool, I stood dripping at the table. I held my shoes in one hand and my shirt in the other. Stuart's face was invisible, Marianne's slightly reddened behind burning cigarette, and Edsel's a dark mingling of hair and evil intent. It was as if he had split me open and shined a flashlight inside, then extricated that core of human sin we all spent lives working to contain.

"You and your filthy ogre shit. Your victorious filth and what have you got. You dick. You ogre dick piss shit cock suck. What's it all now? You fuck. You fucking fuck. Ass fuck you in the fucking mouth you shit."

Marianne stood from the table and laid a long finger onto Stuart's shoulder. Together they stepped into the pool house without a word, while Edsel remained seated, comfortable in his certainty that nothing I did could ever cause him harm. Such dedication to personal ascent, such drive. Such dedication to himself, dominating. Amazing to think we were technically the same species. So terribly *big*.

It took an hour to retrace my route home. It would be several more before the sun came up, but I had no interest in opening the door and climbing those familiar stairs. I stood in the driveway looking at my car. Zoe's Jetta was missing, out for Friday night rampage of teen carelessness, throwing herself around like some rubber ball. Maybe parked somewhere with Jeff. Luke.

I drove to the Rocket Slide. I parked facing the playground and reclined my seat, breathed deeply until the grinding sound had subsided enough that I could fall asleep.

I woke to the screams of children. I sat and listened to their yelps, marveling at their agendaless play. They circled in the gravel and scaled the structure, hollering at no set interval into the morning air.

Both of my elbows were covered in mosquito bites.

It was Saturday, a normal workday for the men and women who tended to the city's network of roads. They were likely out there already, wearing their orange vests and hats and collecting their generous hourly wage. What I lacked today in invoices and a map, I could make up for with the duties of a surrogate big brother. I unreclined my seat, turned the key to bring the car to life, and checked the clock. Yes. It was indeed a fine time to visit Ian.

I found him sitting on the concrete steps with a piece of paper held in both hands in front of him.

"Yesterday I was out here reading this book we're all supposed to read for school and a van pulled up and this man got out."

"Did you run inside and scream that you were calling the police?"

"No. I forgot everything. I just sat here and made like I didn't see him and I was still reading my dumb red-fern book."

"What was he wearing?"

"I don't know. Pants and a shirt."

"You should try to remember clothing. Also height and hair color and race. If you can guess age, that's important too. Age can be hard. So can height if you're sitting down there. So be sure to stand before you make your approximation."

"All he did was walk over and hand me this letter from my mom, then he drove away. And how am I supposed to read this stupid book now?"

"I'd better take a look," I said.

He looked at me and then over at the yard where the kids had played but today were not. He began to bite his lower lip. The idea of secret mail carriers sounded familiar, but I didn't know why. Nor could I explain my faith that the letter contained a thinly veiled code that, together, the boy and I would try and uncover this afternoon, sitting together on his porch with pencils, solving the puzzle.

"She says not to show it to anyone."

"She means strangers," I said.

"No she doesn't," he said.

three

I said it like, why not, Dad. Suggestion from couch to computer, where he was sitting and working. I downplayed my severe inner turmoil and distress. Why not hey let's just why not go to the Arch or something? Out of the house, father and son.

It cost us six dollars to park on the slanted cobblestone of the levee. I followed my father to the river's edge, where we stood for a minute watching driftwood pass quickly from our left to right. The intermittent noise of mud-water sloshing onto the brick shoreline lent something to the moment, I wanted to call it naturalism, and it was tough not to appreciate the Mississippi for her onetime role as national lifeline, this huge muddy bitch of a river.

Beginning uphill, we climbed the two long flights of stairs up to the Jefferson Memorial Park and Gateway Arch. A thin crowd milled about the lawn and aimed cameras into the sky; park rangers on horseback posed and smiled with tourists. I went to one leg's base and ran fingers across the etchings that scarred the steel close to the ground.

"Catenary curve," he said. "The same wide as tall. People forget that."

I did not ask for his help just yet.

We descended a sloping walkway, through metal detectors and into the sprawling subterranean Museum of Westward Expansion.

While my father went for tickets, I walked among the exhibits. I peeked into replica tepees and mud huts and listened to animatronic actors describe the rigors of the prairie. I was looking closely at a stuffed buffalo when he appeared at my side.

"Eighteen dollars for two adults. I don't remember it being so expensive."

Not yet, I thought.

We followed a set of painted dash marks to an area in front of a closed elevator door. When the doors opened, we squeezed with two women and another man into an egg of apparitional whiteness with modular plastic seating. A siren blew and we began to climb.

"Remember to swallow so your ears don't pop," he said.

One of the women offered gum, which I declined. Our capsule climbed for a bit on the angled track, then straightened, and again, continually adjusting for the rondure of the monument's legs.

"The ride is shorter going down," my father said.

At the top we were welcomed by a man in park-ranger green who proudly rattled off a sequence of facts so extensive you had to wonder if he'd ever been laid. The structure was designed to sway eighteen inches in strong wind. The average speed of the elevator trams was 3.9 miles per hour. The capacity of the observation deck was 140 people.

The windows were wide and squat and low enough that you had to half-crouch to see through them. Facing west, we saw that the clouds had cleared, and from here our tranquil hometown looked big and severe, alive in that fabled eight-million-stories sense of a living city. The sky's simple mixture of pale blue and big, Super Ball sun pulled the city upward, into it, and this levitation brought with it movement and life. Below us—cars, bricks, and stone. Busch Stadium, a patch of green engulfed by red seats, neat rim of white around the top.

Begin simply, I thought.

"One of the things I liked so much about school, Pops, was finding myself surrounded by people who didn't know about Freddy drowning while none of us was watching."

"That was not your fault, son."

"One of these people was a girl who exemplified everything I could ever come up with to want. We grew very close very quickly and revealed dreams and compared fears and mocked gently and occasionally told lies, but nothing bad. The sex, I'm sorry, Dad, but the sex was unlike anything I believed might someplace exist. I remember lying with her in bed and touching her thigh and thinking, *My God. This is the reason I grew hands in the first place.*"

My father nodded slowly. I stared out the window and didn't move a muscle. It might have been the whole city I was addressing—from these junior skyscrapers and beyond, out to the bulging seams.

"I fell, as they say. Into love. I practiced saying it, first to myself, in my head. I believed in it. I did. I thought *love* and I bought it completely. I was excited by my belief but was careful not to let this excitement influence or manipulate the belief in any way. The belief had to be pure. So I said it to her, I love you, and she said it back. And this was our contract. We treated the words seriously and respected that they came with implications."

What's scary about looking out the Arch's windows is that through some mystery of refraction, you are able to see directly below your feet, and see that there is nothing there. On the lawn, tiny heads spotted against green. And now, as if by some earlier agreement, we crossed to the windows on the Arch's other side.

"Look at that," he said. "There's a reason that place has the reputation it does. Several, in fact."

Changing the subject for a second was okay. Minus the garish riverfront casinos and strip clubs just beyond, everything in East St. Louis rests between dirt-brown and the loneliest shade of gray. Highways were pale streaks spread like medical tape across the country's wounded heart.

"The love had a strength, Pop. And part of that strength came from my faith in the strength. *Look how strong,* I thought. I had no doubts that I would continue to love her in this manner for the rest of our lives."

"I understand. You look at her and are filled with something grand and complex. With your mother I loved her so much I was given visceral pause. You should have seen her back then, son."

"That's right," I said. "Grand and complex. You say *love* because people believe in the word, it has a shared meaning and demands respect. It makes the strength stronger. But the strength can be unpredictable, it can gain a life of its own and turn on itself enough to make love into something too strong, this massive force. Something horrifying, brief flashes, this same strength."

I pressed my hands flat against the window like a kindergartner stenciling a turkey. It was frigid cold inside the viewing area, but the windows were warm. So much more to say. I had to make it through the Audrey part to get to the part where I ended up on top of Derrick Hoyne's daughter.

"But sometimes, still, I needed to be elsewhere, away from Audrey. I didn't understand. I pushed her away and found myself behaving in a way that didn't align with *love*. I snapped at her and I lied. I lusted after her best friend and committed indiscretions. But why would I do these things if I loved her, Dad?"

"I hope I have made absolutely clear, Potter, that I did not ever, ever cheat on your mother."

I stood from the window. We moved back to the other side of the deck. I followed the highway to the west, through the deep green of Forest Park, all the way to Clayton. There I spotted approximately where my parents' home should be.

We said *I love you* so many times it lost all meaning. We may as well have been saying *I gerbil antacid* or *penguin Boston pole vault.* I had to wonder if I'd been using the word wrong the whole time.

Where did the word even come from? Whose was it? And I began
to suspect more and more that the word was part of a schematic
that had been laid in place long before I came along. A system
that, like all systems, should be regarded with caution. Now I was
doubting not just myself, subject of the phrase, but the verb itself.
It was only a matter of time before Audrey, object of *I love you,* removed herself from the sentence altogether. And told me to
work on the verb. And I came back here. And. Well.

The park ranger welcomed another group off the elevator.
People filed into the elevators for their return to solid ground, six
hundred thirty feet below. Eggs and eggs of people, coming and
going in an endless mechanical ovulation.

"I've made some mistakes, Pop."

"Let me tell you about the things I know, son. I love you and I
love your mother. What else do I know. I love my work and I love
this city. I have always believed that this would be enough. We
cannot account for surprise. It comes out of nowhere, by its very
nature. I wonder now whether I should have made adjustments.
But who can say? No one can say. And what options remain? Do
you run away to some tree in the woods? You've read *Walden;* let's
not pretend that's upbeat stuff. Plus he walked into town twice a
week to buy eggs and flour. You stay and you try to make things
better. That's what you do. You do not give up like a twerp. You
do not walk away. You work, Potter. You work at the commitment you've made. Otherwise, what's the value of commitment."

I couldn't say it. *Help.*

Back in the elevator, I leaned forward on the edge of my plastic
so my elbows rested on my thighs. As promised, the descent went
faster than the climb.

It was all fraud. Once the day's deliveries were complete, I stood
in the warehouse among the great racks of bottles. I moved
slowly down the aisles, passing from the walls of turquoise caps

into a corridor of red-capped Purifieds. I turned a corner and was flanked by walls of deep-blue caps, the Premiums. The nature of the business all but guaranteed fraud. Water, but not *just water*. This was special water, wink nudge wink, trust us.

I left the racks and moved to the bottling machine. The conveyors were still, the whole thing silent and charged with potential. At the end of the belt were three boxes, each open, containing rubberized caps. I sunk my hand into the red caps and heard the voices of drivers in the break room, grumbling over paperwork.

A big part of this enterprise was psychological. The sweaty man at the door with a bottle on his shoulder. The service, the acts, delivery and removal, the peace of mind. The extra charge for Premium over Natural Spring, the mollifying of some basic yearning to have the best. The Summer Special, three bottles of your choice. *Choice.*

I opened the door to the break room and stood against the wall. Various sorts of bullshit flew about the room, equal parts blame and excuse. As soon as Dennis noticed me he began ignoring me, laughing at something, then topping it with his own tale or joke.

"It's all the same water."

A few of them turned to look at me, but only for the splittest of seconds. Dennis glanced in my direction and I took a couple steps toward him, though I'm not sure what I had in mind.

"Right?"

I hadn't planned on yelling. More heads turned. Fine. The problem here wasn't about the water lie but that we all pretended it wasn't a lie. Why not just admit the whole thing? Instead of lying to them, lying to ourselves; meanwhile, Freddy watching everything, spotting my lies from above. I saw Dennis get up from his chair. My voice came out loud and shrill.

"No reason to pretend, is there? I'm not wearing a wire. I'm one of you. But let's just toss it onto the table and look at it. The truth, I mean. The water's all the same."

"Alright. You're done," Dennis said, standing.

His hand latched on to my arm and dragged me from the break room into the main office, which by now was deserted. I realized for the first time that I could be in some danger. He kept pushing until we were at the office door, which he unlatched and opened before shoving me through. He followed me outside. I prepared to defend myself, then saw nothing but dull ambivalence in his face.

"You're fired, don't come back, get the hell home and explain this to your daddy. I bet you he's surprised you made it this long."

He walked back into the office and latched the door behind him. What he'd gotten totally wrong was that *this was hardly a blip on the radar of shit that would surprise my father*. I looked to the sun overhead, burning through haze. Christ, but I was thirsty.

My mother didn't ask why I wasn't at work. After breakfast, I stayed at the counter and read the entire local newspaper from front to back, something I'd never done. My mother moved about the house with a sense of purpose I envied terribly. I went to sit in the rarely used sunroom and found several pieces of luggage on the floor. I nudged one with my foot and it was heavy and full. I could hear Carla moving about the house, going from the kitchen to the basement, then to sit in Richard's office. I moved to the kitchen and tried to listen to her phone conversation but couldn't make it out. By the time I thought to sit on the living-room couch, she had finished talking and begun watering the houseplants. When she was finished with that, she came and stood between me and television.

"How are you for clothing, son?"

"I could probably use some socks."

She handed me the keys and I backed us out of the driveway. I concentrated on traffic, braked early, and accelerated gradually. We parked in a huge concrete structure and took a colored flyer on our way to remind us which level. The walking bridge set us at roughly the midsection on the Galleria's top floor, next to Brookstone. Above us, latticework of glass and painted steel gave the false impression of natural lighting. My mother and I began walking.

Even now, years since this place had been the center of my social universe, a residual unease plagued this visit with my mother, a violation of its adolescent sanctity. It felt crowded for a weekday afternoon, full of laughing families and pods of cool teenagers. The marble floor was polished to a sheen only slightly less vibrant than the store windows. I sped to walk at my mother's side, proving to us both that I wasn't ashamed to be with her. We passed Eddie Bauer, then the Gap, and she asked if I needed any sweaters. She stopped walking before I could answer.

"One hundred degrees outside and I'm asking about sweaters. How completely silly."

When we made it to the mall's end, an escalator took us down a level. On the ground floor now, we walked in silence, pace determined. There was a lot of mall to cover. We walked among pairs of women pushing baby strollers, wearing colorful shoes and form-fitting workout fabric.

"How come no outreach to the poor and elderly today?"

"The program directors ask us not to volunteer more than twice a week. They have concerns about people getting too attached."

"Them attached or you attached?"

"Oh. I think it works both ways," she said. "Doesn't it?"

Soon we saw the atrium, a great yawning chasm. The escalators were here to help, to make clear the appropriate movement. We rode down to the food court.

"Are you hungry?" she asked.

"Not really. But should we eat? I feel like we're here for a reason. Maybe you're hungry?"

"I could use a coffee."

We checked what movies were playing, then took another escalator back to the first floor. Falling back a step, I saw something in my mother's shoulders. There, in the way her arms pinned the purse to her side. I had up until now thought of it as weariness, lack of full satisfaction. But this was more active than that, real *sadness*. Blocking out what I could of the consumer chatter around us, I focused on her feet and heard it in each shuffle and pat of her steps. Sadness; my mother besotted by sadness. And yet moving nonetheless, lugging her body like some burden, her burden like some natural part of her body. She had adapted to the sadness and made a series of adjustments to accommodate its presence. Over time. Her movement through the house was quick and purposeful; it was difficult to detect sadness among scurry.

At the central fountain, children tossed coins into reflective water, then held greedy little palms out to parents for more. I followed my mother to the fountain's edge. Watching her sit, I was reluctant to stop moving, fearful of the sheer massiveness of this place overtaking us.

"Sit for a minute, son. I'm beat."

I did. She reached into her purse and pulled out a small bundle of bills.

"Take this, please."

"Five hundred dollars is bit much to throw in a fountain."

"I wish I could give you more," she said. "I'm not sure how much money I have. It's the strangest thing, to walk through the house and wonder what belongs to me. It's like a totally new set of things. Some of the furniture I had to talk him into buying. But so much is his. The computer. I mean, if we're being literal here, everything is his. Money. I've never thought so much about ownership before. What can I say is mine? My car? The washer and dryer? The garden is mine, of course, but you can't move that. The sunroom. Your father never wanted the sunroom. Potter, take the money."

"I really don't want any more money right now."

I watched her fold and unfold the bills, creasing and then rolling them and unrolling and folding the bills into halves. Not even close enough to pay off Edsel.

"Please. Take it from me."

I did. I could hold on to it and use it for an emergency motel room in some distant but drivable location, some Floridian beachfront peach stucco demilitarized zone. I looked at my mother's profile, the bone of her nose. She blinked but was untroubled by the attention I was paying her.

"When did you know? Was it a moment after an event? Some night you woke up and knew? Or was it more like a slow rolling wave?"

"I can't say, son."

"Start with a time. Please, serious. This is a reasonable and fair question. When did you know you were unhappy and that the only way to change any of it was to leave?"

I waited.

I said, "Alright, then. But can you describe the other side? For all the years? Something made you stay. A force. What was the force? Describe the force. Start with an adjective."

"Okay, Potter. Okay."

My mother stared at the floor and I put the money into my pocket. She reached one hand into the fountain and cupped some water she brought back to her lap. She rubbed her hands clean while drops fell onto her thighs and the marble floor beneath.

"There are some things, and I believe this, that are too big to understand. I don't mean God or the universe or those. But things that happen here on earth. And Potter, what's mindboggling, truly miraculous if you stop and consider, is that these things, these trials, are happening all the time, every day all day long they're happening to *normal people,* and they talk about them, we get together and talk and cry, thank God there are people who listen, and slowly, gradually, they get better. The trials turn into memories. And we make progress and go forward. But nothing ever, ever goes away completely." She turned to face me. "Do you remember what I used to sing? *No-thing goes, a-way all the way.*"

I looked away. A group of teenage girls passed in front of us, wearing tiny little clothes and squealing into their cell phones.

"The other day when you mentioned Freddy, it made me realize how long it's been since we talked about him. He was a wonderful, caring little boy, and sometimes I think how unfair it is that you never got to know him. He would kiss your head. He loved you. He'd kiss you and sing to you. We sang together. Your father couldn't believe how much Freddy loved you. We weren't sure how he was going to react to a little brother. You worry about that. And after the accident, Potter, in a lot of ways your father and I grew closer. My God, how much we doted on you and loved you. How badly we wanted you to have a brother or sister. Do you know that we tried? We did for a while."

Again she paused, and the din of the mall carried on with one fewer instrument. I shut my eyes and waited.

"How long ago? When? I could say six months or I could say twenty years. How much easier it would all be, yes, I want this, I wish I could point and say *here*. Your father is honest, and he is fair, and kind, and he loves you so much that still to this day he'll tell me, he'll turn to me in bed and say how much he loves you. Like something new he just discovered. We laugh about it. All these years. He is a good man, Potter."

I kept my eyes closed and let her voice come and go.

"We got through it, we did. Jesus, I remember, we cried all the time, we spent entire nights crying together. Your father grew that awful beard, and we fought and cried. He sang to you all the time, your father. He filled in for me and Freddy. And one night I remember standing there changing you, and we were both perfectly quiet. You were watching me. And I remember your father saying something behind me, and I hadn't known he was in the room. I asked him to repeat it. And he said it again and I started crying and thanked him. He came over and we hugged, and I swear, Potter, you started laughing, you laughed at us there on your back. And a month later we were out of the apartment and into our house, and we were healing, and you were babbling your little sounds."

"What did he say?"

Somewhere to our right a child was crying.

"That he forgave me," she said. "But why in the world would he have to say that, Potter? And why ever would I thank him for it?"

We couldn't risk sitting anymore. I stood and she must have understood, because she stood too, and picked up her purse, and smiled a tiny smile and began walking.

She moved quickly. We reached the end of the first floor and took an escalator back up, where we waded through another stream of people traveling in both directions, clutching handled paper bags that hung to their knees. I struggled to remain at her side. Then we were standing outside Brookstone, the store where I'd bought every Father's Day gift I could remember, back where we'd begun.

"I'm going to get that coffee," she said.

"You should. If you want coffee, then definitely."

"I think I will."

She moved forward slowly with the line. Sandwiched between more teenage girls and two large men. Was this how she looked when I didn't see her? This was my *mother*, Carla Mays who was once Carla Gingerich, just a child herself who'd grown to a mother and wife whose doubt had eventually crystallized into something absolute, something fist-sized and beyond. She was *sad*. But what could I offer? I was her son. I could surround her with my forearms and callused hands. Her grown son. The physical act of embrace as some base therapy, wordless and meaningful, the absolute least I could give.

But not here. This temple of mass commerce and popular whim. Here, my hug was nothing, would be trivialized, cheapened, end up in some promotional photo on the mall's Web site.

We crossed the bridge and descended to the yellow level. I reversed out of our parking spot and maneuvered slowly and deliberately through the structure, accelerating and braking with extreme prejudice, doing everything within my minimal power to ensure my mother's coffee wouldn't spill.

four

I used my car key to cut through ancient packing tape and then ripped, creating a small cloud of dust and stickless glue residue. Box flaps peeled back to release more dust into the attic's minimal light.

And lo.

I hooked a finger through a ring of big colorful plastic keys and lifted them toward my face. I set the keys down and picked up a bright yellow toy truck, dump truck, yellow Tonka dump truck. I set the truck down and reached back into the box. Little worker men wearing little helmets and overalls. Once everything was out of the box I spoke to my brother.

"This explains why you only appear in the attic. Some paranormal system or like statute of conduct. You, dead brother, are anchored to these toys. Right? My reference points here are mainly literary. Like Dickens."

Across the room, Freddy stood over the toys I had excavated from another box. He wore an old two-piece swimsuit from some era that connoted sepia. A modest, turn-of-the-century costume.

"I'm here because you are my brother and I love you and yes these are my things yes and go right ahead if you want you're welcome to look at them touch them hold them."

"Have you tried appearing somewhere else?"

"You keep missing the point this is my home and your home it's our home that's why we're both here."

I glanced to where Freddy had moved by the window and noticed for the first time that he had no shadow. I reached into a box and pulled out a plastic telephone with oversize buttons.

"Oh, but soon enough we'll officially rupture," I said, "and scatter about. Mom will go one place and Dad somewhere else—Dad probably into a loft downtown, a new urbanist act of solidarity. Mom's hard to say. She'll need green space, obviously. A small garden outside some town-home duplex thing. New construction."

I could feel him watching as I dug into the next box.

"Movement you didn't listen movement Potter is part of love a big part of love. Wherever they go whenever it happens Mom is still Mom and Dad's Dad and that's what I've been trying to tell you about love but it's not working. I'm not doing a good job."

"There's that word. I was talking to Dad about this. It's so soft when you say it, like a shallow depression in space, a natural exhalation. Listen to me: *love*. Not as good."

"Why do you think I'm here Potter why would I be here? Because of the toys you don't really think that don't be a twerp."

"The ball was bobbing there in front of you. And you reached for it and nicked it with your fingers, and I bet this made you want it even more. And you fell in, and somewhere in my infant mind this connection was formed between wanting and dying."

"They're still Mom and Dad will always be my mom and dad and you're my brother always look I died Potter and you're still my brother. You think love means staying still that's why you can't do it right you keep looking too hard at it like some thing sitting there but it's moving and you have to stop looking and start moving with it."

"One in love does not create pain for the object of that love. True or false? True, obviously. Nor does one abandon the beloved or fail over many many years to forgive. Love. Shared phantom concept." I looked at him. "Phantom."

Because who was I even talking to here? A GHOST who had lived all of five years. Who was, if we're going to be frank, quite possibly a FIGMENT. What with the emotional turmoil, mood liability, and confusion. Psychotic symptoms occur because of inadequate coping mechanisms or as an escape from a trying psychological situation. No point ignoring the facts at hand.

"You have to let it be something big Potter big and moving and bigger than what your eyes can see at once let it contain all of this and more like a mystery you can't see all of it at once."

I stared at him resolutely and watched him lose definition, growing dimmer and dryer until he was gone completely. Inside the next box was a child's blanket, chewed and drooled upon, faded and old. Wrapped inside the blanket was a shoebox. I peeled tape and lifted the top half. Shapeless piece of textured rubber, dried by years and the Midwestern cycle of seasons. I dropped the box to the floor and stared at the deflated rubber ball in my hands. I squeezed it and tried to rip it and failed.

I heard landscapers going to work in a nearby yard. I had crossed into whatever day was to come next.

It was everywhere, streaming along the gutters of our roads, hovering like a weather system. *Belief.* We took two of three from the Phillies, gained a game and a half on the Cubs. The team began playing small ball, moving runners with abandon. The city celebrated this newfound aggression—reminded everyone of the mid-eighties. They double-stole second and third and bunted for singles. We beat Houston in the bottom of the twelfth on a suicide squeeze. By the cleanup hitter.

I drove to find Ian standing in front of his house with his back to the street. He threw his baseball onto the roof, waited as it rolled up then down the shingles, bounced off the gutter, and fell into his bare hands. Then he did it again.

At the slam of my car door he turned for a second, looked at me, then returned to the game. I took a seat in the grass. On every fifth throw or so a little bit of roof came down with the ball. I picked up a blade and tried unsuccessfully to make it buzz. I watched Ian for a while longer, then shifted onto my back with hands behind my head, closed my eyes, and listened to the ball hit the roof, clunk off gutter, clap into hands. This continued for twenty-nine more tosses. When the sound stopped I sat up and saw that he was sitting on the porch.

"I tried to break in one of my gloves with some oil and it fell apart. Now I only got one glove. What's even the point of having one glove?"

"You could've used it just now."

"No, because of the way that other one fell apart I feel like I should get used to not having any glove. Because who knows when the other one's going to fall apart or get lost or explode."

How was this goddamn kid so goddamn *smart*?

"The Tower Tee batting cage is hands down the best batting cage in the city. The old machines, the old netting and fences. The sounds and the smells. The whir and creak of ancient machinery. Come on. I'll drive."

It had been years since I'd been to the cage, and I hadn't made the connection that it was so close to Ian's house, just a few miles. The sign for Tower Tee was tall and yellow, jarring out here among the many trees and grass and so many other trees. Upon turning into the lot, I was overwhelmed by the most pleasant sub-section of memory. The last time I was here I would have been fine-tuning my swing, sheer repetition, confident in the causal chain between work and success. They still had the old Fanta machine.

We finally had our break in the heat. Daily temperatures had fallen to the upper eighties and the chill had lured people outdoors; there were cars overflowing the slim strip of parking lot onto grass. Among them I saw the familiar pinched snout of an old silver Datsun 280Z, much like my father's. The car was backed into its spot just as he would park, almost always, a memory of Richard lifting his arm to my seat's headrest and glancing over his shoulder, eyebrows up, a bit of paternal showmanship justified by a valuable lesson when we left—look how much easier to get out.

And now I saw him up there, standing over a section of Astroturf at Tower Tee's driving range. He was wearing dark pants and a plain white undershirt. At his feet sat two mammoth wire buckets, one halfway empty, the other overflowing with cheap range balls. Just across the lawn, fifty feet away.

What day was it? Was he even in town officially? Had Edsel sent him the pictures? Only now did I consider that there would be no warning when he did. No courteous heads-up alert. I looked to the main Tower Tee building over by the putt-putt course and batting cages. Was I the type of son to pretend like I hadn't seen him here? My own car was parked not far away.

"We should go say hello to my dad."

"Oh," Ian said. Then he sighed, and I wondered, should this go on record? Age eleven, sighing like a sixty year old.

We walked past three high school football players dressed in practice uniforms, legs still padded, seeing who could come closest to hitting the fence at the far end of the range, a good four hundred some yards away. Absolute brute force and laughter. The singularity of what was happening here, the one-way propulsion of objects into a void. The sounds were *fwip*, then *clin-nuk,* as clubs cut through thick air and caught a bit of turf along with ball and rubber tee. About halfway down the line of golfers was Richard, with one club and two buckets. We stood behind him for several minutes, unnoticed. Ian climbed onto the park bench and watched from there. We might have stood there all day long.

"That's a lot of balls, Pop."

Sudden laughter from Ian because balls, yes, *balls are funny.* Kids and their comedic carte blanche: balls, farts, midgets, monkeys. Richard turned and took the two of us in for a moment before leaning the club against the divider, smiling, and stepping toward the boy.

"Hello. I'm Richard Mays. What's your name?"

"Ian." They shook hands. "How come you're not at work? Did you get fired like him?"

"Nobody's been fired," I said.

Richard glanced at me briefly before raising a hand to the glare and grinning at the boy.

"We can all use a day off from time to time. Gives me a chance to work through some physical motions, move around a little." He tapped a finger to his temple. "Good for the noggin."

"My dad runs a jackhammer for the city. He works six days every week plus some holidays when they pay double."

"That's mighty important work, Ian. The city would be in trouble without people like him. I bet he uses one of the big ones too. The eighty-pounders."

"He says it makes your teeth jiggle. I could ask if you could do it too, if you want."

Richard's eyes shut briefly as the grin expanded. "May just take you up on that."

The longer the exchange went on, the more worried I became. At fifty-two, my father was in fine shape, but slight. He had a long-married lawyer's physique. Ian's father was a force, as I remembered him stomping into his house. This comparison must have been going on somewhere in Ian's head, even if subconsciously. Connections forming, spreading in a network of dots and lines.

"Dad here grew up in South City, right, Dad? You should tell Ian about the trouble you used to get into. All the fights."

"I don't think that's necessary, Potter. You ever play golf, Ian?"

"Nope."

"Would you like to learn?"

"I guess."

"Wait a second," I said. "Swinging a golf club is about the

worst thing you can do for a baseball swing. You start dropping
your back shoulder, throws everything out of whack. He'll start
popping everything up."

"I think it'll be fine, son."

"Alright," Ian said. "Sure."

He hopped down and took the club. My father illustrated the
basic grip and outlined the simplest components of the swing.
Arms go here, then here, then through here. Nothing beyond the
general sort of tips that floated across airwaves and radio, waiting
for anyone to take and apply. Feet about shoulder width, head
down, don't overswing.

"Keep your left elbow locked," I said.

Ian spoke to my father. "So I just hit it when I want? There's no
signal or something?"

"Whenever you're ready."

"What if I mess up?"

"You're going to mess up," Richard said, teeing a ball before
stepping back to stand beside his unemployed son. "That's why
people come here. Mess up as much as they want."

Ian's prestroke routine was impressive. He shuffled his feet
into position, opened and closed his choked-up grip. I could see
an envelope poking out from his back pocket, the letter from his
mother that he had refused to share. His first swing missed. Back
into the routine like nothing happened. On the second swing he
sent the ball spinning wildly off to the right. He bent down to tee
another and began the routine over.

I could tell he was looking at me, underdressed father of mine,
untucked shirt, tired eyes looking at me.

"When I first saw you there with him, I had no idea what was
happening. I couldn't place you. That's my *son*, I thought. For
some reason my son is standing with a blond boy."

"It's like that Big Brother program. I met him during a delivery.
We played catch. I'm not sure what else to say."

We stood two paces behind the turf, far enough that our role was clear and defined. Ian took swing after swing, each more composed than the last. He caught one squarely, sending it fifty or so yards, and we clapped. He continued with mechanical focus.

"Is that true about your job?"

"The company has suspended operations under suspicion of widespread fraudulence. I have a feeling Debbie Dinkles is going down hard."

"I don't understand how I didn't know that," he said. "I've been out of town recently, but that's no excuse."

"I forgot that you wear V-necks."

I sat on the bench and my father sat next to me. He raised both elbows to the backrest, allowed his legs to spread naturally, while I kept mine crossed at the knee to conceal the idiot cock that had gotten me into this mess. Ian hit another ball cleanly and teed the next. The envelope in his back pocket was pushed a bit further upward.

"It's a good thing you're doing for this kid."

I stood from the bench but stayed where I was. A ball-collection buggy drove along one side of the range, then turned into the middle. The driver was encased by a protective cage of metal latticework as he drove from one side of the range to the other. Every so often a ball clanked off his buggy, adding yet another sound of collision to this place, all the more special for its infrequency.

"Have a seat, son."

Throat clearing. Ian hitting balls, each a little better than the last. My father's arm around my shoulders.

"Things happen. A big part of parenthood is watching your child make mistakes. I'm sure you can imagine the dilemma here. Do you step in and fix the problem? You could. Or do you let the child fail? Failure guides us, it hardens and teaches. It also causes damage and leaves a mark. So there's a choice to make, every time. Hands on, hands off."

Sweat. Repeated blinking. I imagined myself folding into a compact little ball and being absorbed into my father's gaping armpit. The buggy driver maintained his course despite the football players now making a point of aiming for him.

"Your mother and I have worked like yeomen to not blame each other over the years. Sometimes we have found success, other times less so."

By now it was apparent Ian was aiming for the collection buggy as well. He tracked its movement left to right, angled his feet and shoulders to where the buggy was going. My instinct was to rush over there and smother the jock-asshole mentality before it took over his worldview. But the kid! He was killing the ball! A stroke fluid and smooth, right in every way. He narrowly missed the buggy, then rushed to tee up a new ball for the next shot.

"I want you to promise one thing for me, Potter. No matter what happens, where any of this leads us. Promise to call me on the telephone. A father derives something huge and uplifting from a phone call from his son. You and I don't speak on the phone often. We never have. But I can't stress this enough, every single phone call will make me happy. I promise to be happy to hear from you, wherever you are, until the day I die. This is a promise I can make with the straightest of faces. Because the love I have for you eclipses anything you can fathom at your age. Know this much, Potter. We are a selfish species. I am outrageously selfish. I bet you don't know that. You want an explanation for almost every one of the world's problems? Overlapping selfish instincts. Name it. The only thing that breaks this selfishness is family. Especially your first child. People like to believe marriage is the big hurdle in terms of selflessness, but they're wrong. You are still two people with two sets of interests. A child, though, shifts the whole paradigm."

Ian teed a ball, lined up his stance, checked the progress of the cart, and swung calmly.

"And of course it goes without saying that you have to call your mother."

I watched the ball shoot skyward, hang for a second, then fall.

Ian leaned left. Breeze blew and a bird chirped. The ball came down squarely in the middle of the wire mesh protecting the driver's head. Ian gave a tiny hop, then turned to face us on the bench. He held out the club and smiled hugely.

"Your turn, son."

I took the club and stepped onto the turf, teed a ball of my own. Ian sat on the bench next to my father. I loosened with practice swings and tried not to think about my arms or shoulders. I lined up my shot, inhaled deeply. I was going to OBLITERATE this ball.

My swing came in too low, caught more of the turf than it should have. The ball barely moved, trickling less than ten feet into the range. The club's head went much, much farther. In strobe motion I watched it detach from the shaft and soar end over end out into the grass, spinning in a way that could have even been beautiful if it wasn't my father's ancient seven iron. I stood for a second with the suddenly lightened club in my hands, then began after the club head, into the range. I walked off the turf, stepped over and through the initial batch of mis-hit balls, then continued deeper into the field. Beginning my passage into the void. The first sign of opposition was the kid driving the cart, who had shut down the engine and was waving his arms in the tight pattern allowed by the protective cage. He was screaming. And here was something new: the balls made noise as they flew, a steady whiz buzz whistle. Now there were screams behind me too, screams of *whoa* and *hey* as people noticed the young middle-class adult white male taking large, determined steps into the range.

"Man on range! Man on range!"

I reached the approximate area I thought the club had landed and began to circle. This was a land of palpable neglect, untrimmed and lumpy, the antilawn. There was no telling how fast the club had been going, what kind of bounce it had taken. I was standing in a plot of grass that had been deemed RECEPTACLE.

The kid in the cart continued screaming, and I thought about grass as its own kind of medium, a venue for such varied goodness in the world. Now I looked from clumpy green driving range to fat smooth seamless sky. I spun to the tees and saw a wall of people moving toward me, everyone converging from their partitioned bits of turf. Three football players and the couple to their right and a horde of single men in shorts and belts.

"Turn around," I told them. "There is no problem. It's here somewhere and I'm going to find it. Seriously, leave me alone."

But still they came, moving in a scattered line toward where I was standing. Behind them I saw Ian standing next to my father on the small square of turf, watching as the crowd of would-be golfers formed a giant circle around me and tried to help.

The buggy found it. The club's head had churned through the ball-retrieval system and came out chopped and dented to shit. My father stood by his car, holding the headless shaft between two fingers. In a few hours he was boarding a flight to Baltimore to examine their waterfront urban-reclamation project. His eyes looked like ashtrays and I knew: he had seen the photographs and they had reminded him of his own erstwhile desires and the restraint he had exercised without fail, every single time. The plot had spread itself outward and was implicating those around me. This man of virtue who shook Ian's hand and told him to keep swinging, then shook my own hand quickly before driving away.

Standing in the parking lot, we were so very close to the batting cages. They were right *there* and yet could have been somewhere in the Dakotas, so removed were we from their effect. The kid leaned against a Buick and ran one shoe across the top of the other.

"Let me see the letter, Ian."

"No."

"I can help."

"It doesn't even say anything! She doesn't say when she's coming back. It's so stupid! Everyone always runs away but nobody explains why. Or, or if they do say why, the reason is always so dumb there's no way it's the real reason."

"It can be hard, sometimes, for people to find the words to fit the reason. Even when it feels obvious, things get jumbled between your head and mouth. It's language. Sometimes language is insufficient."

"Like what happened to your girlfriend? Why did she go away?"

"For that there are branches and lists, diagrams. It's. It's a big complicated issue."

"What's her name?"

"Audrey," I said, and it was the first taste of the word on my lips all summer. "Audrey. Audrey needed evidence that I still loved her."

"But that's so easy!" the boy said. "Even when my parents would throw things at each other, I could tell my dad wasn't throwing as hard as he could. That's how come I knew he loved her."

I had to sit down for a minute.

"What are you doing?"

"You should give me the letter, Ian."

"Get up!"

I turned my head and saw the grille of a Chevy Cavalier staring me down, turn signal going, and I knew I had sat down in the middle of the lot. But still the car did not honk, oh no, no, not in this town. Too rude.

Ian yelled, "Fine! Fine, here, just get up."

I stood and took the envelope from his hand.

He moved back into the grass in front of the parked cars and I followed. I did not remove the letter from inside and read it. I did not do anything except notice the absence of a return address and the absence of a stamp or any official postmark, just a single word typed across the envelope's back, single tiny word saying *Irenia*, right before the kid grabbed the letter back.

"And if hard work is gonna save us all like she says it is, why couldn't she work hard to be with my dad?"

"I don't know."

"Why wouldn't she?"

"I don't know."

"I don't want to do any of this. I want to go home right now."

The sun on the drive back was blinding. I lowered both of my car's visors and also held up a hand to my eyes. Ian played with the radio until he found a local sports call-in show, then fell immediately asleep.

He awoke as I made the turn onto Waldwick Drive. On the radio, the Cardinals center fielder said, *At this point you don't ask why. See the ball, hit the ball. That's all we're doing out there.* We sat at the curb for a minute before he turned to face me.

"I don't think you should come over anymore."

He dropped out of the car and I watched him walk the path to his house and I saw a weight to each of his steps, a sluggishness, and knew at least some of that weight was compliments of me.

five

at home the next day, I stood facing the kitchen phone, flip-ping through my mother's day-calendar on the counter. Perhaps the progression could be tracked in these pages: her anger, her loneliness, and finally sadness, her sorrow. In today's calendar box were the words *Lunch w/ Nancy*. Potential explosion of my plot nestled within bland but crucial peer support for my mother. If not now then soon.

I opened the junk drawer directly below the calendar. It had not always been this way, junked. Over time mess had trounced order, the frenzy of collected objects. I reached a hand inside and rummaged through the assortment of clothespins, scissors, bat-teries, old photographs, markers, and safety pins. How in the world would they decide to apportion all this shit? I came upon a photograph and lifted it from the drawer. Warped, corners bent and peeling, it retained its central image, which was me standing next to Audrey. Tough to discern our condition by looking. My arm was around her waist. We were smiling, standing next to a fountain in an obscure courtyard among the school's academic buildings. Our school and its myriad fountains. My mother out for a visit during sophomore year. Or was it junior? Frame the couple, press the button. The fountain was four cupid angels spit-ting streams that crisscrossed as they arced into the pool.

Anger comes first, but only in bursts because anger is exhausting. Loneliness, though, is effortless, a passive state. And from
lonely, the slide to true sorrow is polished smooth, all but automatic.

Who were these two people in the picture? My only memory
of this fountain was from a few months prior. February: a point
in the saga when both Audrey and I worried openly, abandon-
ing completely our pretext of joy derived from fortitude and
longevity. It was almost eight o'clock, that hour when the desert
chill settled down for the night and the campus burbled with
quiet activity: the genius Asian and Indian premeds living up to
their parents' rigid expectations; the broad-shouldered basketball
players, like Zeuses among our bespectacled and scrawny major-
ity, walking sorely from practice to private, late-hour meals in the
dining hall; the light-skinned alcoholic sons and daughters of outrageous privilege, rolling bocce and pounding cans of Busch; the
shy, bookish lovers tangled atop blankets in the quad. The future
somethings of our great nation.

Valentine's Day, and we had plans for dinner in a few hours at
the cramped Italian joint we defaulted to for most occasions. Our
paths happened to meet in this courtyard. Which made no sense
whatsoever; we both lived on the opposite side of campus. But
there we were, facing each other by the spitting cupids, arm's
length apart, eyes dodging then settling into each other as the bell
tower chimed.

"These angels keep on spitting," she said.

"Today's a big day," I said.

No solution. Not then and not soon afterward, and not now,
still. I'd given her not a single word for how many months? And
why not? The phone was right here in front of me. The potential
of her voice, right this second. How long? Despicable silence.

I lifted the phone from its cradle on the wall and ran my thumb
lightly over the sequence of long-known numbers. This was
presuming she'd returned from Europe. Presuming she'd gone

home. Presuming she wasn't living in Vermont or Boulder or God could only say where else. Presuming she wasn't with Carmel or someone else, some new foreign person. You can feel panic's arrival; it descends like heat. Where was Audrey? I could have written. *Asked.* The phone became extremely heavy in my hand and I let it fall to the counter.

What I had seen in my mother at the mall was what I had seen in the courtyard, in Audrey, the physical expression of tremendous disappointment. Ian's sluggish steps.

There was a beeping, some pulsing noise I didn't understand. A powerful and terrible squawking. I saw the phone off the hook and realized this was the old alert to warn us that if we didn't do something soon, the house would be cut off from the outside world. In other words, the alarm.

Anger was sharp.

Lonely was hollow.

Sad was the giant, the cloud or earth or ocean, the elemental force.

The beeping eventually stopped. I went back into the junk drawer with a hand. Most likely it would be my mother, or would they clean together? My father scooping the whole stinking mess into a garbage bag and carrying it out to the curb. Dispose, discard, rid the house of things.

My hand came across the extra set of keys to my father's car. Which I clenched tight in my fist. I removed my cell phone from my pocket and tossed it into the drawer. Which I shut.

The injustice was that it only worked one way. The past reached forward and meddled, played its stained fingers across the present. But the present had no such dominion. An old complaint, fine, but made new by the specifics of what had been lost: love, marriage, dear friend, innocence, status as law-abiding non-rapist. Brother.

So the present. Yes. The boy could still be saved. I knew the route, not thirteen miles from here. I had been there only yesterday. I could return and fix. Had the route memorized. Knew the solution. I took the Audrey photograph and an old Cardinals magnet and stuck them to the fridge on my way to the garage.

Together we flew, me and the car my same age. Work had opened this city to me, folded back flaps to expose the depths within. I had been into these homes, stepped over piles of dirty laundry. Into the bare back halls of these businesses, the gloomy cubicles previously known to me only in movie satire. Never had I been more aware of the peopling of a place. Pulses throbbing below the veneer of society's inanimates.

Ian's house was how it always was: dirty and dark, lit by syndi- cated programming and daylight through the screen door. I knocked. No answer. I called out and the television went mute.

"Go away."

I spoke into quiet darkness: "I never told you about baseball camp. Every summer from sixth grade until sophomore year. Down at Mizzou. We stayed in the dorms and ate in the cafete- rias, and each day felt like it was part of something special. We ran drills and scrimmaged and worked on bunting technique. They filmed us swinging, and we sat in the coaches' office and an- alyzed the video. They call it the *trigger,* some thing each of us does to start a swing. Me, I lifted my left foot just barely before setting it back down again. Of course, before the video I had no idea. But there it was on the screen in slow motion. Then you'd see the hips shift as shoulders open slightly. Hands coming down- ward through the zone. 'Down the slide,' they called it. *Down the slide.* Keep your back shoulder up. *Down the slide.* Come on. Let's go to the batting cage."

"My dad's in the back working on something. You should go. I told him about you taking me to Tower Tee and he got real mad. Hurry and go before he comes back inside."

"Your dad is at work. His car isn't here."

"He had to leave for a minute, but he'll be right back any sec- ond now."

"Wait. Is that true? Are you saying to me what you're supposed to say to a stranger?"

"Just 'cause they took away your van doesn't mean you're not a kidnapper."

"Come see the car I'm driving. It's a 1978 Datsun 280Z. It's before your time. Nissan used to be Datsun. Istanbul was Constantinople."

I heard the television come back to life. I turned and saw the hyena kids emerge from their home and begin playing in the yard up the street. Their mother sat in a lawn chair in the shade of the house. I knew I had role models growing up—I must have. I needed to think who they were. My father, of course, and an old instructional VHS tape of Ozzie Smith saying *stay down, don't let the ball play you*.

I called back into the house over the volume of the TV: "I don't see the problem here."

"That's because you're crazy! It's like you think I can't tell!"

"Hold on a second. Sometimes we say things we don't fully believe." The lock was a thin metal rod extending from the frame, hooking into a loop in the door. "It's easy sometimes to get carried away. The heat doesn't help. But we don't want to say anything that could ruin our friendship."

"If anyone's ruined anything," he said, "it's you. And it's everything."

Like tossing unsharpened darts into an endless black void. How many times did I tell her *love*? Her name spoken in my sleep, unconsciously, chanted like some reenactment of an ancient tribal rite, actors in face paint. Skeptics all of us, there were times we all needed proof.

I yelled through the door that I would be right back.

My feet and hands could have belonged to somebody else; they worked clutch and gas and steered and shifted in reflexive concert. Passing and merging, decelerating off Highway 40, turning onto the thinner, curvier country road and going south. It was Saturday, early afternoon, and the Datsun on 94 was like a warm razor through butter. In Defiance, the two bars with outdoor decks were packed with people in red hats. Families: goddamn miraculous and fragile and absurd.

I took comfort in having a plan. Back under the canopy now, the road was dense with winery-bound traffic. Gradually the pack broke apart, until finally I was beyond Mount Pleasant, and alone, me and my spear and this landlocked beach, ocean of countryside stretching straight and endless in front of me. Reaching the sign for Irenia Winery.

The plan was to find Ian's mom. The plan was to locate Ian Worpley's mother and convince her to return to her family. To isolate the semi-former Mrs. Worpley, sit her down, palpate and find the pulse of motherhood thumping beneath whatever was keeping her from her family, stare fiercely into her eyes and say *you are being selfish*. Whatever she was doing out here, working or living or both or whatever it was, Ian was locked inside that dark house with only a television to raise him, and *motherhood has no expiration date*. I was going to find her, sit her down, and speak words that appealed to her most human ingredients. Hope my words might still have meaning.

At the door to the main building, a thin hairless man whom I did not recognize from my last visit examined my driver's license. He wore the pale-blue collared shirt tucked into flat-front khakis.

"Hello there. Welcome. It's good to have you."

Inside the front door was typical retail outlet built around a central, circular counter. A few customers sat at stools as men and women wearing pale-blue collared shirts poured tastes of wine. The plan was to scope the place out, case the joint, and form a general feeling, then get busy finding Mrs. Worpley. I moved nonchalantly through the store, stopping occasionally to pick up an item and examine it. In this manner I would infiltrate the winery without arousing even the slightest fractional suspicion.

"Good afternoon."

A woman stood before me, wearing the same pale-blue sexless collared shirt and flat-front khaki pants. I nodded hello and set down whatever bottle I was holding. Smiling, I backed out of the aisle and moved quickly across the store, through a door, onto a brick patio where tables huddled in the shade of large pale-blue umbrellas. I took a seat at an empty table overlooking the vineyard below. Do this thing for the boy, call on the love of a mother lion for her cubs, jaws that could demolish fragile skulls. That was maternity.

The woman from inside arrived a few minutes later carrying a leather-bound wine list she set open in front of me.

"Can I get you anything? Something white, chilled enough to fog your glass when I pour it? People have been enjoying the sauv blanc."

She sat down next to me.

"I'm not sure I feel like talking about wine," I said. The plan required a certain amount of toughness and resolve.

"Oh?"

"Wine intimidates with the language it evokes. Same with stocks and racehorses. I ask you about a wine, you tell me of its nose and hints of pencil shavings. You mention pear. And then I taste the wine and nod and you win."

"Win this competition we're having," she said.

"Just that wine is a field based on saying the right words at the right time."

"Okay," she said.

The umbrellas made for pods of shade in the otherwise bright afternoon. I noticed quite a few women in the Irenia work outfits buzzing around the patio, approaching and leaving tables with bottles and empty glasses.

"What's your name?" I asked.

"What's yours?"

She wasn't looking at me. She was looking off into the valley, toward the dropping sun. I waited for her to say something else.

"My name is Opal."

"As in the birthstone of October."

"I like how it has two levels. Oh." She paused. "Pull."

It was a cult. Pow. That was it, the nebulous something I felt about this place. Boom. And I was at once pleased with myself for solving the mystery and suddenly concerned for the safety of my mind. This *cult,* den of would-be converters and persuaders, insidious group-huggers. Kablow. We hear or read about such places, these closed worlds of unregulated faith. The attendant metaphor of washing a brain, not so bad a concept in itself.

"This is a name you chose, Opal?"

"Sometimes coming to a new place is a good opportunity to try new things. Leave old things behind. If you want."

Her visage still and balanced, unreadable, she faced the vineyard. Hair brownish, body skinnyish, not too. Fair skin. Eyes the color of—what?—the fake wood grain of my 4Runner's dash. The point was to do something good for the boy. A gesture backed by substantial concern and goodwill and selflessness, a mother retrieved. A testament to the reaches of love, mine and hers.

"I should make clear that I'm not here to enlist in whatever you have going. I need to find a woman with the last name Worpley. I don't know her first name. Do you know her?"

"Why do you need to find her?"

I looked away. Pretty much the full extent of what I knew about cults was: cults hold on. This was how it happened. First they acquired, then they *retained*.

"Just to chat," I said.

"Keep the menu just in case. I'll be back in a few minutes. No rush."

The woman *cultist* had left me at the table. Here was how it happened. They approached in a time of vulnerability. They casually walked alongside the overweight goth girl or the sad sci-fi kid and they spoke of gatherings, meetings where a few of them hung out, no big deal.

Down in the vineyard, I saw blue-dressed cultists leading small groups of normal people along long rows of grapes. They went slowly, the guide stopping now to speak of a vine's characteristics or let dirt fall dramatically through his fingers.

I would have to tread more carefully than I had initially thought. The plan required singularity of purpose and minimal ruffling of cult feathers. I imagined a bearded figurehead wearing robes and white Keds. I pulled over a chair so it sat in front of me, in the sun. I took my shoes off and rested my feet on the chair.

The woman appeared from behind me and took her seat again at the table. It occurred to me that any wine I ordered might be dosed with something.

"You want to know what you remind me of?"

"Yeah, I've decided no wine. I need to find this woman, and if you're not going to help me I'd like to be referred to someone who might."

"Okay," she said, and shifted her gaze to the valley. I looked at my shoes on the ground. I had known the plan was not going to be easy—the plan required focus and fortitude. The plan was to.

"What do I remind you of?" I asked.

"The way a dog looks at you sometimes and you know it wants something but you have no idea what."

"Or a child," I said. "A baby."

She shrugged. "That's a real *man* thing to say. I don't mean that badly, but babies only want two or three things. The hardest part is birth. After that it all gets easier."

"So you have kids?"

"Look at the sun," she said. "It looks like one of those Super Balls."

I had become distracted. I focused on the plan.

I picked up my shoes and walked to the edge of the patio. A long brick stairway led me down into the valley. Row upon row of plants. I began down one of these rows of neck-high plants, walking a strip of grass only a little wider than my shoulders. The ground was harder than I expected and felt too dry to grow anything. I almost never went barefoot, and my feet against the grass looked suspiciously like hands.

Some of the men and women here among the vines were crouched, holding shears. Others carried buckets of grapes in each hand, passing me with a steady smile and a nod. I saw a woman stop at one of the grape pickers and hand him something from out of a canvas bag. Water. I recalled the work of my most difficult delivery of the summer, unloading those bottles into the cellar with those two men in pale-blue collared shirts. I thought of their willingness to help and the diligence with which they'd worked.

The grapes hanging from vines were alive with dust. A trellis system supported the vines, anchored by stakes set into the earth at regular intervals of exactly two natural steps. I kept going. I saw a tour group coming toward me and cut across a row to avoid the sound of their crass, outside-world chatter. I smiled at two cultists who were categorically not Ian's mother, working on an irrigation system. I kept walking deeper into the vineyard and soon reached what appeared to be a perimeter of sorts, where the rows of plants stopped and a field of barely kempt grass began. Turning back, I saw the Irenia building far in the distance, along with a figure slowly making its way down the aisle. Sun perched up there like some massively dispersed searchlight. Of course it was Opal coming toward me, a propane lamp in one hand. I considered my plan and turned back to the western reaches of the property. There was activity out there; I could see tiny bodies moving out in the field, a truck approaching them from the north.

"It's okay," she said. "You're allowed to go out there."

Plans, what they say about them. I had hoped to find Mrs. Worpley in the Irenia building, somewhere closer to my car. Stepping into the field of grass would take me one ring farther from escape. Opal's eyes were deer eyes, wide and vague, but without suspicion.

"There has to be a leader," I said. "Someone who sleeps with the women and runs the meetings."

"That's a bit crass. Nobody here has to sleep with anyone unless they want to."

With her head cocked she looked younger than I'd initially thought, and this was the sort of thing on which one could easily dwell, and there was no time for dwelling. If the sun was to be trusted, it was getting on into late afternoon.

"I need to find Mrs. Worpley. You don't seem to want to help. Fine. But I have to think whoever your leader is might."

"You're wrong. I want to help. He's out there working with everyone else. He's the hardest worker I ever met. That's the point. But he's also willing to speak. He'll answer your questions."

Somehow I had entered into a world of assumed names or sheer namelessness. *Opal* this woman and her talk of some man, only *he, he* the professional noun. Perhaps she deemed his name unutterable. Or she wouldn't say the name out loud for fear of tarnishing it. Or if she said his name once, she was required to say it two more times.

"What would it take to make you say his name?"

"Who?"

"The leader. Your leader."

"Rich? His name is Rich."

We hadn't moved. I looked at Opal again and reminded myself that the point was to do something for another human being. Help the boy. Selfless gesture of love.

"Come on," she said.

Luckily I had been trained for this. Adaptation, applying several fields of knowledge to solving a problem. Liberal as derived from *liberalis,* Latin, meaning *for free men.* As opposed to *servile* arts. Trades. Opal stepped into the grass and I slipped back into my shoes before following. The field was huge and encased by trees. North of us, the trees climbed to a wall of bluffs, topped by some nature of radio or other such tower. West and south were more gentle hills rising with the forestry.

"Tell me something," I said. "How did you come here?"

"I don't want to answer that, so I'm not going to."

We stepped high over an arid expanse of sparse, tall grass. The people we were approaching all wore the pale-blue cultist raiment. Once we'd walked twenty or so yards into the grass, Opal stopped.

"Of course you can ask about the past if that's what you want. But you're going to find that a lot of people here don't want to talk about it. It's all the same, anyway. So what's the point?"

We were walking slowly now, side by side, toward the activity in front of us. Everything was open out here; endless sky, ground stretching outward as far as trees would allow, we creatures standing still. The occasional insect fluttering between stalks of grass, buzzing. When she spoke next, her voice had an energy to it, the charge of conviction.

"People out there? Everywhere you go, people are real good at giving reasons to do things. But if you stop for a minute and look at them, the reasons can be so crazy. Like you love God so you do this. You know?"

I would speak to Rich the Cult Leader and tell him a lie about heart disease. I would say, *Look, man, I respect what you've got going out here, but a boy is dying. He is emaciated and losing his hair and coughing blood and all he wants is one last glimpse of his mother's face.* I would say his name, *Ian,* and this would humanize the disease. I would promise to have her back by nightfall.

Opal and I came to a stop close enough to the workers that I could make out faces. Next to us was a fallen tree on which she sat, and I soon sat next to her. And it wasn't physical as such, the thing I felt. No terrible urge to press my chest against her waist or taste her biceps or any of the other normal desires for flesh. But this thing included those, somehow, and was bigger, somehow. I reminded myself what I knew about cults.

"They have all the contracts and signatures they could ever need. But people still lie and people still cheat. All over the place, all the time." She paused and turned to face the field. "Look out at them."

I counted somewhere between twenty and thirty people moving around the base of what would someday soon turn into a building. Currently it was no more than a knee-high wall of stones forming a perimeter wall, about fifty feet wide and a bit less deep. I looked at Opal. There were things I could have said, and there were things I could have admitted to myself about what was going to happen next.

"What do you think is going on?"

"Normal cult activity," I said.

"Don't be silly. What do you see?"

"The rocks are brought here by that truck over there, then unloaded by those people. And then these people take stones from the pile over to a place on the wall, where these other people lay the stones and then fill them in with some kind of concrete."

"It's limestone from the quarry."

"So what is it? What's the project?"

"A building," she said.

"They're building a building," I said.

"The body wants to work. That's what I learned here. That's biology. Think of your cells working. The cart comes and goes from here to the processing station, where the limestone from the quarry is cleaned and broken up. Right now people are down there mining rocks."

"Work," I said. "The point is to work."

"Yes! Some days you carry and other days you mine and some days you drive the truck. You lay concrete. Because in times like these, hard work is the only thing that can ever save the world."

"So why aren't you working now?"

She smiled. "The body also wants Recess."

I had seen her smile before, along with these dents on her cheeks. The shape of a human face, all the similarities.

"There are three stations. This one is called Building. The other stations are Farming and Marketing, but we usually call Marketing *the House*. Farming is about the earth. You open it up and refill it and move it around. You water it and accept what it gives. At the House mainly what you're doing is selling. It's a different kind of work, but it's still work. That's the point. We rotate stations once a month. Marketing for a month, then Farming, then out here for Building. A month's just long enough to settle in. Then you switch and do something else."

I moved my right hand down to the log just behind her and leaned forward enough that the inside of my arm touched the outside of hers. I leaned back because this was obviously too much but kept my hand where it was.

"Are there guns here, on the premises?"

"Of course," she said.

"Are they being stockpiled?"

"This is the United States of America."

We sat quietly on the fallen log and took in the movement of the workers. One time my father returned from a business trip with an ant farm, carefully pouring the sand, sending away for ants by mail. The point being: a child requires role models who are, above all, diligent. I looked again at Opal, and this time I was a little more sure than the last.

"It's not work alone," she said. "It's why. Because they work out there in the world too, but it's always for someone else or some piece of paper. Here the work is for you. Six workdays a week and everyone has one full day of Recess built into their personal schedule. Everyone here is really great."

I looked at her again and tried very hard not to know but knew anyway.

"Can I tell you something?" I asked.

"Of course," she said.

"I've been devoting a lot of focus to my hands. Examining them and thinking about them." I raised them in front of me, palms away. "They're changing all the time. Growing and thickening or acquiring new scars. The hands I have at twenty-two are not the same hands I had at eleven. You ever seen an eleven-year-old boy's hands?"

"I might have," she said.

"At eleven, hands are growing faster than any other part of a boy's body. When we're old, it's the nose and ears that keep growing. At eleven, though, hands are an indication of who the boy will turn into. There's that X-ray they do to know how tall you'll grow. That's all the *nature* side of the story. There is still nurture to consider."

Her smile remained. I had completed the first step of the plan. Here she was, right next to me. The next steps were less clear. I could try lifting with my legs and carrying her back across the field, through the aisles of vines and past the building to my car. Drive her back to the dirt path and the porch, unlatch the screen door and complete the miracle.

"You're still his mother."

"You know what I remember? On my wedding day, I remember all of us going into that room in the back and there was that piece of paper. I honestly thought they were joking. Then they gave me a pen and I understood, and I remember sitting at the table and crying, just bawling over the baby inside me and the wedding on the other side of the door and this piece of paper with the places to put our names. I see your eyes. You already made a decision about me. It's okay. I could tell you every detail and you still wouldn't understand. But I know who I am and I know my boy. I know he's okay. Nobody knows what's going to happen to anyone, but I know he's going to be okay. And so right now, today, I'm not going anywhere. Look. Here comes Rich."

I recognized the bald man approaching us, recalled his skill at carrying water, his energetic assistance. Now he was sweating heavily and the thighs of his khaki pants were streaked with dirt. He nodded as he approached and raised a hand in greeting.

"Well, I know this guy! Decided to come back and see us. Good. I'm glad to see you."

He took my hand into a firm American shake, held my eyes, then nodded to Opal. I hadn't remembered him being so handsome. Out here in the grass, working with these others, context, context.

"You helped me with the delivery a few weeks ago."

"That's right. I was working the house with Tall David when you came with all the water. Receiving donations is a big part of Marketing. Had a feeling you'd be back sooner or later."

"He's come to take me away," she said.

"Oh, now, that sounds kind of silly, doesn't it?" he said.

I watched Opal leave us and move off into the grass. Here is what a cult does: it passes you among people who appear to care. Their language was one of interest and concern, inclusion. The key was to see behind the words. To spot the mechanisms within, the wheels spinning. I allowed myself to be led a few steps away from the log, toward the building project. Rich stood at my side.

"So what's on your mind?"

"Mrs. Worpley. Opal. I came looking for her. I have to speak with her about motherhood."

"What about motherhood, exactly?"

"What the term entails as far as extent and duration."

"Huh. Didn't know she had a child."

I had no idea how much he knew. Presumably everything. He knew that I'd made it here and that my quest was partially complete. Presumably he would use this partial completeness against me somehow, lull me into a state of contentment. Rich began to massage his shoulder with a hand chipped and scarred with toil. Behind him in the distance I saw Opal bent over in the grass, picking up a piece to bring to her mouth and blow, making it buzz.

"What's it for?" I asked. "The building."

"Depends what you mean. Right now, it's for Building. Once finished it'll be something else. Housing, most likely. Storage. Eventually it will be for tearing down. Some machine will tear it apart. That all comes later."

"Someone could come along in a few years and buy you out.

Turn the house into a Gap or Wal-Mart or something. This field could be paved over, some roadway or parking lot. And this would be a gas station."

"Then it will be a very well-made gas station."

"It's selfish," I said. "All the work."

"Our family is no different than any other family. Except we acknowledge the selfishness. We know denying it is just one more level of selfishness, if you follow."

Between our words came the grunts and heavy breath of the blue-shirted workers. We stood for several minutes before I checked on Opal and saw her stick a piece of grass into her mouth on her way back to the log. The workers moved in concert, the many extremities of this body. So quiet out here, only the clatter of labor against the peace of fading light.

"So you've found her," he said. "You found your mother."

"What? Not my mother. The mother I was looking for. I mean, for whom I was looking."

Opal was sitting again on the log and I wanted very much to join her, I realized. So, too, did I believe she wanted me on the log next to her. Impossible to be sure, though, here inside this place with its agenda. Or even out there; always impossible. Rich smiled at me.

"There she is," he said. "Nobody has to stay here any longer than they want. You want to convince her to leave with you and go back out there, you go right ahead. Keep in mind she's been living this lifestyle for a time now. Legs want to move and hands want to lift. The human back wants to carry weight. It's natural, and these explain why we've got the body parts in the first place. To work. Just because so many have forgotten this doesn't make it any less true. You know this already, I bet, working with the water. If you want my advice, it's this. Listen to yourself. Nobody here is going to rush you into some decision about staying or going. We're happy to have you as long as you want to stay. There's work to be done. Plenty. We could use a man like yourself."

Here again he took my hand and shook it like this meant

something to us both, then left to cross the field. I turned and
moved back toward the log, where Opal sat with her hands in her
lap. Hair pulled behind ears. I sat next to her and listened to her
hum some tune and then stop. Cicadas and crickets all around us
singing or rubbing legs or whatever it was they did to find mates.

"I want to say something."

"What kind of mother. I know. Because I broke one of the
biggest rules there is. But I don't stop loving him just because I'm
not there. And he's with his dad, and do you know his dad loves
him too? He does. And he is a good man overall. Just because I
don't love him doesn't make him a bad man. They go to baseball
games together."

"How long will you stay here."

"I don't know how long."

"Set a time. Stay that long, then go back."

"Why are you here? Really?"

What profound appeal there was to being seen through. Her
thumb went into my waistline and I could feel the shift. There
were creases in her face and I liked them very much. Her entire
face, origin of Ian's. Same beauty. Here on our log I thought of
the other fallen tree and Stuart's return to the pool house, his trip
for cake mix and his new love Marianne and my old new love
Audrey and where I was, developmentally, when I met her. I
moved my hand to the small of her back, damp with sweat. The
sun had left us. Still the workers kept going in what I wanted to
call the *gloaming* but wished I didn't.

"You can come back with me," she said.

"That's my line."

"Unless you want to stay here. Or unless you want to leave."

What was out there, anyway? Emaciated catalysts like fatherly
pride, suspicious urges to please your mother. Here there was the
job, the task, the work of callused hands. I could recover my calluses. There was only lifting, and carrying, and building. Wanting
and working. I watched a man crest the hill carrying at his waist a

stone the size of an overweight cat. This simplified little society, removed from the distant exasperations of the twentieth century. They had outsprawled sprawl itself.

"I'll show you my room," she said.

"I'm to believe that this is something you desire. *Want* in the strict common sense of the word."

"Come on."

We walked quickly across the grass and back among the grapevines. By now, the evening sky had bled off its light and Opal's lamp framed us in a yellowish bubble, anchored by the steady hiss of gas. Around us were other lights, flickering their way up the hill, shadowing pairs of contented workers. I followed her through the vineyard until the main building appeared up ahead. She led me up the hill, across the patio, and into the building, pushing with a small palm against a portion of wall that was actually a door.

Inside was the kind of warm soundlessness that fills ears like a wet finger. A long hallway with many doors we passed along the way. Lighting was mounted on walls. We met people as we walked, similarly dressed cultists who flashed meaningful smiles in passing.

"This way."

We turned a series of corners, descended a short staircase. The building was much larger than it appeared outside. I had the sensation of going deeper, always turning down a dimly lit hallway that would lead farther inward. Disorientation like liberty. The air was damp and odorless and still as a stalled car. At the bottom of another staircase was a door, which we stepped toward. She stopped short, turned, and gestured with an open palm.

"We're here," she said.

six

Windowless room lit yellow by propane lamp in the corner. Twin mattress on the floor, no furniture, no nothing. Seen from above, shape of two people could be one. Tangled. The young man and the older woman on the bed.

She and I on the bed.

You wake and think, *Wait just a goddamn second. These are not living quarters. There are no dressers. No closet. This is the sex room.*

It was time for reevaluation. I looked at her face, older than she was before. Her naked woman leg touched my own boy-man half-tanned skinny leg, and I thought, *All of this has become wrong. You. All your mistakes. Fucking.* I saw her hand on my chest rise with my breath.

First thing was to get OUT of the BED.

I moved her limbs and slid myself away from Ian Worpley's mother. I crawled on the floor and found the jeans from that morning years ago when I'd put them on, but no shirt anywhere, anywhere. And now from this angle, maybe that was a dresser outlined against the wall.

As I stretched her pale-blue polo over my head, Opal rolled onto her side and mumbled something.

"No more room."

That was all. I breathed quietly and prepared for what was sure

to follow: pursuit. Running through dim hallway labyrinth, sconces
of light blurring with speed, find the door and stumble outside. I
would run to the waiting sports car and stomp the accelerator.

I cracked the door and pulled it shut behind me.

Halfway down the hallway, the panic of disorientation. I
reached a fork and went right, climbed a set of stairs, then turned
several more corners. I reached a door and pushed and felt the ick
of late-August night.

Darkness, thick, cut by one circle of towering parking-lot lighting. Two men stood in the gravel lot, good-natured bald men
wearing our same shirt. They threw a Frisbee back and forth that
glowed in the dark. One of them raised it in offering, and I shook
my head no and walked. Good-natured shrug and back to their
game. I eased the Z out of the lot.

Here was Potter Mays, failed lover, taking Highway 94 like a
tear down a cheek. They said you could pass, they gave permis-
sion, and you felt obliged. He glided into the left lane, then went
back to the right.

What was good about the road were the headlights that passed
just inches on my left, the constant chance of collision. My speed
plus their speed times weight of automobile plus adjust for fric-
tion, gravitational constant, physics, and the irrefutable edicts of
the universe. The sound that lucky survivors of horrible wrecks
try to describe but can not, crumpling of metal and shattering of
glass, the thunderous fall of that grand supernal gavel.

I had stayed in that bed for too long. At this very late hour, most
of the city's traffic lights had abandoned their normal cycle for
the blinking of red or yellow, colors of summer. No traffic to
speak of. I came to a stop at the first light in a long stretch of
downhill road marked with a series of red dots. I turned and soon

found myself tracing the edge of Forest Park, past the huge old antebellum mansions. Here the lights ran with no regard for time or traffic patterns. I pulled alongside a snub-nosed Honda with shiny shiny rims, dropped low to the ground. Couple of boys with a girl in the back, kids all of them, children maneuvering the city late at night. Glimmering purple paint job, ground effects, and a decal of Calvin pissing onto Cubs logo.

I wondered if they knew Zoe. They could have had lockers in the same hallway. They could have sat next to her in class and stared.

And what force of nature! A pretty girl's smile, regardless!

The light blinked, and neither of us moved. The Civic pulled slightly forward and I recognized this as a moment when things could begin.

The Civic lurched and I dropped the gas.

Varoom.

I was winning. Then I saw in my mirror that the Civic had made a U-turn, brake lights now shrinking into darkness.

The garage light turned on, the in-dash clock said 3:52. Shoes went here, by the front door. House: dark, still but for the sound of my father snoring.

I opened the door to their room and inched past their bed and into the master bath. Still sharing this bed despite it all, sleeping as if at peace. Only explanation was this: Carla would require substantial aid, something far stronger than her usual warm milk. Two sinks, hers here with the cotton swabs and swiveling makeup mirror and the amber plastic canisters for prescription pills. I held them up to the streetlight through the window until I found the label that said, *Take one pill one half hour before desired sleeping time.* My father snored steadily. Poured a number of pills into my hand and replaced the canister.

I stood at the foot of my parents' bed. They were both here, both parents. Look how huge, this bed. Two bodies slid by mutual agreement to farthest reaches of the mattress, the valley between. I thought of the mess of limbs in which I had awoken and brought one of the pills to my mouth and swallowed it.

A half hour later and I was still watching them sleep. My mother had shifted slightly and my father had rolled over when his snoring had woken him, then settled back into his rhythm of breath.

For me, sleep was some destination miles from here, a full day's drive to the coast, the endless waves that washed you inward while the undertow beneath pulled forever out. If it was everyone's fault at once, that would imply nobody's guilt—and this was the terror of it all. I swallowed a second pill.

I remembered going with my father to sandbag against rising floodwaters in 1996. Service. All the money I had taken from my pockets over the years and dropped into a homeless man's hand. The homeless women with children. Phone calls to grandparents. All the apologies for those names and numbers and faces I had forgotten. How many apologies? Small to large, the limitless wrongs. Stealing candy from the five-and-dime as a boy. Sorry. The lies, from incremental to grand; caught lying, I'm sorry. A liar and doer of wrong. Nonbeliever and ogler and arbiter. Disbeliever.

My father kicked at the blanket. I moved to my mother's side of the bed and saw she was wearing earplugs. For her: silence. No husband, no apologies. I bent and looked into her closed eyes.

You were or you were not remorseful, and if you were not, you were a robot or sociopath.

I whispered to her face, "I am sorry," then again, having crossed to his side of the bed, kneeling among the saw of his labored breath and knowing, things equal, the man before me would as soon forgo this rest in favor of work. Whispered, "I am sorry," and swallowed another pill.

And were they awake, surely they would have answered in kind.

It was for these moments that we had designed language, all the rules and games. Wild-card piece, the chute or the mousetrap or the Sorry. Other cards in the game: I am waiting; I am happy; I am in love. No assurance the state will last beyond the saying of it.

This was the time I stood at the foot of my parents' bed, watching them sleep. That man had never successfully forgiven that woman, though he had claimed to. THOUGH he had tried very very hard and was still trying to this day. And said he did forgive. She would never forgive him for failing to forgive her or failing to see how hard she was trying to forgive herself. Though she, like him, had, was, and would continue to. Try.

I was not tired in the least. I swallowed another pill.

The alarm radio came on and I hurried from their room and climbed the stairs to the second floor.

She did not ask how I knew of her son or if he had grown. This was an ethical mistake, mine, involvement. Her balances unhinged. Young man arrived, and she took hold with her language of community and labor and led me inside. But for what desire? What vacancy or need of that failed mother-woman? Trouble. Call the thing *desire* and blame the body. Obey the body, invent the why at your leisure. Apologize.

This was the world of codes and guidelines. These were the mechanisms.

The day arrived seamlessly. There was a noise above me, what might have been something moving in the attic. It was now a bit past seven o'clock. It was now eight. It was now nine-thirty, and my mother left the house.

I ran through a series of basic stretches I remembered from baseball practice. I swung my arms in small circles, then reversed direction. I swung large circles. We would stand in a circle, a bunch of young men twirling our arms and lifting one foot as if this was a perfectly normal thing to do.

I was still wearing my jeans and Opal Worpley's too-tight shirt.

I went downstairs. At the sight of my green Pine Ridge polo, folded neatly by the front door, I began to cry. I cried silently and reluctantly until I remembered that the house was empty, and then I began to wail. Things I'd done with my body, the loyalties betrayed, expectations failed. I dropped to my knees and sank my face into my worthless hands.

I dried my face on the Irenia shirt, then took it off and put on the green polo.

It was a cereal-box morning: cloudless, sun big and sharp and impossibly round.

By the time I reached my car, I was sweating considerably. But this was not sweat. Nothing like it.

Submersion. I wanted submersion.

I found him shirt- and shoeless in his driveway, wearing a knee-length, loose-fitting skirt. He was bent over the ad, painting a splotch of what looked like bird shit onto its curve. The car was covered in dozens of these splotches, some with tails dripping downward, others with purple in their middles. The skirt he wore was gray with thin black vertical stripes.

Stuart looked at me and squinted. "Potter?"

"I need a quick jump in the pool. Take five minutes."

"Now's not good, actually."

Something was missing from the driveway. I did a quick count of cars and came up short.

"Where's your car?"

"I gave it to Edsel."

And yet again: didn't know what to say. I watched him paint bird shit and tried to understand what he stood to gain by giving

Edsel his car. Why my dear friend would abet my blackmailer, driving assholishly across the city, weaving and cutting off and running his errands and did he even have a license?

"You shouldn't have done that, Stubes."

"As long as this American fairy tale lasts, I can give away a Ford Explorer whenever I damn well please." He wet the tip of one finger to touch the center of a splotch, then looked at me. "You should go."

He was looking past me. I looked at the skirt. Blackmail aside, the skirt had to be mentioned. I turned and saw Marianne at the end of the driveway, walking toward us. Thirty seconds, no more.

"We have to go over what you're wearing. Unless I'm insane, that's a skirt. This girl has you wearing a skirt, Stubes. She's got pants on. There is no way you miss the meaning here."

"We're all wearing costumes, Potsky. Welcome to reality. Sometimes it's hard."

He set the paint down on the hood and went to meet her. The paintbrush jutting upward from the can looked like a. The brush he left submerged in the paint could have been. I saw the brush and thought of.

Stuart and Marianne kissed in the driveway.

Southward, winding roads and midday traffic. Posted speed limits. Lights. Yellow sign peering over trees, Tower Tee.

The man in the hut smiled smoker's teeth and asked how many tokens he could change up for me.

"A whole lot," I said.

Handed him a fifty and he laughed and filled me a plastic cup's worth.

"Careful," he said.

The bats available were old and dented, with browned, old athletic tape for grip. The helmet I picked up smelled almost sweet. Nine cages altogether, counting two at the far end for softball. It would have been busy even without the pizza party, for which I had no patience whatsoever. Groups of men and children stood crowded outside the middle cages, leaving free only the slowest cage, to my right, and the fastest cage, a ways to my left.

I stepped into the slowest cage and dropped a token into the slot. The red light above the machine lit, and soon the first ball came slowly toward me. I watched several pitches, settling in. These were not baseballs but yellow, dimpled, more like *field hockey* balls that were lighter, with a bit more elasticity. Behind me was a thick rectangle of black rubber hanging from two corners by rope. I hit a few ground balls and watched them strike the fence before draining down the sloped concrete into the retrieval system. My trigger was lifting my left foot and setting it back down. The red light went off and I inserted another token.

After a while, the balls hardly appeared to move at all. They waited for me and I obliged, crushing them back to the machine. I formalized the technique of my swing. The hips, the shoulders, the hands coming downward through the zone. More tokens. More swing. But there was only so much satisfaction in conquering that which was presented on a platter. When the red light turned off, I took my plastic cup and stepped out of the slow cage.

I sat holding a can of Fanta in each hand, cold metal easing the blisters already forming on my palms. Calluses gone, hands soft. A few men were discussing this afternoon's game. We had apparently called up a catcher from our Triple-A Memphis affiliate to fill in for the starter, who was suffering from back spasms. Poor old crumbling veteran catcher. Explanation for spasms likely that he spent his whole professional life *crouched*. His replacement was twenty-two years old and had spent four years in the minor leagues. I sipped a Fanta for Derril Brandt, the rookie, his first day in the Show, then walked into the only other available cage.

Token in, red light on, I stood waiting. The ball rocketed out of the machine, and I watched the hanging rubber square shudder. Watched a token's worth of balls slung toward me with enough backspin that I could see the pitch climb on its approach.

A group of construction workers took turns in the cage next to me. Hourly wages, laughter, recreation. Between tokens I watched. I admired but no longer envied. Work alone would not be my salvation. I dropped a token into the machine and waited. I felt my trigger and swung, missed, and saw the shadow of the rubber padding swing. The sun had crested and shadows were growing longer.

The balls thudded against rubber, then gathered at my feet. Another token and I began to catch up. My hands were being rubbed raw. Finally I caught a piece of ball, just a nick, a tip, fouling it off into the fence. The light went out.

"Zooming, ain't it."

A man was standing outside the cage with his arms crossed. A big but I wouldn't say tall man, flat wide face, eyes pinched close and shaded by the barely curved brim of his ball cap. He could have been any of a number of coaches I had known in my life, those authoritarians who barked help but could also chatter for days. Watching the kid who can't seem to catch up with a single pitch.

"It's like I can't swing early enough," I said.

I had to go down the slide. I had to make sure my top hand rolled over the bottom hand on my follow-through. Had to minimize the stroke. I had to calm the bat head while waiting. I kicked the balls forward and fed another token to the slot.

"You're lifting your head," he said. "You're backing out of there; you're scared of something. Got to stay over it."

He was absolutely right.

"You're right. Thank you."

"Don't thank me," he said.

More tokens, more missing. What had been pain in my hands faded to complete numbness. There were natural mechanics, that which the body did instinctively, versus that which was learned, forced, trained. The towering overhead lights flickered on and I thumbed another token into the slot. I hit a few weak ground balls. The other cages had cleared out. But there was no point going back to anything slower now; I was catching up.

On the next token, I found the rhythm. My trigger went earlier and my timing fell into place. To hit a ball square was a satisfaction unlike any other in life. And when I caught one a bit out in front of me and pulled it into what would be left field, the cheap bat responded with that clap sound like *fwap*, solid, and the dimples whizzed into the fencing.

"There you go," the man said. "There you go."

The most wonderful rhythm. After a few more of these it came to me; I knew what to do. I would immerse myself in the ethos of our national pastime. I would chew tobacco and coach some kind of team, Little League or Legion ball or anything I could find. *Yes.* I would lug bags of equipment and clap encouragement and say things twice. Speaking with them as this man spoke to me.

"You see what the Redbirds did today?" I asked.

"Yes sir. This kid Brandt might could turn into something."

"That's what I hear. Good for him," I said.

Let this be the point. The rhythm of amicable speech, common interest between strangers. I would find a wife. We would attend the church of her choice, another weekly rhythm. I would grow myself a mustache, mow the lawn, and listen to sports radio. I would have children by former wives with whom I would maintain contact via the language and ritual of baseball.

The man said, "Left too many runners on base, though. Again. It's what I been saying all summer. Keep swinging the bats like this, and we're going nowhere."

"The bats are starting to come around," I said.

"I got my doubts about the bats. Bullpen's getting tired also."

"You said it. You nailed it with the bullpen."

I would advocate the use of military force abroad to protect our national interest and pastime. I would buy a home buried somewhere deep in the county, a place west enough that my commute would be long, an important portion of each day, and I would appreciate my car.

"How many more coins you got in there?"

"Just a few more," I said.

"You know, back when I played we used to drill a hole straight through a ball, run a piece of string through there, and tie it off, then take our cuts from a tee. Nothing like this place. Didn't even know it was here until yesterday. Came by yesterday, then back today."

The allure of the cage, a place where arms swung or stayed comfortably crossed.

"Then what happened sometimes was the string would break. You hit it so hard the string would tear apart. Or other times the knot would rip clean off. Always felt like you did something right when it happened. You'd see the ball go fly off into the distance and think maybe you were due some kind of reward. Then you realized the only reward was having to go get the damn ball."

I laughed through a swing, then let two pitches go while I refocused. Once more, the sun released its hold on the day. The etymology of *token*, the satisfaction of it disappearing into the slot. Aside from two young women in one of the softball cages, everyone else was gone. The pitching machine churned, the red light came on, I swung, the red light went off.

" 'Bout time for you to wrap it up."

I looked at the man outside my cage. His arms were no longer crossed. One of the overhead lights flickered.

"Is it closing time?"

"I'm getting real tired of waiting out here."

"Oh hey, I'm sorry," I said. "Got so wrapped up in my swings I didn't realize you were waiting. I don't mind taking turns."

"Not waiting for the cage," he said. "Waiting for you to step out."

A man all shoulders and chest, jaw prominent. He pointed a finger through the fence.

"You got some serious pain and harm coming your way."

I stood holding the bat in two hands rubbed bloody by athletic tape. My shoulders ached fiercely. I glanced down at my green Pine Ridge polo shirt, drenched with perspiration, then looked back to the man across the fence.

"There's a lesson to be learned in what's coming. Take heart in that. Lesson is stay your ass away from other people's kids unless you're looking to get beat real real bad."

The girls were gone. Just like that, nighttime had returned. Where had I been all day? Here? The machine waited for a token.

Mr. Worpley crossed his arms and leaned closer to the fence. Colors in the fluorescent light were harsh and cold. Eyes that appeared black. Eyes like shotguns, face of fire. My hands trembled around the cheap bat and I forced them to grip tighter. If he came at me I would have a weapon.

"At least now you know. Tonight's the night you're gonna find a bad corner of life. Soon as you step out of that cage. How's that feel, knowing?"

"Difficult to say."

"Smart mouth, ain't you? Well, you can count on this. It's gonna hurt, true as the rain and the dark and every other god-awful fact of the world. And it won't change either, talk all you want."

I could, of course. Talk to perpetuity. But any words at my disposal had been systematically drained, rendered insufficient. What nouns? What verbs?

"You might not even be a pervert. I sort of doubt you are. I don't know who you are and I don't care either way. Come around my house and this is what has to follow."

I had wronged this man terribly. One minute my face pressed to the wife's chest, her fingers tearing into my back. Then she was above me and I was reaching up to her face. I remembered the bat and looked down at my hands, pale skin flapping over raw patches of blood. The mistake was approaching Ian without any of society's established blessings. The boy and his alien world I couldn't hope to understand; sympathy versus empathy. I lifted off my helmet and leaned the bat against the fence. Anything I'd done to Ian I had also done to his father. But I was not a pervert, as far as I knew. I wanted to say something, tell him about purity of intention, innocence, and a desire to help. I lifted the latch and stepped out of the cage.

"I never touched your son. Or hurt him on purpose. And there's something else I should say, regarding your wife. I shouldn't have slept with her. It's just. It's all very."

The first blow was a sweeping right haymaker that caught me just below my eye. I stumbled, then hovered for a moment while the jolty echo knocked around my skull. Lost balance and fell forward to my hands and knees. Then the sidewalk, which I was relying on for support in this dire moment of need, shot a slab of concrete up into my chest, spinning me onto my back. Like nothing I'd felt. Kick. It was a kick. Then he was standing over me, rocking back and forth as he leveled more kicks into my ribs and abdomen.

My left eye closed of its own accord. Halfway there. T. Worpley stood over me like an actual giant, fairy-tale notion, the boy's mythical father. And perhaps this was all the proof I needed. He stopped kicking and I saw his boots move a few steps away. He stopped. I thought to stand up, but this was impossible. I heard a long series of heavy breaths. When I saw him step back toward me I thought to try harder, then thought to play dead, then thought of the time Audrey and I went to the zoo, how she hated the zoo but I dragged her along because, I tried desperately to explain, it was while watching monkeys cavort that I best understood mankind.

He knelt over me and pummeled downward, so now gravity was in on the act as well. Each punch gathered steam in those

terrific, round shoulders, then spread in compact, economic motions to his arms and fists. He punched my chest and stomach and
I tried to roll and lift and he punched my face and now I was all
the way on the ground now, for good.

He ran a jackhammer, this man, and not one of those pussy
forty-five-pounders. City would be in trouble without him, as my
father had said to Ian. He was talking through clenched lips, and
if I concentrated very hard I could almost make out his words,
the passwords and whatever he could have taught me.

Each impact made for a cluster of floating candles out on the
borders of the world. This was probably for the best. Get me off
the streets. I smiled into his fist. Dancing candles floated out there
but not as far anymore. I heard a terrific crack, and the candles
got too close.

labor day

W hen our progress slowed enough to see and understand the faces around us, we knew we had become part of the thing. A winding line like a pilgrimage of deep conviction, our procession to the New West County Mall. The traffic was everything the media had predicted, but also good-natured, in a sense; a self-selecting club of we who had been duly warned and had come anyway. Eventually we made it off the highway and found police in white gloves playing conductors, the new traffic lights not yet fully operational. They pointed and waved and chirped whistles. I felt pain in my cheeks, the bruises, which meant I was smiling. I turned to see Audrey in the passenger seat next to me, smiling back.

"I feel like you always kind of wanted a broken nose," she said.

"I kind of did. You're right."

She was wearing jeans I recognized and a shirt with tiny sleeves that left her arms bare. She was tanned a deep olive, her face freckled astronomically. Pretty Audrey come to visit her college boyfriend.

Nine days since waking, I still felt some residual, lingering sense of wonder for the dimensions of the world, common enough among those who brush against death. I was enjoying it. There was a hot-air balloon floating above the parking lot. The police passed us off to attendants in orange vests waving orange flags, and soon we were walking, crossing the blacktop slowly while others passed us by, moving with the quick, gaping strides of anticipation. I was happy to have Audrey at my side. As we neared the structure we saw clowns painting faces and ponies being led in slow circles through hay. There was a radio station broadcasting live on location with a mixture of their morning hosts and their afternoon hosts. My face began hurting again.

It's easy to imagine a parallel world wherein she was there when I awoke in the hospital, her face gleaming above me, tanned and present. In reality, my mother, back home after a lengthy stay at my bedside, heard the cell phone ringing in the junk drawer, saw Audrey's name, answered, and explained. She had then gone to the computer in my father's office and booked her a ticket. Between waking in that bed, flanked by a parent on each side, and Audrey's arrival, I was given a week to prepare. On top of the entire summer. Driving to the airport was my first venture from the house, and I waited for her outside security. There were people all around me. I observed their shapes and motions, their interwoven desires and individual contingencies, and it made a solid kind of sense. She had lied about shaving her head. Funny girl.

When we made it into the mall, we approached a large display map surrounded by a crowd of the overwhelmed and stimulated. Squeezing through while I watched over shoulders, Audrey pointed one finger to a large purple square, then squeezed back out, and we walked as a pair to the toy superstore, through a great jingling maw of moving parts and gesticulating robots. I secured a shopping cart while she watched a man in a giraffe suit pose for photographs with frightened children. Pushing our cart along the aisles, I took time to read the backs of boxes and kept only the toys buttressed by what I considered sufficient narrative history, those with some role in a grander story, however ridiculous. Pieces to some whole, armies of good and evil and a war that crossed the galaxy to land on our planetary doorstep.

I had explained that I wanted to make a donation, and she had smiled, and nodded, and left it at that. I hadn't asked her many questions either, so the facts I knew were only those she had shared without prompt. She and Carmel were joined first by a writer and photographer from London, male, whom she referred to as the scribe. There were three Australians, trolls in disguise, from whom they were eventually forced to flee under the cover of Italian night. The search for the faeries began after meeting two South African witches, benevolent, who had tracked them (the faeries) across the better part of Europe, until finally uncovering a herd of them in Budapest. It was soon after finding the faeries that Audrey split with the robot and the others, spending the rest of her time alone, moving at will and whim, sometimes boarding trains for the sole reward of watching field and hills scroll by. She'd been home since the middle of August.

To make things fair, I told her of the covetous ogre driven by American myths of success and fulfillment, skilled in the equally American arts of manipulation and selective ethical disregard. I mentioned the wingless angel who lived in town (location ambiguous), who learned and taught the meanings of certain important words. And I spoke of a half-orphaned boy to whom I had spoken Audrey's name, and my failed hero's quest to locate and retrieve his mother. I mentioned a ghost only in passing. She allowed every abstraction, shrugging aside the euphemism and glaring holes of my story and focusing, instead, on what moral I could take away from the summer. If it was a story, she said, which it should be, then there would be a moral.

"Otherwise what's the point?"

"Alright," I said. "One thing would have to be about history, and that when you and the people around you ignore the history you share, or shove it aside to some dark corner of a dark room, you do that history a grave injustice. Meanwhile, we're always searching for answers that we presume must be hidden somewhere. And the desperate faith that answers do in fact exist, the frustration of this search, might explain why we're always beating and clawing at one another, like what's inside you might remedy or at least explain what's inside me. And so we become tangled and implicated in each other's lives in ways we maybe shouldn't be. That not everybody wants your help. Or maybe, simply put, the moral is all things change. All meaning all. *Staying the same* only means changing in parallel, and is a kind of miracle when it lasts. Oh, and also that the center of a place, of any community, is desirable in a way that people who reside on the edges won't ever understand. My father is right on that. I buy it completely."

She said that was nice, then was silent for a minute before saying hers had to do with movement, with borders and how they define, or fail to define, and also how the world is overflowing with men who have no idea what to do with a full-size penis.

We drove with the toys to the Goodwill office downtown, following one-way alleys until we found the donation dock. There, teams of men wearing thick leather gloves unloaded furniture from a flatbed truck. To begin the process, I handed over an envelope containing the five hundred dollars my mother had given me at the mall. A woman with a clipboard asked if I wanted a receipt. I said no thank you, then Audrey and I began removing toys from my trunk. Call it atonement or call it generosity. Poorly veiled selfishness. Call it buying my way out or really call it anything at all. I focused on a thought of a boy or girl holding a new toy. The unloading went quickly with two of us, and soon we'd filled two industrial laundry carts with shiny and sharp-edged boxes, everything but the two baseball gloves I asked her to leave in the backseat.

There was no sex. What brief physical contact we had was for photographs, plus a few passing touches to a wrist or a shoulder to confirm presence: a refresher course in object permanence. Sex, as I'd come to understand it, was driven primarily by speculation. Our bodies by now had adjusted to a certain distance between them, and they had learned that desire for sex brought about the consequences of sex. Although, had she chosen to cross the hall late one night from the guest room, certainly I would have loved her.

For the most part, our time together was passed in loaded, but not unpleasant, quiet. When she first arrived, our timing was stuttered and awkward, but with each hour we settled into the shape we'd cleared over the course of the summer, one of comfortable mystery. Only once did I look at her in a way designed to convey the remorse I felt. In her return look I saw that she neither expected nor desired further apology, nor *nor* did she especially want to apologize for anything of her own. Her immediate plan was to spend time in Portland before even considering what to do next. Settle into her familiar role as youngest daughter. I mentioned that I'd been thinking about moving to Louisville, Kentucky. She laughed and asked why. I said no real reason.

On her last day we drove north, across the Missouri River to Elsah and along a road that bent with the path of the river. We stopped to watch levees fill and empty, found stores that called themselves antiques stores, and ate fried catfish at a riverhouse of dark impressive wood. We posed for an on-site photographer, leaning against a railing on the second-floor deck so that the wooded bluffs, and the river, and the whole country could be seen behind us. Two prints cost us nine dollars, buy one copy get a second half price.

And then she was gone.

Someday soon I will figure a way to get the last of the toy-store purchases into Ian's hands. Anonymously, or under the veil of a third party, so he will accept them for what they are. Two baseball mitts and nothing else.

Audrey's departure set into motion the household activities everyone saw coming. Cardboard boxes began accumulating in the sunroom, my mother's possessions ready to go even if she was not. There is a condo in Webster Groves, a renovated two-bedroom unit in an old six-flat building heavy on charm. She and

I walked through it together. For now, my father has taken over
the guest room. The snoring is nothing after the squirrels. While
it hasn't been stated explicitly, it is clear that whatever ultimately
happens, they need to abandon this house. At some point it will
appear on the market and sell immediately to a family with truck-
loads of strange furniture and flatware and abundance. There
doesn't seem to be much of a rush; parents behaving like old
friends, teammates in this grim but not crippling preparation.
And at the same time unrestricted in their sadness, allowing it to
spill into the open freely. Tears at all hours, my mother padding a
box with crumpled newspaper, pausing to cough strange laughter into her hands. The curtains in the family room came down
one afternoon, and the new levels of sunlight made us wonder
why we'd needed them in the first place.

On the day of the grand reopening ceremony for the Union
Rock Bridge, I stood in my bedroom, listening to the silence of
the attic above me. Boxes up there and nothing more. I was to
dress presentably and get to the site, ten minutes upriver from
downtown. This was a project my father had been spearheading
for several years, an old truss bridge that had once been part of
Route 66, now a cornerstone of the new River's Edge Bike Path.
A late-afternoon ribbon-cutting and dedication. Would my mother
be there? Yes, she told me, of course she would. By the time I arrived, the refreshments tent was deserted, everyone already on
the bridge aside from a few caterers and my old friend Stuart,
who stood with both hands submerged in a tub full of ice. I approached and stood next to him for a few minutes, trying to or-
ganize the gratitude I knew I owed him, along with an apology
for so gravely misunderstanding why he had given Edsel the
Explorer.

In the swollen clarity of my hospital bed I had come painfully
to suspect that Stuart's gift was not to the ogre, but to me: a car
provided to settle half of the formal blackmail demands. Several
days later, during my recovery at home, a postcard arrived from

Harrisburg, PA, scrawled in stickish handwriting I knew without doubt was Edsel's. The photo was a young blond girl, a child in a yellow dress, standing on the front porch of an old home with a mansard roof. The message was two short lines: *Game over. Thanks for playing.* I tore the postcard into small pieces and understood. The car, a gift to take the ogre away from here, Harrisburg or anywhere else. A wonderful thing Stuart had done for me. But in the days that followed I had still not thanked him. Why? Other, subdermal bruises, perhaps; pride and ego.

But before I said anything, Stuart began detailing a fight he and Marianne had had during the night. He said that at one point their voices got so loud they became tangible. He'd been awake since. He shifted his hands in the ice and described taking the ad to a church parking lot at daybreak, dousing it with gasoline, and setting it on fire. An hour later he'd stumbled upon a newspaper with an article on today's event and decided to walk here. I had never seen him like this, skin hanging from his face, eyes the red of new brick, voice whispery and thin.

And would it be too much to say that my heart opened to my old friend and that I found myself forgiving him for everything? As he handed me a bottle of Evian from the tub, I tried again to thank him. I said I appreciated what he had done for me, the car the money the generosity, and that I could never repay him. I spoke slowly and clearly and looked straight into his eyes. Before I finished, he grabbed me around the arm.

"My God, Potsky. The blackmail. I'm sorry, man. I should have helped but I didn't really. When he came over and asked for the Explorer it was just like he'd asked a thousand times before. To be honest I forgot all about the blackmail. He said something about he'd gotten a job in New York and that he needed the car to get there. So I thought, *Take the fucking car.* What's a car? I was sick of hearing him ask. You know, he's really an asshole, that guy. Some job in an investment banking firm. Hoedecker and Cohen. No idea how he managed that. North tower south tower, who knows. Potsky, I'm sorry. I shit the bed on this. I really did. I didn't help you."

I could see him there, Edsel, in dark slacks and a white button-down shirt, a tie, they would require a tie. He would be man of the times, lewd and powerful, built like an oak. In the morning he would board his train, groggy-eyed and swaying, one hand on the head-high railing for support, among the writers and designers, students and teachers, the lonely and strung out, the nervous and confident cheats and priests and lawmen in blue, lawyers and lawyers and bankers. A downtown train that would sift passengers as it rumbled on ancient tracks, growing more financial, more singularly aimed with each stop, until those who disembarked were near uniform in their devotion to capital. Edsel among his rightful kith, exuberant and insatiable.

We began walking to the bridge. You could still smell the paint they'd used to cover the old rusty I-beams, bright blue, and the new plastic of safety railing and fence. We stopped at the back end of the rows of folding chairs, facing a temporary stage just beyond the bridge's halfway mark. A woman at the microphone was speaking about the value of recreational trails for a thriving city body. A red ribbon stretched between two metal poles in front of her. Stuart and I stood along the southern railing at the bridge's defining quirk, a twenty-two-degree kink designed to help boats align themselves on their way downriver.

I turned to Stuart and said that it was going to be okay. He squinted back at me.

"With Marianne, I mean."

"You're right. Thank you. Her thing is—Jesus, man, what happened to your face?"

The official record would show that I had been beaten by a crazed, anonymous batting-cage patron. One broken nose and much bruising, deep bruising. Swelling and overwhelming tenderness across my face and chest. I saw my friend's hand on the railing, gap of bright blue where a finger was missing. Living through the trials that defined who we were, my face and its fragile smile. I said I'd tell him about it some other time, and he nodded.

The seats were full, at least a hundred people here along with a small press corps. Richard sat on stage, flanked by several men I recognized for their demeanor of local power. I spotted my mother along the aisle in the front row. She had gotten a haircut, so now instead of bushy it looked darker, straighter, harder. I loved her for diving so brazenly into this realm of bodily control. My father was as I would remember him: forceful and static, a man forever occupying the middle of his element.

He was looking at me, my father, up there among these round-faced men of local celebrity, these powerhouses of law and finance and regional clout. The mayor and the current district attorney. Each with his own narrative of ascension. Former Senator Dunleavy stood at the microphone, bald and iconic, philanthropist and heir to massive old wealth. The man sitting to my father's left was a St. Louis native, Washington University Business School grad. Mark, I thought, Mark something, who had spent much of his career in New York before returning here to the Midwest as *St. Louis Hooray!*'s chief financial officer. These men on stage. Mark leaning now to say something into my father's ear while my father held our eye contact. Mark who had been convinced to come here, at least partially, by a hearty meal around my family's smudgeless glass dining-room table. To leave his position at Hoedecker and Cohen, a serious handshake upon agreement. A hearty slow-motion smile from them both now. Hoedecker and Cohen. My father's gaze still fixed, sailing over the audience to where his son stood at the blue railing over the brown river. And *thank you* alone wouldn't do a thing.

Richard Potter Mays, risen to a certain level of influence and a certain kind of might. A good man who loved his sons enough, and loved his wife enough, and loved himself enough, to do whatever he could to protect the one son who didn't drown.

I thought of Audrey's island, and her spear, and knew without

doubt that if there was to be love in this world—and there was—
it had shed all name and could only be considered and spoken of
as gifts. Here was a bridge, gift from the city to the city. Two baseball gloves sat in my car. There was a starfish. Crippled, yes, and
gone forever, but a gift.

Stuart said, "Man, this morning, after the ad, on the walk over
here, you know what I kept thinking about? *Go crazy, folks.*"

"Nineteen eighty-five," I said. "Ozzie and his miracle to beat
the Dodgers. To this day I hear Jack Buck's call and shiver. Six
years old, and I remember sitting in front of the TV with my dad.
Ozzie hangs over the plate. He's not the long-ball threat from the
left side."

"Trying to handle the smoking Tom Niedenfuer. Big man
from the North Country. Minnesota. First baseman and the third
baseman guard the lines."

"Smith corks one into right, down the line. It may go. Go
crazy, folks, go crazy. It's a home run. And the Cardinals have
won the game. By the score of three to two. On a home run by
the Wizard."

"Sixteen years," Stuart said.

"Go crazy, folks, go crazy."

I heard polite applause from the chairs, then a male voice re-
questing a warm welcome for the man without whom none of
this would have been possible, St. Louis's own Mr. Richard Mays.
I began to clap. As did Stuart. And at this point the polite applause
grew, and stacked, and evolved into something loud and powerful
and hearty enough that we all seemed impressed by the applause,
everyone in the small crowd clapping, hands chest-level or higher,
including my mother, who wasn't *the* but was among the first to
stand before others joined, and still others, until every single person on the bridge was standing and clapping for my father. And
also for themselves, clapping for the success of the clapping, an
ascending spiral. Stuart and I watched and clapped. We didn't
stop, and soon enough my father began clapping back, seated at

first and then standing, moving to the lectern, his hands in front of him, completing the circle. Those standing from chairs turned to either side and seemed to clap for their neighbors. This was the beauty of applause, its lack of defined object. It was sound alone, a celebration, a noise that would continue for as long as we made it. Sound of human percussion. I continued clapping.

acknowledgments

To . . .

Roger and Terry Beachy, Noah Eaker, Susan Kamil, Jennifer de la
Fuente, Carol Anshaw, Janet Desaulniers, Sara Levine, Margaret
Chapman, Odie Lindsay, Thomas King, Jake Cosden, Tommy,
Todd Rovak, Kathryn Corrine, Violet Brown, David Cohn (I may
be a writer, but I'm no Serengeti), Janie Porche, Robert Fulstone,
Liz Cross, Cait, Andrew Yawitz, Eric Nenninger, Tracy Marie,
Sarah Aloe, Eden Laurin, Pomonans, skateboarders, and the ma-
gicians from whom I thief. The St. Louis Cardinals and the great-
est defensive shortstop to ever play the game. And then back to
Roger and Terry Beachy, Roger and Terry Beachy, repeated to the
point that I can no longer speak.

. . . Thank you.

about the author

Kyle Beachy lives in Chicago. This is his first novel.